Proof of Life

BlackThorpe Security

Book 4

Kimberly Rae Jordan

THREE**STRAND**
P R E S S

A CORD OF THREE STRANDS IS NOT EASILY BROKEN.

A man, a woman & their God.
Three Strand Press publishes Christian Romance stories
that intertwine love, faith and family.
Always clean. Always heartwarming. Always uplifting.

1

ALEX THORPE pressed his hand to the scanner outside the entrance to the BlackThorpe training compound and waited for the gates to open. He wasn't sure if he hoped he'd run into Justin Morrell while he was there or not. It had been an agonizing few weeks as he'd watched one of the strongest men he knew struggle to keep it together. Justin had always been known for his physical prowess, but it was his inner strength that now had Alex in awe of him.

But he just had no words anymore. How many times could you tell someone you were sorry for their...loss? It wasn't even a loss really because they still didn't know—despite hours and hours of following leads—what had happened to Alana. Even the cops had come to a standstill in their investigation. He knew from personal experience that the not knowing was the most difficult thing, but even their ordeal with Melanie's kidnapping had only lasted two weeks.

Slinging his bag over his shoulder, Alex pressed through the door of the building that housed the gym and the shooting range. He'd convinced Marcus Black to meet him there for a sparring session because they both needed to work out their frustrations. Marcus was more on edge than he'd ever seen him, and that was something considering they'd been friends for over fourteen years.

As Alex stepped into the large gym, his gaze swept the room looking for either Justin or Marcus. Seeing neither, he went into the changing room to get into his workout clothes. He dropped his bag on the floor and sank down on the long bench in front of the lockers.

Leaning forward, arms resting on his thighs, Alex stared at the tiled floor. The knot in his stomach hadn't eased at all since the night the news had come about Justin and Alana. If this was the work of whoever was behind the other attacks on the company, the person was now digging deep into the pasts of people. He would have had to get through several layers of security to find out about Alana's ex and the threat he posed to her.

And that concerned him more than a little. Alex had a secret that wasn't buried anywhere nearly as deep as Alana's, but if the person was looking to cause problems, dredging up his past would surely do that. Not for the first time, he wished he'd taken care of things differently.

Alex reached for his bag and unzipped it. After he pulled out his workout clothes, he changed into them, a bit surprised that Marcus still hadn't shown up. Figuring he could use some of the machines until the man arrived, Alex shoved his bag into his locker.

When he stepped back into the gym, Alex realized that Marcus had arrived, he just hadn't come into the changing room yet. The man stood facing away from Alex, watching something going on in front of him.

As Alex got closer, he noticed that Justin and Than had also arrived. Justin was down on his knees holding a large punching pad. A little boy, who Alex recognized as Alana's son, Caden, stood there with gloves on his hands. Than was using sign language to interpret what Justin was saying to the deaf boy, instructing him on how to hit the pad.

Seemingly oblivious to Alex and Marcus, Caden focused on Justin and then landed a weak punch on the pad.

"Harder," Than said as he signed. "You won't hurt him."

Caden landed another punch with slightly more weight behind it.

"Harder," Than said again when Caden looked at him.

Justin nodded when Caden focused on him again. *Punch.* Justin nodded. *Punch.* Another nod. Each punch Caden landed held more confidence. Pretty soon he was hitting the pad at regular intervals.

Alex glanced at Justin and felt as if one of Caden's punches landed in his gut. Justin's expression was drawn and stark with pain. Every punch seemed to push him closer and closer to an emotional edge. When he looked back at Caden, Alex saw the emotion on Justin's face reflected there.

The punches began to fly as tears flowed down Caden's face. Over and over he punched the bag until he suddenly sagged against it, clearly physically spent, but as Justin tossed the pad aside and gathered the boy into his arms, Alex knew the emotions were just beginning to flow.

Justin crouched with Caden wrapped in his arms, his sobs as heart wrenching as the boy's. Alex felt tears sting his eyes, and he had to look away and take a deep breath. Than came to stand next to him but unlike Alex, he allowed his tears to fall. Alex knew that Than was close to Alana's son because of his ability to communicate with the boy through sign language.

The scene playing out in front of him hit Alex on so many different levels. Anger. Fear. Regret. Guilt. And as he watched Justin with the boy who would one day be his son, Alex prayed that God would protect the woman who meant everything to them.

"I'm going to change," Marcus murmured before turning away from Justin and Caden.

Alex moved to sit on one of the benches that lined the one wall of the gym. Than followed and settled down next to him.

"Was that what was supposed to happen?" Alex asked, his gaze still on the man and boy.

Than nodded. "Caden hasn't been letting anything out since his mom was taken. Justin thought maybe encouraging him to express himself physically might help with the emotional side."

"How's he doing?"

Than rubbed a hand on his thigh and shook his head as his jaw tightened. "I don't know how he's holding it together, man. If it had been Lindsay who was taken..."

Even though some of them hadn't known Alana as well as others, her kidnapping had hit everyone hard. The atmosphere within the company was not what it would normally be at this time of year. With less than a month until Christmas, usually large amounts of decorating would be going on, and Christmas music would be playing on each floor. But instead, it was as if no one felt comfortable moving into the festive part of the year with one of their fellow employees experiencing so much heartache.

By the time Alex left the gym a couple of hours later, his physical state matched his mental one. Totally and completely drained. Maybe tonight he'd actually be able to sleep.

Fog lay low over the city Monday morning as Alex made his way to the BlackThorpe offices. As he did most days anymore, Alex spent the drive praying. He'd believed in the power of prayer from the moment his sister had been returned to them alive. And looking at Melanie now, he knew that those prayers were once again being answered as she blossomed with the love she and Tyler shared.

Now he prayed for the return of another woman. A mother. He just couldn't let himself believe that God would allow anything bad to happen to Alana. Caden needed her. Justin needed her.

Please, God, place angels around Alana to protect her from the evil of the person who has taken her and bring her back home soon.

Alex hit the button to lower his window as he neared the secure entrance to the office compound. A guard approached him and ducked down to look at him through his open window.

"Mr. Thorpe, we've had a young man here since seven-thirty saying he needs to see you," the guard said with a glance over his shoulder.

Alex frowned. "Did he give his name?"

"No. He's refusing to talk to anyone but you." The guard straightened and pointed to a spot not too far from the gate.

The foggy morning didn't reveal much beyond a figure hunched against the cement wall that surrounded the compound.

"Okay. Let me park, and I'll come back out to see what he wants."

When the gate slid open, Alex guided his truck into the parking lot. Usually, he parked in the underground parking lot, but for now, he pulled his truck into the nearest empty spot. Gripping the wheel with both hands, Alex let out a long breath. He had no idea what this newest situation was about, but he really hoped that it was something that could be easily resolved.

It could be someone looking for help with a loved one. It wouldn't be the first time a person had approached them out of the blue to ask them to help a family member. Usually the person needed the help of the BlackThorpe Wellness Center. If that was the case, he'd refer them on to his sister, Melanie, since that was her department.

But as Alex made his way toward the guardhouse, the thought played in the back of his mind that this could be something set up by whoever was behind the attacks. After Justin had been attacked and Alana taken, it would be foolish to dismiss anything out of the ordinary without first assessing it for a threat.

The security guards nodded to him as he stepped into the room where they monitored things when they weren't dealing with people coming in and out of the compound through the gate.

"Can I get one of you to follow me? Stay back a bit, but be ready for anything," Alex instructed as the guard who'd spoken with him initially followed him through to the other side of the gate.

Fog still hung heavy in the air as he paused for a moment, taking in the man where he sat on the sidewalk, his back pressed against the wall. He wore a backward ball cap, and his head was bent forward. His legs were drawn up, and his arms rested on his knees. It was hard to assess much more from a distance, so Alex took another deep breath and let it out as he headed in the guy's direction.

Something must have alerted him to Alex's approach because suddenly the man was scrambling to his feet, pulling the strap of a backpack over one shoulder. Alex stopped a few feet away from him. He didn't bother to glance over his shoulder to see if the guard was there, confident that they were doing as he'd asked.

"I'm told you wanted to see me," he said, keeping his hands in the pockets of his long coat. He was armed beneath his coat—they all were after what had happened to Alana— but he didn't want to tip his hand if this person was a threat.

When the guy shuffled his feet nervously, Alex looked at him a bit more closely and realized that he was more of a teenager than a man.

"Are you Alex Thorpe?" The guy's voice trembled as he spoke.

"I am. Is there something I can help you with?"

"Can I talk to you?" The kid's gaze flicked to the guard behind Alex. "In private?"

Alex stared at the teenager. There was something familiar about him, but he was positive he'd never met the guy before. He was on the slender side, and the jean jacket he wore didn't look like it was doing a very good job keeping him warm. "What's your name?"

"Jordan."

A knot began to tighten in Alex's gut. Surely it was a coincidence that this kid's first name was his middle name. It was a fairly common name, after all. "Jordan what?"

The kid shifted his weight again, both hands going to grip the strap over his left shoulder. "MacKenzie. Jordan MacKenzie."

Air whooshed out of Alex's lungs as the blood pounded in his head. He turned on his heel and approached the guard.

"Have someone bring him up to my office. Bypass security, but send a guard with him. I'm going to park my vehicle underground and will meet him in my office." Without waiting for the guard to acknowledge his instructions, Alex strode back through the guardhouse and headed for his truck, coat flapping as he walked.

Without thought, he got back in his truck and started it up. He didn't look back to see if the guard was bringing the boy as he'd requested. Right then, Alex was trying to figure out what was going on. Was this kid really who he thought he was? But that was impossible.

Wasn't it?

Alex stepped off the elevator when it reached his floor and briefly greeted Kelsey as he walked by. Momentarily, he wondered if it had been a good idea to have brought the boy—Jordan—into the office. Maybe he should have taken him somewhere else to figure out what his story was.

But before he could come up with a new plan, there was a rap on the door of his office. The guard stood there with Jordan in front of him.

"Thanks," Alex said to him. "I'll take it from here."

The guard gave him a nod then stepped out of the office, pulling the door closed behind him. Alex finished taking off his coat and hanging it on the rack beside the door. He turned to find Jordan watching him, his face expressionless.

"Have a seat." Alex gestured to the chairs in front of his desk as he rounded it to get to his own.

Jordan hesitated for a moment before sinking into the

chair nearest him. He put his backpack on the floor between his feet but kept a grip on the strap. Still he didn't say anything.

"Are you hungry? Would you like something to eat or drink?"

When the kid only shrugged, Alex picked up his phone and punched a button for Kelsey's desk. "Hey, Kels, can you do me a favor? Can you get a hot chocolate and a coffee from the deli for me? Also an assortment of muffins. Thanks."

He didn't really want to get into anything only to be interrupted by Kelsey, but they could hardly just sit there staring at each other. And there was a part of Alex that had no idea what he'd do if the kid confirmed his suspicions.

"How old are you, Jordan?" Alex asked as he picked up a pen, unable to keep himself from opening the door from which there would be no return.

"Fourteen." Straightening, the boy pulled his shoulders back. "Almost fifteen."

Alex wrote the number on the notepad in front of him and drew a circle around it. "And your birthday?"

"September twenty."

That got scribbled down on the paper too. Every answer the boy gave just reinforced the conclusion Alex had already arrived at outside the gate.

"What's your mom's name?"

Jordan's shoulders slumped as he shifted in his seat, his gaze fixed on the floor. "Rebecca."

At the sound of her name, memories rushed Alex like a tidal wave. He never allowed himself to think of that time. Never allowed himself to dwell on what might have been.

Drawing on strength he didn't realize he had, Alex shoved all the memories aside. There would be time to deal with them later on. Right now there was a boy sitting across from him with familiar blue eyes and an expression of anticipation mixed with fear on his face.

Before Alex could say anything further, there was a light knock on his door. He pushed back from his desk and went to open it.

Kelsey stood there with a brown paper bag with the deli logo and a tray holding two Styrofoam cups. "Here you go. Need anything else?"

Alex could see the curiosity on her face, but he wasn't in any position to answer her questions when he had so many of his own. "No. Thanks, Kelsey."

With a quick smile, she closed the door. Alex returned to his seat and set the stuff down on the desk. He looked at the lids to determine which one was the hot chocolate then pulled it free. Leaning across his desk, he held it out to Jordan. The boy hesitated before he took it, finally releasing his grip on the strap of his backpack to wrap both his hands around the cup.

Alex looked into the bag to see a selection of muffins. He put the bag on the edge of the desk near Jordan. "Help yourself."

After pulling his cup free from the tray, Alex sat back down and took the lid off. He inhaled the rich aroma, letting it calm his nerves before he took a sip. And then another. Coffee was definitely his addiction.

He watched as Jordan poked out the opening in his lid and took a sip of his hot chocolate. They sat in silence for a couple of minutes, but eventually, the boy set the cup on the desk and reached for the bag. He took out a muffin without spending much time looking them over.

Alex waited for Jordan to take a couple of bites before asking his next question. "Does your mother know where you are?"

Jordan swallowed and lifted his cup to take another sip. "No. I didn't tell her."

"You don't think maybe she's worried about you?"

Jordan shrugged as if he didn't care. "She thinks I'm staying with a friend for a couple of days."

"Are you missing school?" Alex hadn't been to school in a quite a few years, but he was pretty sure that kids were still in class at the beginning of December.

"I'm homeschooled. My mom gave me a couple of days off."

Alex took another couple sips of coffee, wondering which one of them was going to say the words first. As much as he was confused how—given what he'd been told years ago—the kid could be his, there was really no way to deny what stared him right in the face.

Jordan MacKenzie was his son.

2

REBECCA MACKENZIE pushed back from her desk and rotated her neck one way and then the other. Grabbing her phone and mug, she got to her feet and did a few more stretches before making her way into the kitchen.

It was oddly quiet without Jordan around, but at the same time, it was what she needed in order to make this latest deadline. He'd worked hard since the beginning of the school year, so when he'd asked about staying at a fellow homeschooled friend's house for a couple of days, she'd been happy to work with the other mom—who just happened to be her best friend—to iron out the details.

She put her dirty mug into the dishwasher before grabbing a clean one and filling it with a fresh cup of coffee from her Keurig. As she waited for her second cup of the day, Rebecca stared out at the backyard. There was still no snow on the ground even though they were in December, but the forecast was calling for some in the next few days.

It was hard to think that Christmas was less than a month away. Getting this book published had been her focus for the past two weeks, and once that was done—hopefully within the next twenty-four hours—she could turn her attention to the holiday. Her plan was to put the tree up on Friday with Jordan and then start her Christmas shopping. She was woefully behind on that, but only having to buy for one person made it a bit easier.

When the Keurig finished its job, Rebecca pulled the mug out and took a sip. Hot and black. Just perfect. She took one more sip before heading back to the office. She'd just settled into her seat when her cell phone rang. Normally, at this point in a deadline, she'd ignore calls from pretty much everyone, but seeing it was Maureen, her friend where Jordan was staying, Rebecca answered it.

"Hey, Maureen. Are the boys driving you nuts yet?" The beat of silence that followed her greeting had Rebecca frowning. "Is everything okay?"

"I'm not sure, Bec. Jordan's not here."

"What?" Rebecca straightened in her chair. "He went to your place yesterday."

"That's the thing. Apparently, he and Robby had worked something out." Maureen sighed. "Last night around seven, Jordan said he wasn't feeling well and asked if Ed could give him a ride home. Ed and Robby took him home. They watched him go into the house and everything."

"I wasn't here," Rebecca said, her stomach knotting as anxiety built inside her. "I had gone out for a standing appointment. He knew I was going to be away."

"Yeah, apparently that was part of the plan, that we'd each think Jordan was at the other's house. When I asked Robby this morning if he'd talked to Jordan to see how he was, I could tell something was up. It didn't take too many threats to get him to crumble. Jordan told him he needed to do something, but he didn't want you to know. He was smart enough not to give Robby details, so I'm afraid I can't help you out with that, but I know you needed to know what had gone on."

"Where would he go? I don't understand." Rebecca got to her feet and made her way down the hallway to Jordan's bedroom. She pushed the door open, not sure what she expected to find.

"I wish I could give you more info, but Robby said Jordan told him he wouldn't tell him because he knew Robby would never be able to keep the information a secret." Maureen sighed. "Jordan definitely has Robby's number."

Rebecca pressed the heel of her hand to her forehead and rubbed. "Thanks for calling, Maureen. I'm going to try his cell and see if he answers."

As she ended the call with Maureen, Rebecca had no clue what she would do if Jordan didn't answer his phone.

God, please be with my boy wherever he is.

With shaking fingers, she tapped her screen to bring up Jordan's number then pressed the phone to her ear, listening as it rang.

After three rings, a connection was made, and relief flooded Rebecca.

"Hi, Mom."

"*Hi, Mom?* That's all you have to say to me, Jordan Alexander MacKenzie?" Rebecca took a deep breath and let it out, trying to quell the anger that rose up inside her. "Where are you?"

There was silence from Jordan's side of the call though they still had a connection.

"Jordan! Where are you?" Anger and concern continued to battle for top spot in her emotions. "You tell me right this minute."

"Minneapolis."

Minneapolis? Oh no... He *couldn't* know. *How* would he know?

She swallowed hard and tried to keep her voice firm. "What are you doing there?"

"You told me he was *dead.*" Jordan's anger was clear in his voice. "You *lied* to me."

"Jordan." A voice in the background grabbed her attention.

The sound of his voice—still familiar after all these years—took the strength from her legs, and Rebecca sank to the floor of Jordan's bedroom. This was a day she'd never thought would happen. It *shouldn't* have happened. She'd taken steps to make sure that Jordan would never know about the man who hadn't wanted him to even take his first breath. What had gone wrong?

Rebecca wrapped an arm around her legs. "Jordan, sweetie, can you come home so we can talk about this?"

She needed him home—back in Chicago—where she could try to repair her relationship with her son and somehow convince him that he didn't need Alex Thorpe in his life.

"No." Jordan's answer came quickly and with a firmness Rebecca wasn't used to hearing from her fourteen-year-old son. Every once in a while lately, she'd begun to see flashes of his father, and, unfortunately, this was one of those moments.

"Please, Jordan." Even as she said the words, anger rose within Rebecca. She was his *mother*. She'd been there for him every step of the way since he'd been born. Why did she have to beg him to come home? She should be able to just *tell* him to get his behind back where he belonged.

"No, Mom. I need to do this."

Suddenly Rebecca wished she'd told Jordan exactly *why* she had said his father had died. If he'd known the truth, he wouldn't have gone looking for him.

But now what?

"Let me talk to her." Alex's request came through loud and clear.

No. No. No.

"Rebecca?"

Trying to calm the emotions that had welled up in the past few minutes, Rebecca took a deep breath and said, "Alex."

It shouldn't have come as a surprise that Alex was taking

this all in stride. Not much had rattled him as a young man, and apparently that hadn't changed.

"You need to come here," Alex said, his tone making it clear he didn't expect her to argue.

Concern for Jordan had bled away, but now Rebecca found that long-buried hurt was seeping to the surface. She couldn't go there. *Wouldn't* go there.

"Maybe you need to come here," Rebecca replied, hoping her voice wouldn't betray her. "Bring him back home."

"I can't. There's a situation going on here that I can't leave."

"A situation more important than your son?"

There was a pause before Alex spoke again. "I'm not altogether sure you want to go there just yet, Rebecca. I think it would be in everyone's best interest if you came here. Jordan has made it pretty clear he's not going back to Chicago, and I can't leave here right now to bring him back."

"And yet you seem to think I can just drop everything here to go there," Rebecca said.

"Rebecca, please," Alex said, suddenly sounding weary. "The other alternative is that he stay here with me until you can clear your schedule to come."

Rebecca was torn. She had a deadline she needed to meet, but now that she knew he was safe… "You'll take care of him if I can't get there right away?"

"Of course."

Rebecca let out a long breath. "Please let me talk to Jordan again."

"Hi, Mom."

"Jordan. Why didn't you talk to me about this before you went?"

"Because I didn't think you'd tell me the truth."

Rebecca's eyes slid shut. For so long it had been just the two of them. When he'd been born, she'd worried if she'd be able to be a good parent for a little boy. She'd wondered if a little girl would have been easier. But things had been fine. Her brother, Connor, had stepped in to help when he could.

Apparently it hadn't been enough.

"I know Alex will take care of you, but I'll be there sometime tomorrow."

"You don't need to rush."

His words might as well have been a knife to her heart. He was in no hurry to see her. He'd found his father, and she might as well be invisible.

"I'll be there sometime tomorrow," she said again.

"Okay."

"Be good, Jordan." Rebecca hesitated. "I love you, sweetheart. See you tomorrow."

Once the call ended, she sat for a bit trying to figure out how her life had managed to implode over the course of just a few minutes.

"She'll be here tomorrow," Jordan mumbled as he lowered his phone.

Alex was kind of surprised at that. For some reason, he'd assumed she was talking about a few days when she'd said she couldn't come right away.

"She has a deadline she has to meet and then she'll come," Jordan said.

"A deadline? What does she do?" Alex let himself think back to when they'd been together. Her plan then was to become a teacher. Had that changed?

"She writes books and publishes them."

"She always did love to read," Alex mused, as much to himself as to Jordan. "What kind of books?"

"Cozy mysteries. She writes under the name Kenzie Alexander." Jordan looked at him, a thoughtful expression on his face. "I always thought she'd chosen Alexander because it was my name, but I guess it was yours first."

"Your name?"

"Yeah. Jordan Alexander MacKenzie."

So she'd just taken his name and reversed it. "My name is

actually Alexander Jordan."

Jordan's eyes widened a bit at that. "Why would she name me after you? I mean, she told me you were dead, so she clearly didn't want you in my life so why the name?"

Alex found himself wondering the same thing. "That you'll have to ask your mom."

Jordan nodded as his gaze dropped, and he shifted in his chair again. "Are you mad that I'm here?"

"No, I'm not mad at all. Surprised and a little confused, to be honest, but not mad. However, I didn't lie to your mom. I have things going on right now that need my attention. The best I can offer you at the moment is a place for you to hang out until it's time to go home. I have meetings lined up today that I just can't get out of."

"That's okay. I understand."

Alex pushed back from his desk and grabbed the bag of muffins. "Bring your hot chocolate and backpack."

As the kid fell into step beside him, Alex realized that while Jordan wasn't as tall as he was yet, he would no doubt get there soon. He had a build similar to what Alex had had at that age. His short hair was blond which he could have gotten from either parent, but his blue eyes were definitely from Alex. He wondered how many personality traits they shared.

Most men got to know their sons as infants, but he had been handed a teenager. He had no idea what he was supposed to do with him.

Kelsey spotted them as they approached the foyer area. "Hey, Alex."

Alex introduced Jordan to Kelsey without identifying who he was. "Jordan, I'm going to have you wait in the lunchroom. If you need anything, though, you can come back here and ask Kelsey. She'll help you out."

"I sure will," Kelsey said with a smile.

Alex led him the short distance from Kelsey's desk to where the lunchroom was. The one on this floor was smaller than the other floors since fewer people used it, but it still had lots of natural light spilling through the windows and in addition to the tables, it had a couple of comfortable couches and a television.

"Do you have a tablet or laptop?" Alex asked as he picked up the remote from beside the television and handed it to Jordan.

"Yeah. A tablet." He slid his backpack down onto the couch but held onto his hot chocolate.

"Okay. I'll have someone come help you get connected to the network." Alex set the bag of muffins on the table, reluctant to leave him alone, but there was no choice. He desperately needed some time to process all of this and what it meant and how he was going to deal with seeing Rebecca for the first time in so many years. But before he could do anything like that, he had to deal with his day's schedule. "I'll be back as soon as I have a break in my appointments, okay?"

Jordan nodded as he looked around. "Sorry if I've kind of messed up your day."

Alex rested his hand on Jordan's shoulder and waited for him to look up and meet his gaze. "Don't apologize. I just need a little time to sort a few things out and then we'll figure this out. But don't worry about anything. You've got a place to stay tonight, and then we'll see what your mom wants to do."

Jordan stared at him with eyes identical in shape and color to his own. *My son.* It hadn't really sunk in until that moment. This was his son. A son he knew absolutely nothing about. Nothing. Anger burned white hot through him, but Alex squelched it as quickly as it flared to life. In its place came a soul-wrenching sadness. In the end, however, it was guilt that obliterated every other emotion as he acknowledged that he had no one but himself to blame for Jordan's absence from his life.

"I'll be back in a bit. Okay?"

Jordan nodded but didn't say anything as he sank down onto the couch next to his backpack.

Alex took a deep breath and let it out. The sooner he got through the meetings he had scheduled that day, the sooner he could get back here to Jordan. When he returned to his office, he stopped to talk to his secretary.

"Do I have a free hour in my schedule today?"

Lynne nodded. "Eleven-thirty to twelve-thirty and then you're completely free after four."

"Okay. Call Adrianne and Melanie and ask them to meet me here at eleven-thirty, please."

"If they ask why?" Lynne prompted and even though she was the epitome of discretion, Alex didn't give her any details. He just told her to inform them it was personal and urgent.

Before she could ask any more questions, Alex saw the agent from the FBI who had been assigned to Alana's case walking toward them. Given that they'd pretty much confirmed that her kidnapper was her ex from Florida, they were thinking it was likely he'd crossed state lines with her at this point.

Not far behind the agent was Marcus, looking intently focused as usual. As he greeted them, Alex remembered his promise to Jordan to have someone help him with the Wi-Fi.

"I just have to make a quick phone call," Alex said as he pulled his phone out. "I'll be right there."

Alex waited until Marcus had led the agent into his office before placing a call to Trent Hause, who was BlackThorpe's computer network guy.

"Hey, Trent. You got a few minutes to spare?"

"For you, Alex, sure. What's up?"

Not wanting to go into too many details, Alex said, "There's someone in the lunchroom on the exec floor that needs access to the Wi-Fi. Could you hook him up?"

"Sure thing. I'll take care of that right away."

"Thanks, Trent. He's a relative of mine, and his name is Jordan."

After ending the call, Alex stood for a moment gathering his thoughts before going into the office with Marcus and the FBI agent for what was likely to be a meeting where there was no good news.

3

REBECCA STARED at the computer screen. It had been nearly impossible to focus on the file that she needed to format. The words kept blurring, replaced instead by images of her son with his father. How had it gotten to this point? She'd worked so hard to hide Alex's identity from Jordan— even though she'd had a weak moment when filling out the birth certificate and named him after Alex. After all, the man had made it pretty clear that a child was not what he wanted. She had never wanted her son to know that his father had rejected him before he'd even been born.

Her cell chimed a text alert, drawing Rebecca from her thoughts. She picked the phone up, hoping it would be something from Jordan, but it wasn't.

Maureen: Just checking to see if you've found Jordan yet and if he's okay.

Rebecca realized she had no idea if Jordan was okay, but at least he was safe. She sat for a moment, contemplating her response to Maureen. She'd made sure over the years to never discuss Jordan's father with anyone. Even Connor had no idea. She'd wondered if he'd figure it out when he heard Jordan's middle name, but since she and Alex had been so careful to never be seen together, Connor hadn't even suspected it might be his friend from high school.

But Jordan's parentage wasn't the only thing people hadn't known about. No one had known that she and Alex had actually gotten married. They had secretly gone out in high school since her folks had forbidden her from dating until she was out of school. Alex had joined the military just after graduating, but Rebecca had had one more year, so they'd kept in contact through emails and chatting online for the next year. The December following her graduation, they'd received word that he was going to be doing a tour in the Middle East. He'd taken a short leave and come back to Minneapolis.

Looking back now, Rebecca couldn't believe that she'd actually thought that getting married so quickly was a good idea. And not only quickly, but secretly. Their plan had been to have a church wedding once his tour was over. They'd hoped that by that point, things would have settled down with Alex's family and that her own would have been more accepting.

But then she'd ended up pregnant. A honeymoon baby— even though their honeymoon had lasted just over a week. However, it had been his response to her panicked message when she'd realized she was pregnant that had shown her how little she'd actually known about the man she'd married.

I'll send you the money. You just need to get rid of it. We can't deal with this right now.

She'd studied the message so often those first few weeks that it was burned into her memory. Her message to him in reply had been five short words.

I'll take care of it.

And she had. She'd cut off all contact with Alex, which wasn't too difficult since he couldn't travel to Minneapolis to talk with her even if he'd wanted to. When her dad had gotten transferred to Chicago a couple of months later, she'd gone with her family who hadn't yet realized she was pregnant. Later, with her parents' reluctant help, she'd managed to take a course in medical transcription and eventually had found a job that allowed her to work from home. Her dreams of being a teacher were long gone, but eventually, another dream had taken its place, and she'd begun to write.

Her success had surprised everyone...including herself...but Rebecca was beyond grateful that she'd had a means to support herself and her son while still being able to homeschool him. She told people she homeschooled him because she'd always wanted to be a teacher, and while that was partially true, the other part was that she just didn't want to put him into the system where maybe one day Alex might find him.

Given his response to her pregnancy, Rebecca hadn't been too surprised when Alex didn't make any effort to find her. She hadn't buried herself so deeply that, with a little effort, he couldn't have figured out where she'd gone. But he never had.

Which still left the question...how had Jordan found out about his father?

But it was a question that would have to wait. She needed to focus and get this book published so she could give the situation with Alex and Jordan her complete attention.

After taking a minute to respond to Maureen's text letting her know Jordan was safe and sound, Rebecca turned her attention back to her computer monitor.

"Well, what's this all about, Alex? It's not often we get summoned to the exec floor like lowly peons," Melanie declared as she dropped down in the chair next to Adrianne.

It was still a little surprising for Alex to see them looking so much like each other now that Melanie had returned her hair to its natural color and stopped wearing the brown colored contacts.

"Like you're complaining," Adrianne said, a smirk on her face. "You've probably already told Tyler you'll meet him for lunch afterward."

Melanie grinned, and if he hadn't had so much weighing on his mind, Alex might have joined in. Unfortunately, none of his meetings had improved his mood and now he was going to have to reveal his secrets to his sisters. There was no way to hide the presence of a teenage boy in his life.

As if sensing his mood wasn't aligned with theirs, Adrianne's brows drew together as she looked at him. "What's going on?"

"Do they have some news on Alana?" Melanie asked, her smile sliding away.

"No news on Alana." Alex picked up a pen and ran his fingers up and down the smooth surface. He'd tried to figure out the best way to tell them about the events that had unfolded earlier that morning.

"You're starting to worry me, Alexander Jordan Thorpe," Adrianne said, her voice tight.

At the sound of his full name, Alex took a deep breath and looked up at his sisters. "You know how I never date, right?"

"Uh, yeah," Melanie said as she shot a quizzical look at Adrianne.

"Well, I have a really good reason." Alex paused, waiting to see if either sister would say anything, but they remained quiet, their expressions a mix of curiosity and concern. "I don't date because I'm already married."

The looks on their faces morphed into identical expressions of shock. Not surprisingly, Adrianne was the first one to regain her composure. "Say what? Is this some kind of joke, Alex?"

He shook his head and ran a hand through his hair. "No. It's not. I'm married and have been for almost fifteen years."

Melanie's eyes widened. "What? To whom?"

"Rebecca MacKenzie."

Adrianne shot to her feet. "Rebecca *Mackenzie*? *Connor* MacKenzie's sister?"

The tone of Adrianne's voice as she said the names made Alex frown. There was definitely a thread of anger in her words. Even Melanie was staring at her in surprise.

"Yes."

Adrianne's expression was tight as she sat back down in her chair. Her hands were clenched in her lap, but she didn't say anything more. For all that he knew his sister, Alex couldn't figure out what would have caused her to react the way she had. As far as he knew, she'd gotten along with Rebecca even though she'd been a grade behind them.

"Why are you telling us this *now*?" Melanie asked softly, her gaze darting between him and Adrianne.

Given Adrianne's reaction to the first bomb he'd dropped, Alex wasn't sure she could handle a second one. Unfortunately, he had no choice because, at the end of the day, he was going to be bringing his son to their home.

"Well, this morning, a young man showed up and said he was my son." It was strange...up until that point in his life, Alex had never really understood the saying *so quiet you could hear a pin drop.*

Melanie reached out to lay a hand on Adrianne's arm as she looked at him. "Where is he?"

"In the lunchroom," Alex said, recalling the last time he'd checked in on the boy. He'd been staring out the window, his tablet clutched in his lap. Though Jordan had assured him he was fine, Alex had seen the apprehension and worry in the young man's eyes. "Would you like to meet him?"

Though Adrianne didn't say anything, Melanie nodded her head. "I would."

When she got to her feet, she grabbed Adrianne's hand and pulled her up as well. Alex couldn't help but wonder about his twin's reaction to his news. Melanie was definitely taking it all in stride, but Adrianne...he had no idea what was going on in her head. No doubt she was hurt that he'd kept a secret like this from her for so long. But now was not the time to deal with his regrets. He'd lived with them for years...a little while longer wouldn't make any difference.

As the three of them made a silent exit from his office, Lynne glanced up but didn't say anything. Alex lifted his hand so she could see his phone, and she nodded her understanding.

When they reached the lunch room, he spotted Jordan in the same place he'd left him earlier. Thankfully, the room was otherwise empty. Not that that was too surprising since the only ones who used it were those on the executive floor and most only came to get fresh coffee.

The boy's eyes widened as he took in their approach, and he quickly got to his feet, pressing his back to the window he'd been looking out of.

Alex held out a hand to reassure him and smiled. "Jordan, I'd like you to meet my sisters."

Jordan's gaze darted to the women on either side of him. Alex had no idea what was going through his teenage mind, but the confidence he'd had earlier seemed to be slipping away.

It didn't surprise Alex that the first person to move was Melanie. She walked toward Jordan and held out her hand. "Hi, Jordan. I'm Melanie. It's nice to meet you."

Jordan stared at Melanie for a long moment before taking her hand and shaking it. "Uh, nice to meet you too. I didn't know I had an aunt." His gaze slid to Adrianne. "Aunts."

"That's Adrianne," Melanie said with a wave of her hand. "She's actually your dad's twin sister."

"Twins?" Jordan asked, his eyes widening briefly.

"Yep," Melanie said as she stepped to his side and slid her

arm through his. "She's just a little shocked at your dad's news. We had no idea about you."

"Yeah, I didn't know about him—or you—either," Jordan said, shifting from one foot to another but apparently not too uncomfortable with Melanie's nearness because he didn't pull away from her.

"Are you hungry?" Melanie asked. "It's almost lunch time."

Jordan glanced at Alex and then back at Melanie before giving a quick nod. "A little."

"How about you come with me to the deli for some lunch? I think Adrianne and your dad need to talk for a little bit." Melanie motioned to his backpack. "You can leave your stuff here if you want. It'll be safe."

"Okay. I'll just bring my phone."

Alex felt a sense of relief as he watched Melanie take over the situation. At least, Jordan was in good hands. He had a feeling that Adrianne was going to be the first of many difficult conversations he was going to have over the next few days.

"I think we're going to go snag Tyler to come with us," Melanie said to Alex as they walked past. "We'll come back up here when we're done, but phone if you need us back sooner."

"Let's go talk in private," Alex said once it was just him and Adrianne.

She nodded and walked in silence beside him as they made their way back to his office. He shut the door behind them and then went to his chair while she sat down across from him.

"Why didn't you ever tell me?" Adrianne asked as soon as he sat down. Her expression gave away nothing of what was going on in her head.

Alex let out a sigh. "There was so much going on back then. We were all still trying to recover from Melanie's kidnapping. We'd been quietly dating for a while, and after she had graduated, when we realized I was being sent overseas, we decided to elope."

"But I don't understand. It's been years. Why haven't we heard about it before this?"

"Because I did something incredibly stupid. Horrible, in fact."

Adrianne tilted her head. "Did you cheat on her?"

"No." Alex looked away from his sister, not eager to see the disappointment his revelation would surely bring to her face. "When she let me know she was pregnant, I told her to get rid of it."

"Oh, Alex." Adrianne's voice was low, her eyes sorrowful.

The ache that had finally dulled over the years exploded into a breath-robbing pain. He rubbed his chest. "She told me she'd take care of it, then about a month later, after not hearing from her at all, I got a letter saying she couldn't be with a man like me. A man who could so easily dismiss proof of our love. A life we had created together." He paused. "She was right, so when she disappeared, I didn't try to find her. She was definitely better off without the man I was back then."

"So you never got a divorce?"

Alex shook his head. "I didn't know where she was. I suppose I could have found her—especially once we got BlackThorpe up and running—but, honestly, I had no desire to date or remarry, so I just put it out of my mind. If she'd served me with divorce papers, I would have signed them, but for whatever reason, she didn't."

"So what happens now? Does Rebecca know he's here?"

"Yep. We had a brief conversation this morning." Alex leaned back in his chair. "She's going to be here tomorrow."

Adrianne's eyebrows rose at that announcement. "Oh boy."

"Yeah, exactly. Jordan can stay with me tonight, but I'm

not sure where Rebecca will want to stay when she gets here."

"Do you want me and Melanie to get the apartment set up?"

"Could you? I know you're busy too, but I have appointments all day and no time to arrange for anything."

"What about Jordan? Is he just going to hang here?"

Alex let out a sigh. "I'm sure he'll be bored out of his mind here waiting for me to finish. I've cleared my schedule for tomorrow, but there's nothing I can do about today."

Adrianne got to her feet. Whatever her reservations were from earlier, they seemed to have been forgotten. "Leave it to Melanie and me. We'll take care of him. Just be home in time for supper."

Alex pushed up from his chair, rubbing a hand over his face. "Just one thing...no Mom or Dad just yet, okay?"

Adrianne gave a huff. "Yeah, that goes without saying."

Once she'd left, Alex sat in the quiet of his office still trying to wrap his mind around everything that was going on. He prayed that he'd have the wisdom to deal with Rebecca. He knew better than anyone that he really didn't deserve this opportunity to get to know the child he'd rejected. He had no doubt Rebecca would see it that way as well. But now there was Jordan, wanting to get to know his father—worthy or not. And underneath the guilt he carried there was a part of him that cried out to be allowed to have this second chance at fatherhood.

He only hoped that Rebecca would give it to him and that he was up to the challenge.

Rebecca pressed a hand to her stomach as the plane touched down at the Minneapolis-St. Paul airport. She hadn't been back to the Twin Cities since the day her family had left fifteen years ago. There had been absolutely nothing to draw her back in the years since, but today there was.

She'd texted Jordan to let him know what time she was arriving then asked him where he was staying so she could rent a car and get to him. He'd replied that he was staying with Alex but hadn't gotten back to her with the address before she'd boarded the plane. Hopefully, there would be a message waiting when she got off the plane. If all else failed, she would go to the BlackThorpe offices.

The plane had barely come to a jerking halt at the gate when people surged out of their seats and into the aisle. Rebecca considered joining them but then decided she was in no rush. Instead, she pulled out her phone, hoping to see a text from Jordan once she was connected again. Unfortunately, nothing popped up.

Hey, sweetie! Still need an address so I can figure out where I'm going. Xoxo

She kept an eye on the queue of people in the aisle as she waited for his reply. Once the doors opened, the line began to move forward, but Rebecca stayed in her seat, her laptop bag and purse on her lap.

There was still no message by the time the line of people had thinned out. With a sigh, Rebecca slid the phone into her purse and got to her feet. Mentally she began to make a plan as she walked up the jetway.

Get her bag.

Rent a car.

Find a hotel to stay at.

Look up the address for BlackThorpe.

Go get her son.

And see her husband for the first time in fifteen years.

Rebecca closed her eyes briefly. She could have done without that reminder. Gripping her laptop bag handle more tightly, she looked around for information on getting to the baggage claim. It wasn't long before she had exited the secure part of the terminal and was on the escalator to go down one floor.

As she stepped off the escalator and began to head in the direction of the baggage claim, she heard a familiar voice.

"Mom!"

Spinning around, Rebecca spotted Jordan heading toward her. Relief swamped her to see that he was okay—even though she'd reassured herself countless times that he was. As he got close, she set her laptop bag down and wrapped her arms around him, hugging him as tight as she could. Given how he'd been with her on the phone, she was a bit surprised—but very relieved—when he returned her hug.

She stepped back from him and gripped his face in her hands. He had gone through a growth spurt recently and now she found herself looking up at him. So many words tumbled through her head—things she wanted to say to him—but finally she just said, "I love you, sweetheart."

"Love you too, Mom."

As she stood there, relief coursing through her, the realization slowly came that if Jordan was here...so was Alex. The thought made her stomach clench, and she wondered briefly if she was going to be sick. Swallowing hard, she continued to look at Jordan as she gave herself a quick lecture.

I am not that eighteen-year-old girl who was in love with him. He told me to get rid of Jordan. Remember that. I no longer have stars in my eyes where he is concerned. He is not the man I thought he was.

Lifting her chin, Rebecca allowed her gaze to find Alex. He stood several feet away—obviously giving them space—watching them without any expression on his face. There was much that was still the same about him. His height. His piercing blue eyes. His square jaw.

But there were differences too. His hair, once buzzed short for the military, was now more clearly styled short on the sides and longer on top and was a darker blond than she remembered. He'd also bulked up. Even though he wore a leather jacket, she could see that. His lanky frame now seemed to carry more muscles than it once had. He wore a pair of dark blue jeans and a white collared shirt under his black jacket. Even though it was a somewhat casual outfit, there was an air of confidence and authority about him that he hadn't had before.

Rebecca bent to pick up her laptop bag and then watched as Alex walked toward them. She hoped that neither he nor Jordan could hear how her heart was pounding.

Alex kept his hands in the pockets of his jeans as he came to a stop beside Jordan. "Hello, Rebecca."

4

SEEING HER SON with his father was a surreal experience for Rebecca, and she had to fight to keep her focus on the conversation—such as it was. "Alex. There was no need for you to pick me up. I told Jordan I'd be renting a car."

"I know, but that's not necessary. We have a car that you can use."

We? As far as she knew, they were still married, but that didn't mean he wasn't in a relationship with another woman. "I'd really rather have my own car."

If Alex was frustrated by her response, he didn't show it. "How about we just get you out of here and once we talk a bit more, if you want to rent a vehicle, I'll make sure you get one."

Of course, he'd have that kind of control. Part of the

previous night had been spent googling Alex Thorpe, and what she'd read had been enlightening.

She glanced at Jordan and found him watching her expectantly. His expression seemed to want her to just go with the flow. Going with the flow was difficult though since she'd been the only one responsible for herself and Jordan since the day he'd been born. But she had to remind herself that there were likely bigger battles to be fought in the days ahead.

"Okay. Just let me get my bag and we can go."

Alex's brows drew together briefly, almost as if he'd been expecting an argument from her. Without saying anything more, Rebecca turned toward the baggage claim carousels and found the one for her flight. It was already circulating bags, and Rebecca spotted hers right away.

She handed her laptop bag to Jordan and stepped forward to lift the suitcase from the conveyor belt. After setting it upright, she pulled the handle up and turned to face Jordan and Alex. "This is all I have so we can go."

"Let me help you with that." Alex held out his hand to her, and Rebecca had a sudden memory of him doing that and of her slipping her hand into his.

She flashed him a quick smile that she hoped didn't look totally fake. "I'm fine, thanks."

Apparently he was also saving his arguments for the bigger battles because he just nodded and fell into step on Jordan's other side as they walked toward the exit. Thankfully, the weather was similar to what they were experiencing in Chicago so her jacket was sufficient.

"You can just wait here while I go get the truck," Alex said.

Rebecca wasn't even tempted to argue with him if it would give her a few minutes alone with Jordan. She watched as Alex walked away from them, his long strides confident.

Once he was out of earshot, Rebecca turned to Jordan. "Are you doing okay?"

"I'm doing great!" A big smile spread across Jordan's face. "The house where they live is amazing. It has an indoor pool, and he has a gym and everything."

"Who are *they*?" Rebecca asked, letting curiosity get the better of her.

"Alex, Adrianne, and Melanie. They live in a really big house."

Rebecca recognized the names of Alex's sisters. "They all live together?"

Jordan nodded. "It's super cool. Plus they have a place for you to stay as well."

"That's where you stayed last night?"

"I slept on the couch in Alex's rooms. Then today, we went and got furniture and stuff for the place where we can stay now that you're here."

"You're going to stay with me?" Rebecca asked.

Jordan shrugged. "Alex said it would be better if I did. But the apartment is right next to the house so I can see him when I want."

Rebecca wasn't sure she was happy staying that close to Alex for her own sanity, but she was grateful to have Jordan with her. If that was the price she had to pay to have her son back with her, she'd pay it. For now.

When Alex pulled up in a big black truck a few minutes later, it still felt like it was far too soon for Rebecca. She could have gone another ten years without seeing him instead of just ten minutes.

Once he stopped the truck, he hopped out and came around to put her bags in the back seat and then held the front door open for her. Jordan climbed into the back behind the driver's seat. Rebecca looked over her shoulder at him as she snapped her seat belt into place and saw the excitement on the teenager's face. Clearly he loved his father's mode of transportation.

If Rebecca had been worried about holding a conversation with Alex, she needn't have been. Jordan was more than happy to fill the silence with a report of all he'd done with Alex and his sisters since he'd been with them. After her little date with Google the night before, Rebecca was aware that Alex wasn't the only Thorpe who worked for BlackThorpe Security. And she was also aware that there was a fair amount of wealth attributed to Alex as one of the founding partners of the company.

Not that she was poor by any stretch of the imagination. She'd worked hard at each of the jobs she'd had and been frugal with their money. But she was a single parent so she'd always tried to live on the cautious side financially. She could have afforded a bigger house in a nicer neighborhood and a fancier car, but in the back of her mind, she always cautioned herself that should something ever happen where she couldn't work for an extended period of time, she needed a nest egg. And so she'd focused on building that instead of buying more expensive things that they didn't really need.

Though Rebecca tried to stay engaged in the conversation with Jordan, it was hard. Each time she turned to make a comment about something he said, she had to look past Alex and, way too frequently, her gaze snagged on his profile.

Rebecca watched familiar sights go by as they headed out onto the highway. She had no idea where Alex lived now but was pretty sure it wasn't anywhere near where they used to live. Her house had been just three blocks from where Alex had lived with his family. She was a bit surprised to hear that he still lived with his sisters.

There was no denying that she had some nerves over meeting the two women again. Melanie had been a few years younger than her so they hadn't spent much time together. Adrianne had seemed friendly though reserved whenever she'd been around her, and after Alex had left for basic training and then his first posting, she hadn't seen her at all.

What would they think of her having kept Jordan from their family all these years? Had Alex told them the truth?

Rebecca pressed the palms of her hands to her thighs to stop the slight tremor that had started up at the thought of what was about to unfold whether she wanted it to or not.

Alex only half-listened to what Jordan was saying. He'd heard most of it on the drive to the airport so he knew he wasn't missing much by not giving Jordan his complete attention. That was directed at the woman sitting in the passenger seat of his truck. It was a bit of a surreal situation, if Alex was honest with himself. It was also a scenario he'd never allowed himself to consider happening. And he was pretty sure he wasn't the only one.

Tension was radiating off Rebecca in waves. She'd barely moved except to glance back at Jordan occasionally. He could only imagine what was going through her mind...and imagine it was what he'd have to do because something told him she wasn't going to be sharing her innermost thoughts with him anytime soon.

The midday traffic wasn't too heavy so they reached the turnoff to the estate without too much delay. He pressed the button to open the gate as he approached it and then drove through, watching as it shut behind him.

"Isn't that cool, Mom?" Jordan said from the back seat. "The security around this place is sick."

"Is there a reason you have so much security?" Rebecca asked, the question clearly directed at him and not Jordan.

"We've had to upgrade our security in light of a few incidents that have happened recently," Alex said as he guided the truck along the curving driveway to the house.

"Is it safe for Jordan to be here?"

Alex glanced over at her. "I've gone over things with him and as long as he pays attention to what I've told him, he will be fine. Most of this is just a precaution."

"Is this part of the situation you said you couldn't leave?"

"Yes." Alex didn't bother to expand on things. He had a pretty good idea of how she'd react and he didn't really want to have that conversation in the truck with Jordan present. "The girls are at work for a couple more hours, so I'll show you where you'll be staying."

Jordan was quick to exit the truck when it came to a stop, but Rebecca didn't move at all. With a sigh, Alex turned toward her.

"Stay here for tonight. If it's still abhorrent in the morning, I'll drive you to the nearest hotel."

When she turned her gaze to his, it was all Alex could do to keep his mind in the present. Her blue-green eyes framed by long dark lashes threatened to pull him into the past. The past where those eyes had gazed at him with love. With devotion. With adoration. He never saw the look of horror that had no doubt filled them at his demand she end the pregnancy. The look she gave him now was reserved and revealed nothing else of what she was thinking.

"For tonight." She gave her head a jerky nod then turned to pull the handle to open the door.

By the time he got around to the other side of the truck, Jordan had the back door open and they were getting Rebecca's bags out. Jordan seemed to be very excited to show his mom the studio apartment he'd worked with Melanie and Adrianne to prepare.

It had surprised him—even though it probably shouldn't have—how well Jordan had gotten along with his aunts. Melanie, in particular, had jumped into the role of aunt with both feet. At dinner the night before, Jordan had happily answered all the questions she and Tyler had about his life. He supposed he should have been the one asking the questions, but he was still just trying to adjust to the idea of *having* a son.

"It's up here, Mom," Jordan said as he led the way toward the set of stairs that ran to the second floor of the garage.

The small apartment above the garage had been one part of the estate that he hadn't paid too much attention to when he'd bought it. Instead, he'd focused on the main house, but Adrianne, Melanie, and Jordan had tackled it over the past twenty-four hours. Alex was kind of curious to see what they'd done with the place as he had just handed over his credit card and let them go to it.

As he followed Rebecca into the studio, Alex glanced around. Taking in the new furniture set up in the open area, he knew that his card had taken quite a hit. Where there had once been only dusty, empty space, there was now a brand spankin' new couch, love seat, recliner and a dining room set. He moved further into the room and added another thousand dollars to the total in his head when he saw the large flat screen hanging on the wall.

He could only imagine what they'd spent to fix up the bedroom. Alex suddenly found his mind flooded with images he hadn't thought of in a very long time. Images that would not help the current situation and certainly had no place in his mind even if Rebecca was still technically his wife.

Taking a deep breath, Alex focused instead on Jordan's words as he showed his mother around.

Rebecca tried not to be impressed by the cozy one bedroom apartment. Jordan was so excited for the part he'd played in picking out the furniture with his aunts. He had never really struck her as the type of teenage boy who was all that interested in furniture. She was going to chalk it up to him enjoying spending time with his newly discovered aunts.

"We even put a desk in the bedroom in case you needed to do work while you were here," Jordan said, waving his hand in the direction of a doorway on the other side of the apartment.

His mention of work brought to mind her new release. On a normal release day, she would be monitoring the book's sales. Posting to social media about the book being available. It would have had her total focus. It was one of the reasons why, when Jordan had asked to spend a couple of days with his friend, she had readily agreed. He knew how focused she got during those new release days and he'd used it to his advantage.

She turned to Jordan, watching as he talked to Alex about how Melanie had sweet-talked more than one sales person into giving them rush delivery on the furniture. His face was animated in a way she hadn't seen recently. And there was no denying the admiration on his face for Alex. His father.

Which reminded her...

"Jordan?"

He swung around to face her. "What?"

"How did you find out about Alex?"

The question drew Alex's attention. He crossed his arms and stared at Jordan, his jaw firm.

Jordan's gaze dropped to the floor as he shuffled his feet. "Robby and I were boarding at the park when this kid came up and gave me an envelope. He said he'd been asked to deliver it to me."

"By whom?" Alex was the one who asked this time.

"He didn't say." Jordan's gaze shot to Alex and then to her. "I'd never seen the kid. He was about our age, but I didn't recognize him from the neighborhood."

"Did you ask him for any details about the guy?"

Jordan looked at Alex. "No. I didn't realize I needed to ask about that. I didn't know what was in the envelope yet."

"What *was* in the envelope?" Rebecca asked.

"It said something like *your father is Alex Thorpe* and then gave the address for BlackThorpe Security."

"Did you keep the letter?"

Jordan nodded. "It's in my backpack."

"I need to see that letter," Alex said. He nodded his head toward the door. "Let's go get it while your mother settles in." He looked over at her. "We'll be back in a bit. Or if you want, you can come to the main house when you're settled."

"I'll come over when I've unpacked."

Alex gave a quick nod of his head and then turned to leave. Jordan glanced at her, his hands shoved in his pockets. "I'll see you in a few."

Alone in the apartment, Rebecca took a deep breath and then let it out slowly. She stood in the middle of the room for a moment, letting the stress of the day slip away with Alex's departure.

She had done it. She'd faced Alex after fifteen years and hadn't dissolved into a puddle of conflicting emotions. It helped that Alex hadn't shown any emotion when he'd seen her for the first time. It was almost like meeting a total stranger. And yet they weren't strangers at all. Because of their marriage, he knew her in a way no one else did. And back then, even if he presented a stern, emotionless face to the world, his expression had always softened when he looked at her. He made her feel special in a way no one else had.

But today, from the moment she'd seen him, she'd been the recipient of his "other people" face anytime he looked at her. She was angry by how much that hurt. After all these years, he shouldn't be able to make her feel that way. But he was the only one who had ever looked at her like that and now that she was with him again, she found herself missing it even though she knew she shouldn't.

Rebecca pulled her shoulders back and gave her head a shake. She reached for the handle of her suitcase and pulled it toward the bedroom. Pausing in the doorway, she took in the surprisingly large bedroom. There was a queen size bed with a white wrought iron frame against the far wall between two tall windows that were covered with lacy curtains. Sunlight cast a dappled pattern on the hardwood floor.

There was a large comfortable-looking arm chair in the corner with a table and tall lamp next to it. The wall beside it had another large window with a desk underneath it. She spotted two other doors and assumed they led to a closet and possibly a bathroom. It was a beautifully decorated room and very similar to her room in their house in Chicago. Had Jordan kept that in mind when they'd gone shopping for furniture?

She lifted the suitcase and laid it on the bed, leaning forward to grasp the zipper. Once open, she lifted a stack of clothes out and went to one of the doors. Nice bathroom with a large tub and shower. The other door opened into a walk-in closet to die for. Places for shoes. Drawers for clothes. Lots of places to hang things.

Rebecca paused before opening a drawer and setting the stack of T-shirts inside it. She hadn't really thought how long she'd stay. Looking at how the apartment was furnished, it was hard not to wonder if Jordan was hoping she'd feel so comfortable she wouldn't mind staying as long as he wanted.

The truth was, she could stay indefinitely. Her work was portable as long as she had her laptop and internet access. Even Jordan could do his school work here since it was primarily online. But just because their lifestyle allowed them flexibility in when they returned to Chicago, it didn't mean she wanted to stay any longer than necessary.

Abandoning her suitcase, Rebecca walked over to one of the windows beside the bed. A forest of trees greeted her as she looked out. Some were bare—their leaves gone with the start of winter—and others—the evergreens—still had thick green branches. It appeared that Minneapolis had as little snow as Chicago. The gray sky above the trees, however, seemed to promise an end to the snowless state of the city.

Rebecca ran her hands up and down her arms as a sudden chill swept over her. She couldn't allow herself to get comfortable here. This was not her life. This was not Jordan's life. Their lives were back in Chicago. And with Christmas coming, she wanted to be in her own home. Not that they'd decorated or anything for the coming holiday. That had been on her to-do list once her book had been published. Her plan had been to do minimal writing during the month of December so she could focus on Jordan and Christmas.

It would be just the two of them this year. Her parents were in Germany spending six months with her younger sister who'd met her German husband online and promptly moved there to be with him. There was a slight possibility Connor would be able to get some time off to spend Christmas with them, but he hadn't been certain. He'd been maddeningly evasive about making plans to be with them.

With a sigh, Rebecca turned from the window and ran a hand through her hair, gathering it into her fist. She just had to get through this day and then she'd have a better idea of what the next few days might look like. But first, she needed to finish unpacking so they didn't come looking for her.

5

ALEX TOOK THE envelope Jordan held out to him. He was careful to grip just at the very edge of it. No doubt the person who had given it to Jordan hadn't been sloppy enough to leave prints, but at this point, he wasn't going to take the chance of messing it up on the off chance that he had.

He looked at it, taking in Jordan's name on the front but nothing else. Though he wanted to read the message inside, Alex laid the envelope down on the table instead. He needed to get it to the office to have them look it over. His gut instinct told him this was another attack by the person who had targeted BlackThorpe in the past. It hadn't been as damaging as previous attacks, but maybe the person behind it had hoped the revelation would wreak havoc on his life. However, while the timing wasn't great since his focus was needed on the situation with Alana and Justin, it hadn't been the negative impact the man had likely hoped it would be.

Or at least, it hadn't been for him. Likely Rebecca had a completely different view of the latest turn of events.

"Wanna go for a ride to the office?" Alex asked Jordan.

The boy's eyes lit up as he nodded but then his brow furrowed. "What about Mom?"

"Go see if she wants to come with us. I'll meet you back here in ten minutes." Alex waited until Jordan darted out the front door before heading up to his rooms to change. Even though he'd taken the day off, he still felt compelled to show up in a suit in case he was needed for something.

Thankfully, it was only mid-afternoon so the people they'd need to see would be at the office. Still, Alex didn't want to delay getting there too long. After grabbing his briefcase from his desk, Alex went back downstairs. Jordan and Rebecca weren't there yet, so he went into the kitchen and grabbed a large plastic bag. He slid the envelope inside and then put it in his briefcase.

"Mom will be here in a minute."

Alex glanced over his shoulder to see that Jordan had returned. "Do you want to grab a jacket?"

Jordan nodded then took the stairs two at a time before disappearing into Alex's suite where he'd spent the previous night. As Alex shrugged into his own coat, the doorbell rang. Figuring it had to be Rebecca, he opened the door.

"You don't need to ring the doorbell," Alex said as he stepped back and motioned for her to come inside. "I'll give you the code for the lock."

Rebecca hesitated just inside the door, still wearing the black pants and gray jacket with a turquoise scarf she'd had on earlier. Her gaze circled the room before it met his. Once again, all he could focus on was that her beautiful eyes had lost the trusting adoration they'd once had when she looked at him. But he had no one to blame but himself for that.

The sound of heavy, rapid footsteps drew Alex's attention. He looked over to see Jordan heading down the stairs toward them with energy only a teenage boy could have. The kid's gaze moved between him and Rebecca, a hopeful expression on his face and, for the first time, it dawned on Alex that perhaps Jordan was looking for a family. Not just a father.

Alex hated to think that he would see disappointment on that face in the not—too—distant future. After all, he knew his future didn't include Rebecca even if they were technically still married. In fact, now that they had reconnected, he figured it was only a matter of time before he was served with divorce papers.

"So why are we going to the office?" Rebecca asked a few minutes later as he guided the truck around the circular driveway and out to the gate.

"We've been having some...issues at BlackThorpe recently. In light of that, I find this revelation of my identity to Jordan to be a bit suspicious. I want to check the letter Jordan received for fingerprints. It's a long shot, I'll admit, but there's always a chance."

"And these issues have involved revealing secrets from people's pasts?"

"Not all of them, no. But the last one did, which makes it plausible that this is another targeted attack on the company." Alex glanced at the rear view mirror and saw Jordan watching him. "I'm going to have to fingerprint Jordan so that they will know to exclude those prints from any they do find on the envelope and letter."

Jordan grinned when he heard that and Alex couldn't help but grin back. It probably did sound exciting to a teen. Alex supposed he was lucky that the first time his son was being fingerprinted, it wasn't for a crime.

Jordan spent the remainder of the trip asking questions about the process. Alex was happy to answer them, remembering when he'd been Jordan's age, curious about so many things.

The guards didn't hesitate to wave them through the gate, and the security guys waiting in the building's foyer gave barely discernible nods when Alex lifted a hand in their direction before escorting Jordan and Rebecca to the elevator. The curious looks started when they stepped out on the executive floor.

"Hi, Kelsey. Is Eric in?" Alex asked as they approached her desk.

"He sure is," Kelsey said with a wide smile, her gaze going past him to Rebecca and Jordan.

"Thanks." Alex turned and motioned for them to follow him. Thankfully, they didn't meet anyone else as they made their way down the hall towards Eric's corner office.

"Hey, Alex," Eric said when they appeared in his doorway.

"Hey." Alex stepped aside so Jordan and Rebecca could come into the office with him. "How's Staci doing? Pregnancy treating her well?"

Eric grinned as he got to his feet. "Once she got past the first trimester, things definitely got better. Hopefully, it will be smooth sailing from here on out."

"Is Sarah excited about becoming a big sister?"

"Oh, yes. It's all she talks about these days." His gaze went to Rebecca and Jordan then back to Alex. "I see we have some company."

"Yes," Alex said as he motioned to them. "This is Rebecca McKenzie and...our son, Jordan."

Eric's eyes widened but to his credit, he didn't allow his smile to falter as he held out his hand, first to Rebecca then to Jordan. "Nice to meet you. I'm Eric McKinley."

As briefly as he could, Alex explained the situation. "Can you scan Jordan's fingerprints and then run a scan of all the other prints on the envelope and letter. I'm thinking the guy might be using this situation in much the same way he used the information on Alana's ex-husband, only to slightly different results."

Eric nodded. "Definitely a possibility." His brow furrowed. "Hopefully, this particular scenario is now at an end."

Alex nodded, understanding Eric's concerns. "Jordan and Rebecca are staying at the estate with me and the girls so they'll be safe."

"Good." He turned his attention back to Jordan. "Why don't you come here, Jordan?"

"We can sit down," Alex said to Rebecca, gesturing to a couple of chairs next to Eric's desk.

Rebecca stayed quiet over the next fifteen minutes as Eric talked Jordan through what he was doing. He patiently answered all the teenager's questions even though Alex knew that it lengthened the process considerably. Alex was pretty sure the man's unending supply of patience came from his dealings with his own child.

Alex fought the urge to fill the silence between them. Thankfully, it wasn't too awkward since Eric and Jordan's conversation kept it from being completely quiet. Rebecca didn't even glance his way once. She just sat there, dressed in the same outfit she'd used for traveling, legs crossed, hands folded in her lap. Though she still had long hair, it wasn't as long as it had been when they'd married. So many small flashes of memory of the young woman she used to be kept coming to mind as she sat beside him. The young woman who had been his wife.

Alex leaned forward, pulling his cell phone from an inner pocket of his suit coat. He needed to have Rebecca out of his direct line of sight. Her presence was taking him back to a time he'd avoided for a very long time. So much had happened between then and now. Things that had changed them both from the people they'd been back when they'd said their vows. Letting those memories and emotions surface would only serve to muddy waters that Alex needed clear.

Clearing his throat, Alex got to his feet. "I'm just going to see Adrianne for a minute. I'll be right back."

That got Rebecca's attention, and she looked toward him. "Do we just wait here?"

"Yes. I won't be long."

Once out of Eric's office, Alex exhaled deeply and headed in the direction of Adrianne's. If anyone could talk him out of these emotions, it would be his twin. Unlike Melanie, who had embraced his marriage and having a son as something wonderful, Adrianne had been more reserved and not nearly as accepting.

He knocked on the door frame then stepped into her office. Adrianne glanced up from her monitor, her brows lifting when she saw him. "What are you doing here?"

Alex paused before turning to close her door. He sank down into a chair across the desk from her. "I came in to have Jordan fingerprinted. He was given a note that told him that I was his father and where to find me. I want Eric to run the prints on the envelope and letter to see if we get any hits. He needed Jordan's in order to exclude them."

Adrianne nodded as she leaned back in her chair. "That doesn't explain why you're *here*, sitting on a chair in my office."

Trust his sister to cut to the chase. "Just needed a break."

"Having a little trouble dealing with the wife?" Adrianne asked, her tone tinged just slightly with sarcasm.

Alex tilted his head. "What exactly do you have against Rebecca? I thought you got along with her okay."

Adrianne's gaze slipped away but one blink and she was looking at him again. "It's not really Rebecca I have a problem with."

"Jordan?"

Adrianne shook her head. "Definitely not. I would just prefer that their presence in our lives not bring Connor around."

Alex's eyebrows shot up. "Connor? Why?"

"Let's just say that we had a difference of opinion, and I'd be happy to never see him again."

Alex wanted to press for more details, grateful for the chance to focus on something instead of his messed up life, but he needed to get back to Eric's office. "Want to come see Rebecca?"

After a quick glance at her monitor, Adrianne nodded and got to her feet. "Sure. Why not?"

Rebecca shifted on the chair. She glanced at the open

doorway, wondering when Alex would be back. Eric seemed friendly enough, and Jordan was having a blast with the process of being fingerprinted and then having his hand scanned so he could get into BlackThorpe without any issues, but she was on edge. Eric offered to scan her hand as well, but Rebecca had politely declined. She didn't intend to be around long enough to be making regular trips to this building.

"Well, hey guys."

Eric's greeting had Rebecca turning to see that Alex had returned with a pretty woman at his side. Was this Adrianne? She didn't look like Rebecca remembered from fifteen years ago. That Adrianne had been on the heavier side with a bad case of acne and badly permed hair. She'd been reserved, more likely to be seen with her head ducked down.

This woman was none of those things. Her figure still seemed to be more on the curvy than slender side, but her skin was flawless and her blonde hair was straight and hung in a highlighted curtain past her shoulders. But the most stunning thing about the woman was the confidence with which she held herself. Observing her standing next to Alex, Rebecca could see the similarities between them in a way she hadn't been able to before.

Rebecca got to her feet as Jordan approached Adrianne, a smile on his face. "Hey, Aunt Adrianne. I just got my hand scanned."

The tension in Adrianne's expression eased as she smiled up at Jordan. Yep, *up*. Rebecca almost smiled herself. Even though Alex was tall, Adrianne was on the short side. Jordan stood about four or five inches taller than his aunt. Rebecca figured it was only a matter of time before he was towering over her as well. At the moment, he only had a couple of inches on her own five foot six inch height.

"Rebecca, you remember Adrianne?" Alex's words drew her attention from Jordan.

"Yes. Of course." She approached them and held out her hand. The tension had returned to Adrianne's face and though she took her hand and gave it a firm shake, her blue eyes looked at Rebecca from behind a pair of glasses, reservation clear in her gaze.

"Nice to see you again," Adrianne said.

Rebecca was fairly certain the woman was lying though she had no idea why.

"Are we done here, Eric?" Alex stood with his hands on his hips, his long coat pushed back.

"Sure thing." He lifted his hand with his cell phone grasped in it. "But if you do not want to face the curious masses, you might want to beat a hasty retreat."

"Alex, my man!"

Rebecca watched as Alex rolled his eyes. He slipped his arm around Adrianne's waist to move her to the side as he stepped back. "Hey there, Than."

"Thought you were off today." A man wearing a suit much like the two guys came to a stop next to Alex. He looked at Rebecca, curiosity blatant in his brown eyes, and the corner of his mouth quirked up. "And who do we have here?"

Rebecca looked at Alex. This was his territory.

"Than, this young man is my son, Jordan MacKenzie, and this is his mother, Rebecca." Alex motioned to Than. "This is Than Miller. He's part of the BlackThorpe administrative team."

Rebecca glanced over when she heard Adrianne start to laugh.

"Not often I see that look on your face, Than. Sure wish I'd had my phone."

"No worries," Eric said with a chuckle. "I captured the moment on mine."

Than turned to Alex. "Your son? Wow. Never saw that one coming." He seemed to recover and held his hand out to Rebecca and then Jordan. "It's a great pleasure to meet you guys." Then he clapped Alex on the shoulder. "Well, congratulations, man. First Eric and Sarah and now you and Jordan. Wonder what Marcus is hiding. Wait. Does Marcus know about him?"

"No, not yet."

"You might want to clue him in before office gossip reaches him. You're lucky that his head is buried in the sand at the moment so that nothing is probably registering right now."

Alex's head dropped briefly before he nodded. "We're going there after this."

Than's expression sobered. "No more news, just to let you know."

"How's Justin today?"

"Pretty much the same."

"I'll give him a call later."

"They've arranged a twenty-four hour prayer vigil for Alana at their church."

Sadness seemed to have saturated the features of the four BlackThorpe employees and the air was heavy with it.

Alex sighed. "Please send a company-wide email notifying everyone about it once you have all the details. I know there will be some who will want to attend."

"Will do." Than turned to Rebecca and smiled though the teasing look of earlier was gone. "It was a pleasure to meet you. Hope to see you again."

Once Than had left them, Alex turned to her. "Do you mind making one more stop before leaving here? I'd like to introduce you to my partner."

Rebecca nodded, though in some ways it felt like a waste of time to meet these people when she'd probably never see them again once things were settled between her and Alex.

"Let me know what turns up when you scan the prints," Alex said to Eric before ushering them out of his office. Adrianne stayed with them as they returned the way they'd come earlier but then stopped at a desk next to a closed door. The woman there smiled up at them as Alex said, "Is Marcus available?"

A momentary flash of panic ripped the smile off the woman's face. "I uh...I'm not sure."

Was her hand actually trembling as she reached for the phone sitting on her desk?

Alex waved his hand in the air. "Don't worry about it. If he's busy, I'll take the blame for barging in."

The relief that swept over the woman was palpable. "Thank you."

Alex moved forward without hesitation and swung the door open. "Hey, Marcus. You got a minute?"

When Adrianne didn't move any closer to the door, Rebecca also stayed put, her hand on Jordan's arm. She got a weird feeling that they were bearding the lion in his den.

There was a mumbled reply then Alex turned back around and motioned them forward.

The lingering look of fear on the receptionist's face made Rebecca pause. Who exactly was behind the door that instilled such a reaction in the young woman?

"Marcus's bark is worse than his bite, but he still manages to scare away every receptionist we find for him," Adrianne said, her voice low.

Rebecca glanced over at her. He couldn't be too bad if the other woman hadn't abandoned them yet. Slowly, she followed Adrianne and Jordan into the large office.

A man pushed himself up from behind the massive desk that dominated the room. He had dark hair and stood about as tall as Alex. When his piercing gaze landed on her, Rebecca had to fight the urge to step back.

"Marcus, I wanted to introduce a couple of people to you," Alex said as he approached the desk. Clearly, the intense look on the man's face didn't deter *him*. "This is my son, Jordan and his mother, Rebecca MacKenzie."

As the introduction registered with her, Rebecca realized that he never introduced her as his wife even though, technically, he could. She had to admit that she appreciated his discretion with regards to their marriage. Such as it was. Jordan didn't even know that they had been married. Or that they still were.

"Your son?" The man's dark brows drew together over a set of light blue eyes. His gaze went from Alex to Jordan and then to Rebecca.

"Jordan. Rebecca. This is Marcus Black." So this was the Black part of BlackThorpe, Rebecca realized. Business partners.

Marcus rounded his desk and held out his hand to her first then to Jordan. "Pleasure to meet you." He turned back to Alex. "You've been holding out on me, my friend."

"I'll give you a call a bit later to bring you up to speed."

Marcus gave a quick nod of his head. "I'm meeting Bryson Davis this afternoon for an update."

From comments made since they had arrived at the office and the tension in the air, Rebecca wondered what was going on. Would Alex tell her if she asked or would he just say it wasn't any of her business?

"We can head back to the house," Alex said as they left Marcus's office. "Unless you need to stop somewhere, Rebecca."

"No, I don't need anything."

He turned to Adrianne. "See you at home later."

"You cooking supper?" Adrianne asked with a grin.

"Something like that. I assume Melanie and Tyler will be there too."

"Yep. And you're going to have to plan something with Mom and Dad soon. You know they won't be happy if you keep this from them for too long."

Rebecca's hands clenched. She hadn't really thought much about Alex's parents. Jordan's grandparents. Years ago they had been friendly if a bit distant the couple times she'd met them as part of the group of friends who'd gone to the Thorpe home. No doubt they wouldn't be happy to discover that they had a grandchild that they hadn't had the opportunity to get to know. She really hoped that—once they got over whatever their reaction was—that they would be good grandparents to Jordan.

Goodness knows he wasn't really getting that from her parents. His major failing was that he hadn't been born to her younger sister, Cecilia. She knew that her parents' disappointment in her getting pregnant out of wedlock—or so they thought—and then refusing to name Jordan's father officially had damaged an already faltering relationship.

Her younger sister had been everything she wasn't. Even though Rebecca had gone on to have a successful career of her own, it didn't match up to Cecelia's life where she had the perfect businessman husband and three kids. Which was why she was facing another Christmas with just her and Jordan. And maybe Connor if he decided to show up.

Alex's gaze met hers. "We'll discuss that tonight and figure out how best to let them know."

It was made as a statement, but Rebecca nodded her agreement without argument. It was going to be the first of many things they would need to discuss. Even though everything in her just wanted to grab Jordan and catch the next flight back to Chicago, there was no going back to how things had once been. Back to when Alex was oblivious to Jordan's presence in the world. And Jordan had thought his father was dead.

Rebecca continued to hold her tongue as they made their way back to Alex's truck. Jordan more than filled the silence so she didn't have to say anything and that was just fine with her. She felt a bit like she was on a recon mission trying to gather all the information she could about the enemy. Enemy might be a strong word, but it was how she felt right then. Could they ever work together to raise their son? Even with their history between them?

As much as she knew in her head that the right thing to do was work things out so Alex could get to know his son, Rebecca would have liked to settle for limited contact. Jordan coming to the Twin Cities for a weekend every couple of months and spending a week or two with Alex during the summer. Unfortunately, she was fairly certain neither Alex nor Jordan would go for that.

So she played with scenarios in her head, testing out possibilities, weighing the pros and cons of each. It was like when she was writing and delving into the plot of a new story. Only now it was her life she was trying to plot out.

"Mom?"

"Hmm?" Rebecca turned in her seat so she could see Jordan.

"Um..." Jordan's brows drew together as he looked at Alex then dropped his gaze. "He asked you a question."

Rebecca looked at Alex. "Sorry. What did you say?"

He glanced over at her then focused back on the road. "I asked how Connor was doing."

"Last I talked to him, he was doing fine." Rebecca knew she needed to let her brother know what had transpired with Jordan. If her son hadn't already beaten her to the punch.

"What's he up to these days?"

"He's working as a civilian contractor with the DoD in the Middle East. He was in Iraq the last time I heard from him, but he was only on a temporary job. I think he was headed back to Afghanistan after that."

Alex shot her a surprised look. "Did Connor go into the military?"

"Yeah." Rebecca stared out the front window. "He did one semester of college and decided it wasn't for him so he went into the army, but after two terms, he decided not to re-enlist."

"Is he married?"

"Nope. He always said he was too involved with his job to do what was needed to sustain a serious relationship." And that hadn't made her parents any happier with him than they were with her.

"I'd love to reconnect with him," Alex said.

"I'll let him know." When silence followed her statement, she asked a question that had come to her while they'd been in Eric's office. "Was the situation with Alana the reason you couldn't come to Chicago?"

"Yes. Alana is the fiancée of one of our employees and she was kidnapped a few weeks ago."

"Kidnapped? Do they know who took her?"

"We have a pretty good idea." Alex's profile seemed to harden as she watched him. "We're just having trouble tracking him down. It's like they've vanished off the face of the earth."

"That's awful." Rebecca sat for a moment, staring at the traffic in front of them as she played back the different conversations that had gone on while they'd been at BlackThorpe. "Do you think that what happened with Jordan is somehow connected?"

"Not in the sense that it's connected to Alana's kidnapping. It's more that we've had someone targeting BlackThorpe for a while now. They tried to kidnap one of our employees while he was overseas, then we had a hacking attempt on our computer systems. The worst was when they infiltrated a training exercise and shot several of our team." He rubbed a hand against his thigh. "No one was killed, but it certainly took things to the next level. With the Alana situation—and with Jordan—whoever it is has started digging into the pasts of employees and their families. It's like he's trying to stir things up. We don't know why exactly except to maybe keep us distracted. They've definitely accomplished that with Alana's kidnapping. The whole company has been impacted by it."

"And now your life has been even more distracted by the revelation that Jordan is your son."

Alex glanced at her then looked back at the road. His Adam's apple moved as he swallowed. "To be honest, it's been the best sort of distraction. It's been a bright light in the midst of some really dark and difficult things. Whatever harm the person hoped to cause with this revelation never came." One more look at her. "At least for me."

Well, at least he was acknowledging that while this might be a great change of circumstances for him, it wasn't for her. "Are you worried about something worse happening?"

"Certainly that's in the back of all of our minds. This person has made it fairly clear the no one is off limits. And while we've always focused on the security of our buildings and our employees, we've increased all of that even more. That's why we have so many security features at the house. We've upgraded the fence and gate as well as installing perimeter alarms and several additional cameras. You and Jordan will be safe there, just don't go off without letting someone know where you're going."

Rebecca wanted to protest having to account for her movements but held her tongue.

"Oh, and just so you know up front, all the vehicles at the house have a GPS on them so we can track them if necessary."

As if to reinforce his comments about the security at the house, they pulled up to the gate and waited for it to open once he pressed a device attached to the visor in front of him.

"If you don't mind, I need to do a little work," Rebecca said when the truck came to a stop in front of the garage.

Alex nodded. "Jordan can come hang with me while we get supper ready."

Rebecca slid out of the truck into the crisp December air. Large flakes of snow were finally falling from the dark gray sky. She lifted her head to watch for a moment, loving the softness of it.

"See you in a bit," she said to Jordan before heading for the steps that led to where she would be staying.

6

WHAT ARE WE having for supper?" Jordan asked as they walked into the house.

Alex glanced at the boy as he took his coat off and hung it in the closet. "What do you think? Chicken? Steak?"

Jordan grinned. "Both?"

Remembering what it was like to be a teenage boy with a hollow leg, Alex smiled and nodded. "I think we can probably even barbecue."

"It's snowing," Jordan said with a wave of his hand to a nearby window.

"Hardly a skiff. It takes more than that to stop us from barbecuing," he said with a grin. "But first, I'm going to get out of this suit. I'll be right back."

Up in his room, Alex took his time changing out of his work clothes into worn jeans and a long sleeve T-shirt. He sat down on the end of his bed and stared out the large window across the room from him. As he let out a long breath, Alex wondered if he was actually in a dream.

He had a son? He was back in contact with Rebecca? How, in the space of less than forty-eight hours, had his life changed completely?

Unfortunately, with Jordan's arrival in his life, the guilt he'd carried for so long had an even stronger grip on him than ever. Every time he looked at Jordan he felt the guilt of having asked Rebecca to abort him. Every time he looked at Rebecca he felt guilt for not having been the husband he should have been to her.

Alex had never realized the full weight of that guilt until he stared into the bright blue eyes of his son. Even though he'd felt relief that Rebecca hadn't followed through on his demand, all he could think was that he'd brushed aside his son's life like it meant nothing. Over the years, he'd prayed and asked for forgiveness for his words and the intention behind them that he thought had led Rebecca to abort the baby. But still the guilt was there...for fifteen years it had always been there in his heart and mind, lingering, but now it was at the forefront of everything, crushing him.

He bent his head, closing his eyes, thankful in spite of the guilt. "Thank you, God. Thank you for preventing Rebecca from doing what I asked of her. Thank you for bringing Jordan into my life. I don't deserve to have a relationship with him, but I want one so much. Thank you."

Alex knew that there was still more required of him. He needed to ask Rebecca's forgiveness for what he'd asked her to do. And then there was the situation with their marriage. There was no way to ignore that, even if he kind of wanted to.

Alex got to his feet. For now, he'd focus on spending time with Jordan and trying to work out some sort of arrangement with Rebecca that would allow him to build a relationship with him.

Back in the kitchen, he found Jordan sitting at the counter on a stool, his head bent over his phone. He looked up when Alex walked in.

"Keeping in touch with your friends?" Alex asked as he crossed the kitchen to the fridge. He pulled out the chicken breasts and steaks that he'd asked Melanie to pick up the previous day.

"Just my best friend." Jordan shifted on the stool, a guilty look on his face.

Alex pulled out the ingredients for a marinade for the meat. "What's his name?"

"Robby." Jordan paused then said, "He's grounded right now. I kinda got him into trouble."

"How's that?"

Jordan flipped the phone over and over in his hands. "He helped me when I came here."

"He covered for you?" Alex put the meat in the marinade and slid it back in the fridge.

"Yeah. I feel bad about it. He can't use any of his gaming stuff this week."

Alex wondered if Rebecca wanted to punish Jordan for what had transpired in order for him to show up at the BlackThorpe office. At the very least, there had been some lying going on. While he was grateful for the end result, he supposed the process had to be addressed. He didn't want to step on Rebecca's toes in that area, but he would support her if she felt a punishment was in order.

"What do you two usually do together?" He pulled out a bag of potatoes and began to cut them up.

"We like to play basketball with some other guys from our church. The church has a gym so our moms reserve it once a week so we can play ball since we're homeschooled. We also like to play on our game consoles."

Jordan fell quiet, and when Alex glanced over, the boy's gaze was distant as he stared toward the window over the sink.

"What's on your mind?" Alex asked as he added olive oil and spices to the potatoes before moving on to cutting up some veggies.

Jordan didn't reply right away, causing Alex to look at

him again. His gaze met Jordan's as he waited for the teenager to say something.

"What happened with you and Mom?" Jordan asked, his words coming in a rush. "Why didn't you get married or at least stay together?"

Wow. Alex had known he'd have to answer the difficult questions sooner or later, but he'd been kinda hoping it would, at least, be after he and Rebecca had a chance to talk. He had no idea what she would want him to know. Did she want him to be aware of the fact that they were actually still married?

"I understand why you're curious about that, but I think it would be best to wait until the three of us can sit down and talk about it together. You, me and your mom." Alex rinsed his hands in the sink and reached for a towel to dry them off. "You know that status on Facebook that says *it's complicated*? Well, that definitely applies to this situation." He leaned against the counter across from Jordan. "I promise I'm not trying to shut you down. You have questions and you deserve answers, but I think it needs to be all of us together when we talk about it. What happened back then isn't just my story to tell, it's your mom's as well."

Jordan nodded though he didn't appear happy to not have the answers he wanted. "I don't think Mom is going to want to talk about it, though. I mean, she went all these years telling me my dad was dead. Why would she lie like that?"

Alex realized then why Rebecca might not be dishing out a punishment for Jordan. Inasmuch as he'd lied in order to come see Alex, Rebecca had been lying to him his whole life. But no matter how bad a picture it would paint of him, Jordan deserved to know the whole truth. Alex hoped that the revelations the boy so badly wanted wouldn't end up destroying their relationship before it had even started.

Rebecca stared at the email on the screen. Why was she hesitating? The only reason she hadn't pursued this sooner was because she hadn't wanted Alex to have a way to find out about Jordan. Since that was no longer a concern, there was no reason to put off filing for divorce. Hopefully, Alex would see the sense in it. She didn't want anything from him—including child support. All she wanted was a divorce from a man she no longer knew.

Pushing aside the lingering doubts, she pressed the send button and hoped that it wouldn't take too long for her lawyer to get back to her. She wasn't sure if he'd be the one to help her with this, but he'd helped her when she'd set up her publishing company so even if he couldn't handle the divorce, no doubt he knew someone who could.

Not wanting to dwell on it, she pushed away from her laptop and grabbed her phone. She might as well go see what was happening with Jordan. She took a few minutes to change out of her traveling clothes into a pair of jeans and a sweater that were more comfortable.

Though there was a crispness to the day, the light jacket Rebecca had pulled on was enough to keep her warm as she walked from the apartment to the house. She paused before punching in the four digit code Alex had given her earlier. The door opened without incident even though she'd been half expecting to set off blaring alarms and flashing lights.

She heard male voices coming from her left so followed the sound and found Jordan and Alex on opposite sides of the counter. The air was thick with tension, and Jordan sat with his shoulders hunched. As she got closer, Alex's gaze came up and met hers.

Rebecca laid a hand on Jordan's shoulder, not missing the way he tensed further. "What's up?"

Alex looked at her then back at Jordan. "He asked why we didn't get married or at least stay together. Why I didn't know about him."

Rebecca's stomach clenched. She'd known they would have to have this discussion, but she had hoped to talk with Alex first. "What did you tell him?"

Before Alex could answer, Jordan's head came up, and he twisted his shoulder out from under her hand. "He said that it was something the three of us needed to discuss together." He turned to look at her, his eyes blazing with hurt. "Are you guys planning to talk first so you can get your stories straight? Or are you actually going to tell me the truth for a change?"

"Jordan." Alex's tone was low but firm. "I know this is all very confusing for you, but you need to still speak to your mom with respect."

Jordan's head bent forward as he traced patterns on the counter with his fingers. "So, we're all here now. Can we talk about it?"

"No." Alex didn't even wait for Rebecca to say anything. "It's a discussion that needs to be had when we won't be interrupted by other things or people. Now is not the time."

"Whatever." Jordan got to his feet and grabbed his phone from the counter before stomping out of the kitchen.

Rebecca took a deep breath and let it out as Alex moved back to a pile of chopped vegetables. She watched him work in silence. His broad shoulders stretched out the T-shirt he wore, reminding her that he wasn't a lanky nineteen-year-old anymore.

Dragging her gaze from him, Rebecca sank down onto the stool her son had just vacated. She waited for Alex to say something, but he just continued to chop the vegetables. So many words tumbled around her head that wanted to be set free, but too many of them were words of accusation and would in no way lead to a productive discussion about their son.

In the end, the opportunity passed without her saying a word because of the arrival of two people she hadn't met yet.

"Hey!" A slender woman with short blonde hair and striking blue eyes smiled at her as they came into the kitchen. "You must be Rebecca. You might not remember me since I was only fourteen or so when we last met." She held out her hand. "I'm Melanie, and this is Tyler Harris."

The man with a headful of shaggy curls and a friendly smile stepped to Melanie's side and slid his arm around her waist as he held out his other hand to Rebecca. "Nice to meet you. We had a lot of fun with Jordan yesterday."

Rebecca returned their greeting, shaking their hands,

surprised that they were so welcoming considering her role in keeping Jordan from them. Had Alex given them all the details about everything that had happened back then? Had he acknowledged his part in what had transpired between them that had led to her keeping Jordan a secret?

After dropping a kiss on Melanie's cheek, Tyler left her side and approached Alex. "Can I help with anything?"

Alex glanced over at him from where he was putting vegetables onto sheets of tinfoil. "Want to start the barbecue for me?"

"Sure thing," Tyler said, apparently not at all surprised by the request even though there was snow on the ground. He headed toward a set of garden doors on the far side of the kitchen next to what looked like a breakfast nook. He hit a switch on the wall, and lights flooded a large deck. Even though it was barely five o'clock, the sun was already in the process of yielding the sky to the moon.

Melanie leaned a hip against the counter. "Jordan is a great kid. You've done a wonderful job raising him. It must have been difficult as a single mom."

Rebecca wondered if she could take the woman's words at face value or if there was a hidden meaning behind them. A jab at her having to be a single mom because of her actions. Melanie's expression seemed open and honest, so Rebecca decided to reply in kind. "It was difficult at times, particularly at the beginning. Having no one to spell me off when he was waking up every two or three hours at night was exhausting."

Melanie's brow furrowed. "Weren't you with your parents?"

Rebecca found herself tracing similar patterns on the counter as Jordan had earlier. "They felt that since I'd allowed myself to get into that predicament, I was responsible for taking care of him."

She looked up to find Alex staring at her, his expression intense. As much as she wanted to blame him for her having to raise Jordan alone, the reality was that even if he'd been excited about the baby, she would likely have still been on her own because of the length of his tour overseas. And her parents would still have had much the same attitude since they no doubt would not have approved of her marriage to him.

"It got easier as he got older, and I was able to find work I could do from home. He was a good kid, happy to play with his toys most the time. And when he was old enough for Lego, that, more than anything else, would occupy him so that I could get work done."

Melanie smiled. "Gotta love Lego." Then she glanced around the kitchen. "Where is Jordan anyway?"

Rebecca looked at Alex, but he'd turned his attention back to the food. Why wasn't he saying anything? "We...uh...had a bit of a disagreement."

"Oh no," Melanie said with a frown. "I'm sorry to hear that, but I suppose in some ways, this situation is ripe with the potential for a lot of disagreements."

"Melanie's a shrink," Alex murmured as he came to get something out of the drawer next to his sister.

"A psychologist, Alex, or does that word have too many syllables for you?" She bumped him with her hip and grinned before she turned her gaze back to Rebecca. "I am more than happy to just play the role of aunt in all of this, but if you guys do need any professional input, I'm happy to help or refer you to someone else if that would be more comfortable."

Though Rebecca was grateful for the offer, she really didn't think they'd need that much help to iron out the situation. Although once Jordan knew the full story, he might need someone unrelated to him to talk it out with. "I'll keep that in mind. Thank you."

"Barbecue's ready for you, Alex," Tyler said as he joined them once again.

"I'm gonna run upstairs and change into something a bit more comfortable," Melanie said. "Be right back."

Left with just the two men, Rebecca discovered that Alex did talk, just not to her apparently. He and Tyler chatted about work stuff until Alex headed outside with the food for the grill. Before Tyler could say anything to her, Melanie returned with Jordan in tow. Adrianne arrived shortly after and after a quick hello, she also excused herself.

Rebecca was glad to see that Jordan was back to his normal friendly self. She had no doubts that they would be revisiting the reason for his earlier upset soon, but for now, she was going to just appreciate the reprieve for however long it lasted.

"So Jordan mentioned that you're a writer?" Melanie asked as she opened a drawer and began to pull out the cutlery.

"Yes. I write cozy mysteries."

"That is so cool," Melanie said with a big smile then she glanced over to where Alex stood at the cupboard, a large platter in his hands. "We should probably eat in the dining room, eh, Alex?"

"Yeah, we'll be more comfortable there." He went to the fridge and pulled out a couple of containers. Rebecca was surprised at how at ease Alex was in the kitchen. She hadn't remembered that about him, but they'd never had a home of their own so she'd never really had the opportunity to see that side of him.

Melanie held out a handful of cutlery. "Wanna help me set the table?"

Rebecca nodded as she took the cutlery from her. She waited until Melanie had pulled the plates from the cupboard then followed her through the kitchen and the breakfast nook to a large room along the back of the house. Her gaze skipped right over the large table to the full wall of windows facing what she assumed was the backyard. Because it was dusk, it was hard to make out much about the backyard, but she could see the hint of lights dotting the landscape.

As her gaze roamed the rest of the room, Rebecca said, "This is beautiful."

Along the wall opposite the windows, there was a large fireplace framed with stones and a wooden mantle. There was another entrance to the room on the other side of the fireplace which she assumed came from the large foyer area.

The table itself was a dark wood with a floral display in the center. Ten chairs ringed the table though it looked like it was possible to seat more.

"Yes, I really love this room," Melanie said as she pulled open the drawer of a buffet at the other end of the room. "Alex insisted on having lots of windows in here. I particularly like it in winter when it feels like we're part of the outside but have the warmth of the fireplace."

Rebecca watched as she positioned placemats on the table. "Have you lived here long?"

"About three years now." Melanie glanced over at her. "Have you had a tour of it yet?"

"No." Rebecca followed behind the woman as she set the plates on the table.

"Oh, goodie." Melanie gave her a grin. "I'll give you a tour after supper."

Rebecca nodded, not sure how Alex would feel about her seeing all through his home. "It looks like a unique place."

"Yeah, it is. Alex built it with a set of rooms for each of us. We each have two rooms in addition to a bathroom." Melanie plunked the last plate down. "I doubt we'll all live here forever, so Alex has planned to eventually use the rooms here to house BlackThorpe clients or VIPs who need something more long-term than a hotel."

"Glasses, babe," Tyler said as he came in followed by Jordan.

Melanie hurried to take the glasses from him and began to put them on the table.

"This is one big table," Tyler said as he circled it. "Maybe we should have invited a few more people."

Melanie laughed. "Yeah, maybe Ryan."

Tyler scowled. "Should I be jealous that you want to invite my best friend for dinner?"

Rebecca watched as Melanie slipped her hand into Tyler's and pressed her cheek against his arm, smiling up at him. It didn't take long for the scowl to slide off Tyler's face.

Something told her that Tyler wasn't one for too much seriousness.

"I guess he could come for Adrianne," Tyler said.

"Nope," Adrianne announced as she walked up behind Tyler and Melanie. "I am *not* into robbing the cradle."

"He's mature for his age," Tyler offered then promptly started laughing along with Adrianne and Melanie.

As she stood there, arm resting on the back of a chair, Rebecca noticed that Jordan was paying as much attention as she was to the interaction between the three of them. Jordan was probably curious about the family he was only just now getting to know. For her, it left her wondering if she was getting a glimpse of the life that might have been.

She couldn't let her thoughts go in that direction. The past was the past, and all it held was definitely over. Pulling her gaze from where Melanie and Tyler continued to offer Adrianne suggestions for dates, Rebecca saw Alex step into the room. She watched as he made his way to where Jordan stood and said something to him.

Her heart clenched at the smile that grew on Jordan's face as he replied to Alex. Watching them together, Rebecca could see the similarities between them. They both stood, arms crossed over their chests, shoulders straight as they talked. Though she'd been trying not to acknowledge it as Jordan had shot up in height over the past few months, it was hard to deny the evidence when she saw it so clearly now. The little boy she'd raised on her own was now turning into a young man showing many of the characteristics he'd inherited from his father.

Rebecca stood there, knowing that she had no part of this family. Her connection to each of them was through Jordan, and once things were settled between her and Alex, she would rarely, if ever, see them again. She had to remember that. No matter how friendly they were, no matter how welcoming they were, they were not her future. The Twin Cities was not her home. She had her career and a home in Chicago.

"What's everyone want to drink?"

Thankfully, Melanie's question moved the attention back to the meal. It wasn't long before the food was on the table, and they were all seated. Conversation flowed easily around the table with most the attention on Jordan. Though she wasn't thrilled with the turn of events that had brought them to this point, Rebecca was happy to see how relaxed and engaged her son was with Alex and his sisters. If they had to be around Jordan, she wanted them to be interested in him.

"He likes basketball," Melanie exclaimed as she grasped Tyler's forearm. "You have to go to a game with Tyler. He's got season tickets—good ones—to the Timberwolves."

"Really? That would be so cool!" Jordan's face lit up. "Of course, I *am* more of a Chicago Bulls fan."

Tyler laughed. "I suppose I can forgive you for that."

"Isn't there a game coming up against the Bulls soon?" asked Melanie.

"I'll have to check, but I think you're right." Tyler looked at Rebecca. "I'd love to take him to a game if that's okay with you."

After seeing the excitement on her son's face, there was no way Rebecca would refuse Tyler's offer. "As long as it's while we're still here, I'm sure that will be fine."

Rebecca waited for someone to ask when they were planning to leave, but the conversation continued to focus on Jordan. He seemed more than willing to share about their life in Chicago—probably sharing more than she would have liked him to—but she understood their curiosity about him. She knew that soon she'd have to have a discussion with Jordan about returning to Chicago. It wasn't something she looked forward to because she had no doubt that he would want to stay in the Twin Cities.

When they had all finished eating, Rebecca helped to clear the table and clean up the kitchen, but once that was all done she excused herself, citing her need to work. It wasn't a lie, she had neglected her books since being in the Twin Cities. Though the others protested—although Alex wasn't among them—Rebecca stuck to her guns. After telling Jordan to come see her later, she stepped out into the cold night air, pulling the edges of her jacket tighter. She looked up into the sky, surprised to see how clear it was since it had been so cloudy earlier, but now the snow had stopped and the sky had cleared. The sparkle of stars was like diamonds thrown across black velvet. Living in the suburbs of Chicago, there was usually too much light to see the night sky in such a way. Unfortunately, clear skies such as these usually heralded plummeting temperatures.

Tucking her hands under her arms, Rebecca hurried up the steps to the apartment. She stepped inside, grateful for its warmth. After she had taken off her jacket, she hung it on the hook beside the door and slipped off her boots. She made herself a cup of coffee then went to the desk in the bedroom and sat down in front of her laptop. Resolutely shutting out thoughts of what was happening in the large house next door, Rebecca focused on the work she needed to do to follow up on her new release.

7

DO YOU PLAY basketball?"

Alex shook his head, not surprised that the topic had made its way back around to a sport that Jordan obviously enjoyed. "That's Tyler's department. I think he plays each week. Isn't that right, Tyler?"

"Who do you play with?" Jordan asked.

Tyler settled back into the couch with Melanie by his side. "I play with a group of guys from my church. Some of them are in wheelchairs. Some are like me with prosthetics. And the rest have no disabilities."

Jordan's eyes widened as he stared at Tyler. "You have a fake leg?"

"Actually, I have two of them."

Alex watched the expressions on his son's face as he listened to Tyler's story. Jordan was like a sponge, absorbing everything he was learning about them. He was glad for his son's curiosity about his family and knew it was just a matter of time before he had to set up a meeting with Jordan and his grandparents. The only fly in the ointment was Rebecca's apparent unwillingness to involve herself further in his life. Though he understood, Alex wished that she was more open to developing relationships with his family, but he supposed that he should just be grateful she wasn't preventing Jordan from getting to know them.

He had no idea what the next few days held, let alone the future. As long as he was allowed to have a role in Jordan's life, he would be happy.

The evening didn't run too late since they all still had work the next day. Once Tyler had left, Melanie and Adrianne went to their rooms, leaving just him and Jordan in the kitchen.

"I think it might be a good idea for you to sleep in the apartment with your mom tonight," Alex said. When disappointment crossed Jordan's face, Alex continued, "She's been worried about you. I think she needs to have you close by."

"She's fine," Jordan said, an earnest expression on his face. "I'm with her all the time. I've hardly spent any time with you."

Alex laid a hand on Jordan's shoulder. "I understand that, but this is a big adjustment for her too. I think she will be more open to us spending time together in the future if we cut her some slack now."

Jordan's brows drew together in a frown. "I know you guys haven't told me what happened, but I think it's her fault we've been apart all these years. So I think it's only fair that I get to spend more time with you."

"You'll understand more once we've had a chance to all talk together. But in the meantime, I need you to trust me. Spend tonight with your mom, and we'll talk some more about it tomorrow."

Jordan's shoulders were slumped as they climbed the stairs to the second floor. He remained silent as he gathered his things together and shoved them into his backpack. Alex walked him back down to the door and stood on the cold porch, watching as Jordan made his way up the stairs of the apartment and disappeared inside. Even though the cold bit through the fabric of his shirt, Alex stood staring at the apartment, watching as shadowed figures moved across the curtain-covered windows. Though Rebecca would likely say otherwise, he couldn't stop thinking of them as his family. Fifteen years ago he had given up the right to call them that, but hopefully he had a second chance.

At least with Jordan.

Rebecca looked up in surprise when Jordan appeared in the doorway of the bedroom. She had anticipated that he would come much later to tell her good night because even though earlier he'd indicated he would be staying at the apartment with her, she was pretty sure he'd rather stay with Alex. Instead, he flopped on her bed his arms spread wide, gaze on the ceiling. Pushing away from the desk, Rebecca got up and went to sit next to him on the edge of the bed.

She ran her fingers through his hair and looked down at him. "Everything okay?"

Jordan let out a big sigh before turning his gaze toward her. "He said I should stay here tonight with you."

"He? You mean Alex?" Rebecca had noticed that Jordan didn't call Alex by his name. She wondered if her son wanted to call him dad but wasn't sure if that would be welcome.

"Yeah. He thought I needed to spend time with you."

Rebecca wasn't sure what to think. On one hand, she was grateful to have Jordan back with her, but on the other, she was curious why Alex wasn't more interested in spending time with Jordan. Maybe Alex wasn't as keen to reunite with his son as she had initially thought. And though she really didn't want to have to forge a relationship of any kind with Alex, Rebecca didn't want her son to have his heart broken by his father.

With a sigh, Rebecca laid down next to Jordan on the bed, curling up on her side. She remembered doing this when he was much smaller and needed her to talk with him when he was scared. It had been a while since she'd had to reassure him in this way, but she reached out and cupped his cheek in her hand, not surprised to feel the skin wasn't as baby-soft as it had once been.

"I know this has been difficult for you, Jordan," Rebecca said as she looked into his blue eyes, so very like his father's. "I know you have lots of questions. You will get the answers, but I can't promise that they will be what you want. This has been confusing for all of us."

"Can't you just tell me what I need to know?" Jordan asked. "Does he even need to be part of this conversation?"

Rebecca hesitated, tempted to take the opportunity to tell Jordan by herself. But she knew that if they had a hope of working this out, Alex needed to be there when they discussed the past. If, after hearing everything from both of them, Jordan no longer wanted a relationship with Alex, Rebecca wouldn't force it on him. As far as she was concerned, Alex had given up the right to be Jordan's father fifteen years ago. She would only consider allowing that to change now if it was what Jordan wanted.

"I'm sorry, Jordan. This involves all of us, so we need to be together to discuss it."

Jordan let out a long sigh and turned his gaze back toward the ceiling. "I thought he liked me." He ran a hand through his hair. "But tonight it seemed like he couldn't get rid of me soon enough."

Rebecca couldn't believe that she was now in the position of having to defend Alex. "I don't think he wanted to get rid of you, Jordan. He has a lot going on with his business, and he took a big chunk of today off to be with you. I'm guessing that he had work he needed to do tonight. You'll see him again tomorrow."

"Yeah," Jordan said as he pushed to a sitting position. "I'm going to go make the bed in the other room."

Rebecca followed him out of the bedroom and together

they made up the hide-a-bed. Once Jordan was settled on the bed with his phone texting Robby, she returned to her laptop but found it difficult to concentrate as her thoughts kept returning to their conversation. It had been a long time since she had experienced such a tumult of emotions. Fear. Anger. Worry. All of them were twisted up inside of her, warring for the top spot. And there was also a very small part of her—the part that remembered what it had been like to be loved by Alex—that was filled with joy and anticipation. For sure she could not allow those emotions to ever rise to the surface. They needed to stay tucked away where they had been ever since she made the decision to leave Alex and keep their child.

Alex tried to stifle a yawn as he stared at the monitor on his desk. There were more emails to go through even though he had gone through a chunk of them the night before. But he was having a hard time concentrating given how things had ended with Jordan the previous night.

Sleep had been elusive as he had replayed the events of the day, including seeing Rebecca again for the first time after so many years. He had tried to figure out if there was a way for them to put their family back together again, but there was no getting around the fact that he and Rebecca were essentially strangers. Married strangers, but strangers nonetheless. It would take a commitment for both of them to work through what had happened in the past and to get to know each other in the present. Was there still a flicker of love that could be fanned into a flame? Or was that all gone now?

A knock at his door drew his attention from the monitor and his thoughts. Before he could say anything, the door swung open to reveal Marcus standing there. Not bothering to say anything, Alex watched as his best friend and partner made his way to a seat across the desk from him.

Marcus's gaze was intense as he stared at Alex. "A son, man? Do you really have a son? And you didn't know about him?"

Alex flipped the pen he'd been holding onto his desk and leaned back in his chair, lacing his fingers across his stomach. "No, I had no idea."

"I thought we knew pretty much everything about each other," Marcus said, his brow furrowed. "Somewhere along the line, you forgot to mention the events that would've led to the birth of a child. Care to fill me in now?"

Unlike when he'd shared the story with Melanie and Adrianne, Alex spared Marcus none of the details. If anyone could understand Alex's mindset at the time, it would be Marcus.

"So you don't just have a son, you have a wife as well?" Not much took Marcus by surprise, but it was clear that Alex's news did. "How did I not know this about you?"

"Well, the marriage happened before I met you," Alex said. "By the time we became friends, everything had already happened with Rebecca, and I realized that our marriage was over, and there was nothing to tell."

"But still, Alex, a wife and a son? That's pretty epic news." Marcus leaned back in his chair, elbows braced on the armrests and fingers steepled in front of him. "What are you going to do about the situation?"

Alex ran both hands through his hair and pressed his palms into his eyes for a moment. "I have absolutely no idea. I need to talk to Rebecca to find out what she wants."

Marcus huffed. "I think we both know what *she* wants. My guess is she's going to want as little contact between you and Jordan as possible. After all, she's kept him from you all these years for a reason. And likely in her mind, that reason hasn't changed."

"You're right." Alex sighed. "But I would really like to be a part of Jordan's life. He seems like a neat kid."

"What about Rebecca and the marriage? Was the only reason you didn't file for divorce because you didn't know where she was?"

Alex didn't respond right away as he mulled over Marcus's words. The reality was, given the resources at BlackThorpe, he could likely have found her at any point and used that information to file for divorce. "For now, I'm just going to leave the marriage side of things alone. What Rebecca chooses to do, however, is an entirely different matter."

"So what was it like seeing her again after all this time?" asked Marcus.

"To be honest, I have tried not to look at her as the woman I married. Because clearly, she isn't. It just makes it easier all around to view her as Jordan's mother. Not my wife."

"This is some really messed up stuff," commented Marcus.

"Tell me about it," Alex agreed. "And we haven't even told Jordan all about the circumstances surrounding what happened back then."

"Well, if there's anything I can do, be sure to let me know." Marcus leaned forward, his expression intensifying. "Changing the subject slightly... Did you see the email from Eric this morning?"

Alex nodded. He had seen the urgent message when he checked his email earlier. "It's a bit frustrating that the note and envelope didn't yield more information."

"Yes. Very frustrating." Marcus scowled. "But I suppose it was too much to ask that whoever is behind all of this would slip up and leave his fingerprints on a piece of paper."

"So you think that this is all tied together as well? I've been waffling on that myself." Alex grabbed the pen he'd flipped away earlier and rested his elbows on his desk.

"At this point, I am suspect of anything out of the norm that happens to anyone associated with BlackThorpe. Even though, on one hand, this situation with Jordan seems to be a positive one for you, it is serving as a distraction. You can't deny that your full attention is no longer on BlackThorpe business."

Alex knew Marcus was right. From the moment he'd realized just who the young man was standing outside the BlackThorpe compound, his whole attention had shifted from what was going on with Alana and other BlackThorpe things to Jordan. But what else could he do? He wanted a relationship with his son, and if Jordan wanted that as well, he wasn't going to push him away.

"I'm not criticizing you, man," Marcus said. "Just stating a fact that would be true had it happened to any of us here at BlackThorpe. I know your son needs you. But you still need to be alert and aware of what's going on. There's nothing saying that whoever is behind this wouldn't hesitate to use Jordan against you. After what happened with Alana, no one is safe. Make sure the Rebecca and Jordan are aware of that."

"I had been thinking of sending them back to Chicago until everything here has been resolved. But with what you're saying it makes more sense to keep them here where I can protect them better." Alex rubbed a hand across his eyes. "Not sure how well that will go over with Rebecca."

"Well, hopefully, her desire to keep her son safe will outweigh any negative feelings she has for you."

Yes, hopefully. However, given that they were in danger *because* of him, Alex wasn't sure anything would outweigh the negative feelings Rebecca had towards him.

Rebecca was surprised at how much it felt like home being in the small apartment. It had nothing to do with the decorations or the furnishings, but more because of the schedule they were able to keep. When she'd woken up, she'd been uncertain of what the day might hold, but after discovering a fully stocked kitchen, Rebecca started the day as they would have had they been at home.

By the time Jordan woke up to the knock at the door, Rebecca already had a breakfast of bacon and eggs cooking on the stove. She opened the door to find Melanie on the other side, the thick coat pulled tight around her a clear indication of the drop in temperature overnight.

"I hope I didn't wake you," Melanie said. "Alex went into the office early so he asked me to come by and check on you." She smiled as she sniffed the air. "It smells like you've got breakfast well underway here."

Rebecca nodded as she stepped back and motioned for

Melanie to come inside. "I assumed that it would be okay to use the food I found in the refrigerator."

"Oh definitely," Melanie said. "Jordan went with me to the store so we could buy the things that you like to cook."

Rebecca laughed. "From what I see of the contents of the fridge and cupboards, I would say that Jordan helped you pick out the things he likes to eat."

"I did wonder when he told me that you'd like Cap'n Crunch," Melanie said, a wide grin on her face. "We mainly bought just breakfast and lunch food since we all try to eat together at night. Hopefully, you'll be okay with that too."

Family dinners. Something Rebecca had always wanted, but she wasn't sure that this was the best way to get them. "That sounds like it would be okay."

"Alex is hoping to get off early, but that could change if something comes up at the office. He said that he would text Jordan to let him know what his plans were." Melanie pulled a small card from the pocket of her jacket and held it out to Rebecca. "Here's my business card with my numbers on it. If you need anything at all, just give me a call. Do you think you might want to take the car out?"

Rebecca shook her head. "I think we'll be okay for today. Once we determine how long we're staying, though, we may need to make a trip to Walmart or another store to pick up more clothes and toiletries."

"Okay. That sounds great." Melanie opened the door and stepped out into the cold then turned back. "I hope you have a good day. We'll see you a little bit later."

Once they'd said goodbye, Rebecca quickly closed the door, but because of the small size of the apartment, the cold air had already filled it. Jordan lay on his side with the blankets pulled up to his ears, but he was clearly awake.

"You ready for some breakfast?" Rebecca asked as she went back to where the scrambled eggs were cooking on the stove. She pulled a couple of plates from the cupboard and quickly dished up food for each of them.

Once they'd finished eating, they cleaned up the kitchen together and then moved on with their day just as they would have at home. Jordan sat on the hide-a-bed with his tablet logged into his home school site. Rebecca brought her laptop out to the small dining room table and sat there with it going over the results of her latest book release. They worked in relative silence for the next hour until a noise from Jordan's phone interrupted them.

Jordan picked it up and glanced down at it. "It's from...uh, Alex. He says he'll be home around two o'clock."

Rebecca just nodded, uncertain what her response was supposed to be. She wouldn't be surprised if Alex would take advantage of the fact that his sisters were at work in order for them to have the conversation that Jordan wanted. And if he did, she wouldn't object. The sooner Jordan knew the details of what had happened, the sooner they could move forward. She wondered if part of the reason Alex had had Jordan stay the night with her was to keep distance between the two of them, since it was entirely possible that Jordan would reject Alex when he heard what Alex had to say about the past.

She glanced at the clock on her laptop and saw that it was just past noon. Since they both had slept in and had a late breakfast, the morning had slipped past quickly. When she looked over at Jordan, he sat there with the phone in his hand looking at her expectantly. "Okay. Just let him know we'll see him then."

Jordan nodded then bent his head over the phone, typing out a quick message in reply.

"I know we didn't have breakfast that long ago, but are you hungry for something for lunch?" Rebecca asked.

Picking up his tablet, Jordan shook his head. "I want to finish this unit before he comes. Then I shouldn't have to do much more today."

"Sounds good." She wasn't too surprised by Jordan's eagerness to do his homeschool work. He was a smart kid and, for the most part, he enjoyed the subjects he had for school. With the advent of the Internet and the online high school she had signed him up for, homeschooling wasn't the chore it might have been otherwise. Honestly, if she had been left alone to help him through some of his high school subjects, he most certainly would've failed. They were far and above what she remembered taking when she'd been in high school.

As two o'clock drew closer, Rebecca felt her stomach begin to knot. The emotions of the previous night began to take up residence inside her once again. The familiarity of their schedule and having Jordan with her had helped to calm them earlier, but now those emotions were back with a vengeance. She just had to keep her mind focused on the fact that finally laying all the cards out on the table would be for the best. The only thing she really didn't want was for Jordan to be hurt by the revelations that lay ahead.

8

IT WAS CLOSER to two thirty by the time Alex made it home. He took a few minutes to head into the house to put his briefcase away and change out of the suit he'd worn to work. He tugged on a pair of jeans and a sweatshirt then debated on a jacket since it was just a short distance away. But the weather had definitely turned colder in the past day, so in the end, he pulled on his leather jacket and headed to the apartment to see Jordan and Rebecca.

Jordan opened the door in response to his knock, a wary expression on his young face. Alex knew that this was no doubt a result of their interaction the night before. But Jordan stepped back from the door and waved for him to come in.

"Did you have a good morning?" Alex asked as Jordan closed the door behind him.

Jordan rubbed his hands together then crossed his arms

over his chest. "I had to do some school work, but other than that it was good."

Rebecca came out of the bedroom dressed in a pair of black pants and a light purple sweater. Her hair was pulled back from her face and it looked like she wore just a little bit of makeup. She looked even more like the woman he married, and Alex had to fight to keep from letting those memories cloud what he needed to accomplish there.

"Hi, Alex. Why don't you take off your jacket and stay awhile. If that fits in with your schedule, that is."

Though her comment could've come off as snarky, Alex didn't detect anything like that in her tone. He shrugged out of the jacket and hung it on one of the hooks beside the door. He toed off the boots he'd worn over from the house then stood in his sock feet, not sure what to do.

"Would you like a cup of coffee or something else to drink?" Rebecca asked as she moved towards the kitchen.

"A cup of coffee would be great," Alex said and took a seat at the small table.

Jordan joined him, phone in hand, taking the seat across from him. Alex could sense the boy's reticence and hoped that it wouldn't have turned to outright hatred by the time all was said and done.

Rebecca set a glass of chocolate milk in front of Jordan then came to the table with two mugs. After setting one in front of Alex, she sat down in one of the two remaining chairs, cupping her mug in her hands.

Looking at Alex, her expression unreadable, Rebecca said, "I suppose now would probably be a good time to have that talk."

Alex hesitated then nodded. Even though he agreed it was necessary, it was really the last thing he wanted to do. Without looking away from Rebecca, he said, "I'll let you decide how you want to handle this. I'll answer whatever questions Jordan might have, but it's your call what we talk about here."

When Alex looked at Jordan, the boy's gaze was darting between him and Rebecca, clearly as uncertain as Alex about how this would proceed. Rebecca seemed to be the only one who was calm and focused.

"How about I just start at the beginning?" Rebecca suggested.

When Alex nodded, she continued. In an emotionless tone, Rebecca laid out the events leading up to that horrible day. Jordan was quiet as he listened to her explain why they dated in secret. Nodding his head in understanding when Rebecca mentioned how her parents had forbidden her from dating while she was still in high school. His eyes grew round, however, when Rebecca revealed that they had not only dated in secret but also gone on to marry in secret.

"You guys were *married*?" Jordan asked in surprise.

"Yes. When it was clear that Alex was going to be shipped off to the Middle East for a tour, we decided that we would get married before he left. No one in either of our families knew that we had gotten married. We had planned to tell them at a later date and to have a church wedding at some point. But then I found out I was pregnant and knew we couldn't keep the marriage a secret any longer."

"I don't understand," Jordan said, his brow furrowed. "If you guys were married, why didn't you stay together when I was born?"

Rebecca looked at him then and from her expression, Alex knew that she was done talking. He swallowed hard, hating the feeling of being so out of control. He looked at Jordan, feeling guilt well up within him once again, and knew that the look of admiration he'd seen in his son's eyes the day before would soon be replaced by something much harsher.

"That would be my fault." Alex paused, trying to gather his thoughts together, in hopes of being able to justify something that was totally unjustifiable. "When your mom let me know that she was pregnant, I told her she needed to get an abortion."

Jordon's sudden intake of breath made Alex wonder if perhaps he should've tried to sugarcoat it a bit more, but the reality was, there was *no* way to sugarcoat it. It had to be more like ripping off the Band-Aid. No matter which way he did it, it was going to hurt.

Jordan's eyes were wide with hurt and looked suspiciously moist. He swallowed audibly before saying, "You didn't want me?"

"It wasn't you I didn't want," Alex said, once again desperate to find the words to explain to Jordan what had been in his mind. "I didn't know you. In my mind, the baby wasn't real."

"But still. Why would you tell Mom to abort me?" Jordan's hands clenched his cell phone so tightly Alex was afraid he was going to crush it.

"I know what I asked your mom to do was wrong. I have prayed and asked God to forgive me for what I asked her to do. At the time, however, I felt like it was the best thing."

Jordan thumped the table with his clenched hands. "How could killing me have been the best thing?"

Alex took a deep breath and let it out. "I don't want to make excuses for what I did because I know it was wrong. But I would like the chance to explain why I asked your mother to terminate the pregnancy."

He left it up to Rebecca and Jordan to let him know if they were willing to hear what had led him to make that request—demand—of Rebecca. When Rebecca gave him a slight nod of her head, Alex shared for the first time where his head had been.

"Not long before I joined the military, your aunt Melanie had been kidnapped and held by a sex slave ring. We were fortunate that she was rescued when so many around the world are not. On top of that, I had just gone on a couple missions where I had seen things I never could have imagined. Children injured and killed all in the name of religion." Alex tried to keep the images from flooding his mind, but they were all there still the same. So clear even after all these years. "And then there were the child soldiers. Children forced into roles they were too young to play. Forced to fight a battle they didn't understand. And we had to defend ourselves against them."

Alex didn't look at either Rebecca or Jordan as he spoke. His gaze was on the table, but all he could see were the faces of the children who were forced to live in a world so horrible. "Between what had happened to Melanie and what I had seen while on my tour in less than two months, I couldn't fathom bringing a child into that world. I didn't want to have a child who might go through what Melanie had. And though logically I knew that a child born here would never be forced into the situations I saw in Afghanistan and Iraq, all I knew was a fear that I wouldn't be able to protect my child because I'd taken the lives of others. Of course, it was clear someone needed to protect my own child from me. And that's what your mother did."

Silence filled the apartment as neither Rebecca nor Jordan responded to what he'd said so far. But that silence barely registered for Alex as he was once again back in the past. Alex remembered the feeling then he'd had of not being worthy to be a father when he hadn't been able to protect the children he'd seen over there. And now he knew that he'd been right. He didn't deserve to be a father to Jordan. He wanted to be, but he didn't deserve it. He hadn't protected his own child...he'd sentenced it to death with just a few words.

Only it was a death sentence that hadn't been carried out.

Alex pulled his thoughts back from the past. What was done was done, and now all that was left was to move forward. He had a feeling that the future he had first envisioned upon finding out about Jordan wasn't going to be the one that would unfold.

"I want to go back to Chicago," Jordan said, his tone firm.

When Alex looked up, he saw that Jordan and Rebecca were staring at each other. He let out a sigh as he mentally shifted gears from the emotionally charged revelation to the reality of the situation.

"I know this is the last thing you want to hear from me, but I really need for both of you to stay here in Minneapolis."

"Why?" Rebecca asked, her brows drawn together as she turned to look at him.

"After reviewing the details of how Jordan got the note, we believe that the person who revealed my identity to him is the same person who has been behind the other attacks on the company. It's pretty clear from how he contacted Jordan that the person knows all about your life in Chicago. It would be safer for you both if you could remain here where security is tighter." Alex cleared his throat. "I know it's getting close to Christmas, but I hope you'll be agreeable to staying here for at least another week or two. That would give us a chance to delve a little more deeply into the situation. If there is no resolution at that point, I will send someone with you back to Chicago to help secure your home and provide security for you."

Rebecca sighed. "I understand that you're not really responsible for what's happened here, but this has turned into a huge inconvenience for Jordan and me. Our life is in Chicago."

Alex straightened in his chair, pulling his shoulders back. "I'm sorry for how this has disrupted your life, but at this point, your safety is paramount. This person has proven that they are willing to do almost anything to impact the lives of the people working for BlackThorpe. By hand delivering that note to Jordan, he has also shown that he knows the details of your life. That makes him a threat to both you and Jordan. You are welcome to stay here in the apartment, or we have apartments available at the training compound just outside the city. And I will provide you with a vehicle that you can use for the duration of your stay here."

"So basically we have no choice in the matter," Rebecca said.

At that point, Alex would gladly have given up knowledge of his son in order for him and Rebecca to have remained safe and outside the reach of the person who seemed so determined to cause harm.

"I really don't want to stay here, Mom," Jordan said, a pleading look on his face. "I miss all my stuff in Chicago, and I don't have enough clothes to stay that long."

Rebecca looked at Jordan for a moment before replying.

"I need to think about this a little bit before making a final decision. Keeping you safe has been my job since the day I found out about you. That hasn't changed. So if I feel that it safer for us to stay here, this is where we will stay."

Jordan slumped back in his chair, arms crossed and chin pressed down. It was hard to ignore the pain in his chest as Alex saw how desperately his son wanted to be away from him. Though he didn't blame the boy, he hoped that someday Jordan might find it in his heart to forgive him for what he'd asked his mother to do. In the meantime, however, he would make sure that the two of them were safe. He was grateful that Rebecca wasn't rejecting what he told them outright. But as much as he wanted to, Alex knew he couldn't keep them in the Twin Cities if Rebecca made the decision that they would go back to Chicago.

Alex pushed back from the table and got to his feet. "Let me know what you decide. Again, I'm sorry for the inconvenience this has caused you."

Neither Rebecca nor Jordan said anything as he made his way to the door. He plucked his jacket from the hook and shrugged into it before sliding his boots on and leaving the apartment. With each step that he took away from Rebecca and Jordan, Alex resolutely pushed aside all the emotions that had come to life in the past two days. He had a job to do and that job was to keep his family safe, even though, right then, they wanted no part of him.

Rebecca sat at the table, staring at the door Alex had disappeared through. Just four days ago her life had been so uncomplicated. Now she was having to deal with revelations that cast the events of the past in a new light. And on top of that, she and Jordan were now in danger and required security to stay safe.

Part of Rebecca agreed with Jordan about returning to Chicago. But there was another part that was worried about their safety. What Alex had said made sense. Clearly the person who had approached Jordan, even though they'd used a courier, knew enough about him to know where he could be found. And not just that, they must've researched her life enough to know about Jordan. That information would have given them access to her home address and who knows what else.

"We're going to be staying here, Jordan," Rebecca said, bracing herself for her son's response. Jordan was basically a good kid, but as with all teenagers, he could have his moody and stubborn moments. She had a feeling that one or both of those emotions were about to show themselves.

Jordan chewed on his lower lip, his gaze fixed on the table and the phone he held between his hands once again. "I don't want to stay here, Mom. He doesn't want me."

Rebecca ignored the hysterical laugh that wanted to break free at the thought that she was now going to have to stand up for the man who broke her heart. That she was going to have to justify why Jordan should give him another chance. Because she couldn't ignore the joy she'd seen on her son's face when he had interacted with Alex before finding out the truth. And despite what Jordan may have thought, Alex very much did want him—now. She'd seen it in the way he dealt with Jordan the previous day, up until he told him that he needed to stay with her for the night.

"I can't add anything more to what Alex has already said in order for you to change your mind about him, but I'm pretty sure that he *does* actually want you. I'll support you in whatever type of relationship you want to have with him in the future." She reached out and covered his hands with hers. "We have to stay here for now, but I won't force you to spend any time with him. That will be your choice."

It took a little while, but eventually Jordan accepted that, for the time being, they would be staying in the apartment next to the house where Alex lived. Rebecca was a bit uncertain as to how to handle the relationships with Melanie and Adrianne. For supper that night, she just used some of the groceries that were in the kitchen to prepare them a simple meal.

Around nine o'clock, her phone rang, drawing her

attention from the email she was answering.

"Hi, Rebecca. It's Alex." He barely let her reply before continuing on. "I was just wondering if you would be willing to let Jordan meet my parents. They had absolutely no role in my decision back then. My mom, especially, is eager for a grandchild, so I know both of them would be absolutely thrilled to find out about Jordan."

Thinking back to how her own parents had treated Jordan, Rebecca was suddenly anxious for her son to have at least one set of grandparents who were excited about him. "What exactly were you thinking?"

There was silence for a moment, as if Alex had expected her to immediately veto his request. "I was hoping that maybe you and Jordan could meet my parents for lunch tomorrow with Melanie and Tyler. Also, if you agree to this, I will tell them everything tonight, so they don't think it's weird that I'm not there with you."

For some reason, Rebecca found herself wanting to reassure Alex that eventually Jordan would come around, that they would have a father and son relationship at some point in the future. But instead, she just said, "I think that would be okay."

"Thank you, Rebecca. I am well aware that you are under no obligation to agree to anything I ask, so I appreciate your willingness to do this for my parents. I'll call you back a little bit later with the details."

"Okay, that sounds good." She hesitated a moment then asked, "Has there been any more information on the woman who was kidnapped?"

"Unfortunately, not. And the fingerprints on the envelope and the note didn't give us any information that would be helpful, but we will continue to search for this person knowing that, at some point, they'll make a mistake. And when they do, we'll be waiting for them."

After a brief pause, Alex ended the conversation and said good night. Rebecca set the phone back down next to her laptop. She wasn't sure how Jordan would react to the news of meeting his grandparents, but she hoped that he was willing to have a relationship with them as well as his aunts. Relationships of those types were sorely lacking on her side of the family. The only person who paid Jordan much attention at all was Connor, but he was hardly ever around.

Rebecca got up from the desk and went out into the living room where Jordan lay propped up on pillows, his tablet in his hands. He looked up as she approached the bed, curiosity clear on his face.

After settling on the edge of his bed, Rebecca said, "Alex just called to see if we'd be willing to meet with his parents — your grandparents — tomorrow for lunch with Melanie and Tyler."

Jordan scowled. "Do they even know anything about me?"

"They will by the time we have lunch tomorrow. Alex said he was going to call them tonight to tell them all about you and what happened in the past. He said they're very eager to have grandchildren, so they'll be excited to meet you."

Jordan's scowl disappeared, but he still looked dubious. No doubt he was thinking of the relationship he had with her parents. "So you think they'll like me?"

Rebecca leaned forward to run her fingers through his dark blonde hair and smiled. "Of course, they'll like you. What's not to like?"

"Ha ha. Very funny." Jordan's gaze dropped to his tablet as his fingers traced around the edge of it. "I just hope they're not disappointed that I'm not a baby when they meet me for the first time."

"I doubt very much that they'll be disappointed by that. Babies are fun and cute and all, but they'll be able to get to know you right off the bat since you're able to talk. I really think it will be fine."

Jordan sent a quick look her way and nodded, but Rebecca could tell he wasn't completely convinced. She didn't blame him for being a little bit wary, and she really hoped that she was right when she told him that he had nothing to worry about. After she gave him a kiss and told him good night again, she returned to her bedroom and the laptop waiting there for her.

Unfortunately, there were thoughts in her head that would not be ignored in spite of what waited for her on the laptop screen. At least with Melanie and Tyler there the next day, there would be someone else to make conversation should things between Jordan and his grandparents get stilted. She stared at the screen, wondering just how much Alex was actually telling his parents. Would he tell them that not only had they gotten married in secret fifteen years ago but that they were actually still married?

"Are we keeping you from something?" Marcus asked, his voice piercing through the fog of Alex's distraction.

Alex glanced around the large table at the men gathered there. Each of them played a vital role in BlackThorpe and had spent the better part of the morning discussing possible scenarios and theories regarding the attacks on the company, especially Alana's kidnapping. The only person not present at the meeting was Justin Morrell. Alex and Marcus had gone back and forth on whether or not to include him in the meeting, but in the end, they had decided that the men would speak more freely if Justin wasn't present. Because the unfortunate reality was that they didn't know if they would be getting Alana back alive.

He'd been able to stay focused for the first hour or so, but as the clock ticked closer to noon, he found himself wondering how the lunch meeting was going with Rebecca, Jordan, and his folks. Their response when he'd revealed the news to them the previous night had ranged from shock to anger. But when all was said and done, they were thrilled at the prospect of having a grandson. Alex hoped that Jordan would be open to a relationship with them, even though he wasn't keen on having one with him.

"No. Sorry. I've just got a lot on my mind at the moment."

He saw several of the men nod and knew they understood where his preoccupation was coming from. Each of them had also faced their own challenges in their personal lives and were more than willing to cut him some slack as he dealt with his own issues.

"Why don't we agree on the direction we want to take and call it a day? I think we've come up with some possible avenues to pursue even if they do seem a bit like we're grasping at straws. We'll continue to cooperate with the law enforcement in Alana's case, but I think we need to think outside the box in order to bring all of this to some sort of resolution."

It didn't take long for the men to finalize a plan of action and then head back to their offices. Usually one of the first to leave after a meeting, Marcus hung around with Alex after the other men had left.

"So what's happening with you and Jordan?" Marcus asked as he shut the door to the board room then returned to his chair. "I assume he's the reason that you are distracted this morning."

Alex settled back into his chair with a brief nod. As he recounted the events of the past day to Marcus, Alex realized that he wasn't just distracted by how things were going with Jordan. Rebecca had surprised him when they told Jordan about what had happened back when she'd first found out she was pregnant. He had expected a lot more anger and bitterness from her. Instead, she had allowed him to speak without tainting Jordan's understanding of what happened. Of course, he hadn't needed her to do that. His actions alone had been enough to turn his son away from him.

"I'm sorry this hasn't gone as well as you would've liked," Marcus said, his expression serious. "Hopefully, Rebecca will understand the wisdom in staying here for security purposes. It might give you the time you need with Jordan to move forward and build some sort of relationship."

"I hope you're right," Alex said. It was what he wanted more than anything at that point, but he understood that he might never have the sort of bond with Jordan that he wanted. Which was surprising, really, since just a few days ago he would've told anybody who asked him that he wasn't interested in being a father. And while he now had the desire to be a father, he still wasn't convinced that he deserved the title or the role.

"Well, if you need to talk again, you know where to find me," Marcus said as he got to his feet. "I'm going to go give the FBI guy a call to see if anything has changed."

Alex got to his feet as well and followed Marcus from the board room. When he got to the sanctuary of his own office, he checked the time again, wondering how long the lunch might last. Unable to just sit around and wait, Alex pulled out his phone and shot Melanie a quick text message to ask how it was going and if they were almost done.

Her reply came back quickly. *Lunch is going fine. Mom is in love. Will text you when we leave the restaurant.*

Knowing he had to be satisfied with that reply for now, Alex tried to focus on the results of the meeting and the things he needed to do. His thoughts eventually turned to what Than had shared about Justin during the meeting. While Justin had always been the embodiment of physical strength, it was now becoming apparent that he was also a man of emotional and spiritual strength. Alex wasn't sure how much of that had already been in place before Alana's kidnapping and how much was a result of growth since that time.

With his arms resting on his desk, Alex closed his eyes, took several deep breaths, and bowed his head. Too often he allowed himself to get distracted by how complicated things seemed to be. What Than had shared was a reminder he needed that no matter how messy and out-of-control things seem to be, God was still in control. God still had a plan. The devil thrived when they allowed themselves to be caught up in the panic of not knowing what was going on.

In the solitude of his office, Alex acknowledged the emotions within him that the devil could use — and was using — to bring in doubts. Fear. Anger. As his mind went over all the uncertainties they were facing, Alex reminded himself that he could only see such a very small part of the larger picture. God, however, saw everything. He knew where Alana was. And He was there with her. No matter what the outcome was, God would be there also for Justin and Caden and all those who loved Alana.

Alex took time once again to pray for Alana and Justin and also the situation with Jordan. Though he would never have wished that they had experienced all of the events of the past year, he couldn't deny that it was strengthening his faith. But it was moments like this when he was reminded how easy it was to fall back into his old habits of trying to control everything.

After going through a period where he felt like he had no control, Alex had welcomed the role of co-founder of BlackThorpe with Marcus. It had been horribly hard to not have any control when Melanie had been kidnapped. Then that had been followed by his time in the military where pretty much every aspect of his life had been dictated by someone else. The final straw had been everything that had happened with Rebecca and being so far away and not able to deal with it directly. Ever since that time, he'd done his best to keep control of his life and his business. God, however, had apparently decided to challenge that in a big way with him.

The situation with Jordan was challenging in different ways. In some respects, it was a bit easier to let that control go since he wasn't convinced he had the right to be Jordan's father. But it didn't stop him from wanting to control what he could...like the lunch with his parents.

As if on cue, his phone chirped an alert for a text. Alex pulled it out and stared at the message there from Melanie.

9

*E*VERYTHING *WENT FINE. Mom didn't want him to go, but we're on our way back to the house now.*

Alex tapped out a quick message to thank her. Though Melanie had said everything had gone well, Alex needed to hear it from Rebecca. She knew Jordan better than anyone else and would be honest with Alex about how it had gone. Unlike Melanie, Rebecca wouldn't care how it would make him feel if Jordan hadn't enjoyed meeting his grandparents.

I think she wants to see him again soon so maybe we can plan dinner at the house?

Alex sighed. A dinner that he wouldn't be part of. *Sure. Sounds like a good idea. Go ahead and set it up with Mom and Rebecca.*

Melanie didn't reply so Alex set his phone aside to do a little work before he caved in and phoned Rebecca.

This time, when her phone rang, Rebecca recognized the number. She glanced over at Jordan where he sat on the couch with his tablet then walked into the bedroom as she tapped the screen to accept the call.

"Hello, Alex," she said as she settled into the easy chair in the corner of the room.

There was a beat of silence before he responded. "Uh, hi. How are you doing?"

"I'm doing fine. You?" She rolled her eyes at the mundane chitchat. He just needed to get to the point of the call. They both knew what it was.

"I'm alright. Just calling to see how lunch went."

Rebecca rubbed her hand along her thigh. "You didn't ask Melanie or your mom?"

"Melanie texted me that it went fine, but you know Jordan better than either of them do. How was he?"

"It was a lot for him to take in, but I think that he'll warm up to them. He's not used to having grandparents who fawn all over him."

"Really? Your parents aren't involved in his life?"

"No. At least not to the extent that your parents seem to want to be involved with him." Rebecca turned her gaze to the window, staring at the bare branches of the trees. "You remember how strict my parents were."

"Yes. That's why we had to sneak around and hide when we got married."

"Yeah. Well, the marriage was easy to hide, but the pregnancy wasn't. By that point, in my mind, the marriage was over so when they assumed that I'd gotten pregnant out of wedlock, I didn't tell them any differently."

There was silence on Alex's end for a few moments. "You didn't tell them that I was the father?"

Rebecca slid down a little in the chair, resting her feet on the ottoman. Backtracking into the past really wasn't something she wanted to do now that they had told Jordan everything. There was nothing left for them back there.

"To be honest, I didn't consider you the baby's father."

She heard his swift intake of breath but pressed on. "You had rejected the baby, therefore giving up your right to be its father. I told no one about you. About us."

There was more silence from Alex before he said, "I understand." He cleared his throat. "So do you suppose that Jordan would be willing to spend more time with my parents before you guys head back to Chicago?"

Clearly, Alex wasn't any more interested in spending time in the past than she was. "I think he would be. Melanie mentioned something about decorating a Christmas tree this weekend. Perhaps we could combine the two."

"I'm sure that would work. I'll leave it up to you and Melanie to iron out the details." Alex paused. "Thanks for letting me know how it went. I'll leave you to the rest of your afternoon."

After a quick goodbye, Rebecca was left with just her thoughts in the quiet room. It was so weird interacting with Alex now. He was different than the man she'd assumed he'd become. The overbearing, domineering man she'd imagined he would have turned into was nowhere to be seen. Not that he didn't have a controlling edge to his nature—he did—but he seemed to be more in control of himself and knew when to let that side of him come out and when to rein it in. The fact that he'd stepped back when Jordan had needed space had revealed that.

She let out a long breath and closed her eyes, letting her mind drift back to a time she hadn't allowed herself to think of in years. Back then, she'd been so sure that they would make it. That they would be the ones who would prove to the world that just because they married young didn't mean it wouldn't work out. But something told her that even if they had agreed together to keep the baby, things would have required a lot more work than they might have been willing to give at that age.

In her head back then, she'd assumed that they had the kind of love that would make being married and having a relationship easy. She'd believed that the people who struggled with their relationships just didn't love each other enough. So when Alex had turned into someone she didn't know with his request that she get rid of the pregnancy, she'd begun to wonder if you could ever truly know a person. She'd trusted Alex with her heart. She'd thought they'd known each other so well. But when push came to shove, she hadn't recognized the man who had made such a heartbreaking demand.

Rebecca supposed it was one reason why she had never gotten the divorce. She had no interest in a relationship when there were no guarantees that the person wasn't hiding who they truly were. Experiencing that kind of hurt twice in her lifetime was just not going to happen if she could help it.

"Was that him?"

At the sound of Jordan's voice, Rebecca opened her eyes and straightened, lowering her feet to the floor. "Yes. Alex wanted to know how lunch with his parents had gone."

Jordan made his way into the room and sat down on the ottoman. "What did you tell him?"

"That I thought it had gone well and that you'd enjoyed getting to know your grandparents."

Jordan's head bobbed slightly. "They were really nice. I don't think they cared at all that I wasn't a baby."

"I told you they wouldn't." Rebecca shifted in her seat. "So are you okay with spending more time with them?"

"Sure. Whatever," Jordan said with a lift of one shoulder, his gaze on his phone.

Rebecca knew her son well enough to interpret that reaction as being as close to excited as he thought was cool for a teenage boy when it came to spending time with his grandparents. "Okay. I'll talk to Melanie and figure something out."

Over the next few days, Rebecca and Jordan fell into a pattern of sorts. One similar to what they had back in Chicago. Mornings were spent concentrating on school work for Jordan and writing for Rebecca, then afternoons Jordan spent swimming in the pool or playing on the gaming system that had mysteriously appeared in the apartment. She knew he missed his friend, Robby, but, at least, they were still able to do a few things online together like gaming.

She usually didn't take much time off between publishing one book and starting the next. And that was even truer this time around. She needed the distraction of writing to keep her mind off the situation with Alex. And what a situation it was. Alex had managed to make himself scarce over the past few days. Apparently he had taken Jordan's words to heart and had decided not to force his presence on the boy. And Rebecca was uncertain what to do about it.

Since she had never wanted Jordan to know his father, the current situation worked. However, now that Jordan did have Alex in his life, Rebecca knew that somehow they needed to forge a relationship, and Alex keeping his distance did not achieve that. As she stared at the blank page waiting for her attention on the screen of her laptop, Rebecca found herself contemplating how to best bring father and son together again.

"Are you planning to be here tomorrow?" Melanie asked as Alex poured himself a cup of coffee from the coffee maker on the counter. "After we get the tree, we'll spend the afternoon decorating it and then have supper together with Mom and Dad. Do you think you and Adrianne would be able to make it?"

"I don't know about Adrianne, but I'll probably be tied up at the training compound." Alex took a sip of the black coffee, relishing its hot, slightly bitter taste.

Melanie leaned back against the counter, her arms crossed. "Do you really think none of us have noticed that you haven't been around at all this past week? I thought things were going well between you and Jordan, but you've pretty much just disappeared."

"Things were going well," Alex agreed. "But Jordan insisted on knowing what happened between Rebecca and me, and why I never knew about him. That revelation cast me in a bad light—as it should—and he's decided he doesn't want anything to do with me."

"So he's holding what happened all those years ago against you?" Melanie frowned. "But surely he can see that you regret what happened."

Alex set his cup of coffee on the counter and rubbed a hand over his face. "That doesn't seem to matter to Jordan."

"I understand that you might feel giving him space is the best thing, but I really think it's not. He may choose not to speak to you, but I think you need to remain a presence in his life. At least for as long as they're here."

"I just didn't want to make the situation even worse. Jordan was pretty adamant about going back to Chicago, which to me is a pretty clear indication that he wants nothing to do with me."

"He's a teenager, Alex." Melanie rested a hand on his arm. "I have a feeling that over the years he imagined what having a father might be like. The reality hasn't been what he likely wanted, but he can't go back now. Neither of you can. So I think you need to step up and show him that you'll be there for him regardless of how he feels about you. Show him the unconditional love you have for him, not by putting distance between the two of you but by being there. Being present in his life and being there for him."

Alex considered Melanie's words. It was true that there was no going back. They knew about each other now. Father and son. Nothing would ever change that connection. He wanted to show Jordan that he cared about him, that he would always be there for him, just like Melanie said. His guilt had convinced him that giving the boy space was the right thing to do because it had been what Jordan wanted. But now he could see that space would only make the issues more difficult to overcome—should Jordan ever decide to try to overcome them.

"Okay. I will be there tomorrow." He picked up his mug of coffee and took another sip. "What Adrianne will do, however, I have no idea."

Melanie's brows drew together and her lips tightened at Alex's words. "She's been as absent from the house as much as you have been these past few days. I have no idea what's going on with her."

"I'll check in with her at work to see what's going on. I've been so distracted with my own stuff, I haven't been paying attention to what she might be dealing with." Alex drained the last of his coffee and rinsed the mug out before setting it in the dishwasher. "I'll let you know if anything comes up while talking to her."

"Sounds good." Melanie pulled on her jacket and gathered up her laptop bag. "You could actually start things off by being here for supper tonight. Tyler and Ryan are both coming, and Rebecca said something about making lasagna."

"I'll see what I can do, but I make no promises."

Once at work, Alex dumped off his coat and briefcase in his office and went in search of Adrianne. She didn't usually beat him to work, but for the past few days, she'd been arriving before him and leaving after him. He had asked her about it in passing, but she'd said something about a project for a fundraiser that needed her attention, and he hadn't pushed further for an answer. There had been no reason not to take her explanation at face value, but clearly something was bothering Melanie about how their sister was acting.

"Hey, Annie." Alex settled himself into the chair across the desk from Adrianne. "How's it going?"

Adrianne glanced at him over the top of her glasses before looking back at her computer monitor. "It's going fine. How about with you?"

"I've been better." Without waiting for her reply, he went on to explain what had transpired over the past few days with Rebecca and Jordan. "So that's been my excuse for coming into the office early and staying late. What's yours?"

"What do you mean?" Adrianne's gaze held his for a little bit longer this time, then she looked away, her expression unreadable. "I told you I was working on a project for an upcoming fundraiser."

"I know what you told me, but I find it rather strange that this project has come up at the same time as Rebecca and Jordan appearing in our lives. There's been no mention in our weekly meetings of anything that would demand this amount of your time." Alex leaned back in his chair and rested his hands on his stomach. "Do you want to tell me what your problem is with them?"

Adrianne shot him another quick glance. "Honestly, like I told you before, I have no problem with either of them. In fact, I think it's great that you have a son. He seems like a really neat kid. And from the way Mom's been talking, it sounds like she'll be backing off of me. For a while at least."

"So what is it, Annie?" Alex bent forward. "I know something's bothering you. Is it something about Connor? I just wish you felt comfortable enough to talk about it."

Adrianne shrugged and this time when their gazes met, she didn't look away. "It's just something very personal. If I do decide to share, you'll be the first to know."

"I know it seems that I have a lot going on right now between the situation with Alana and with Jordan, but just know that I'll always be there for you. If you need anything at all, if you need to talk, you know where to find me."

Adrianne nodded. "I do."

"So do you think I can talk you into going with us to get a tree, decorate it and then have dinner with Mom and Dad?"

She stared at him for a moment then smiled. "I think I can make room in my schedule for that. When is this happening?"

Alex gave her the details and then left her office for his own, feeling a little bit better but still concerned about what his sister felt the need to hide.

When Alex entered the house from the garage several hours later, he was greeted by the warm scent of tomato and spices. Mixed in with it was the aroma of fresh bread and garlic. His stomach rumbled, reminding him it had been several hours since he'd last eaten. He pulled off his coat and hung it in the front closet before removing his shoes. He could hear voices in the kitchen and headed in that direction, loosening his tie as he went.

As he rounded the corner, Alex took a quick inventory of those present. In addition to Rebecca, Melanie, and Jordan, Tyler and Ryan were also hanging out in the kitchen. From their attire, it was apparent that they'd made a stop at home before coming to the house. Faded blue jeans and sweatshirts weren't normally the dress code for the office.

After a moment's hesitation, Alex veered off towards the staircase. There was no way he was going to stay in his work clothes when everyone else was comfortable in casual clothes. It didn't take him long to switch out his suit and tie for a pair of jeans and a long-sleeved T-shirt. As he came out of his room, he met Adrianne on the landing.

"You planning to join us for supper?" Alex asked.

Adrianne nodded. "I'll be down in a few minutes."

Alex's return to the kitchen was noticed this time. Melanie greeted him with a hug and a query on how his day had gone.

"I sure hope you made lots of that lasagna, Rebecca," Tyler said. "It smells so good, I'd hate to be rationed."

"No worries," Rebecca said with a smile. "I learned long ago to always make plenty when there are men and teenage boys to feed. If I end up with too much, it's always great frozen."

Alex met Jordan's gaze for a moment where the boy stood helping his mother put garlic bread in a basket. Jordan glanced away without acknowledging his presence. A knot twisted in Alex's gut. Maybe this wasn't such a good idea.

He felt an arm slip around his waist and give him a tight squeeze. When he looked down, Melanie gave him an encouraging smile, obviously having caught the interaction between him and Jordan.

Going up on her tip toes, she whispered in his ear. "Remember, you're just here to show him that you'll always be there for him."

By the time the table was set and the food was ready, Adrianne had returned. Alex still wasn't sure what the deal was with her and Rebecca and Jordan, because despite her earlier assurances that she had no problem with them, she clearly wasn't comfortable in their presence. When they were all finally seated at the table in the dining room, Alex found himself between his sisters. Tyler sat on the other side of Melanie while Ryan was seated beside Adrianne.

Alex had anticipated the conversation being somewhat stilted because of his presence, but even though Jordan didn't interact with him directly, the boy happily carried on a conversation with the others at the table. Though he would've liked to have been able to talk with Jordan, Alex learned more about his son as he listened to him talk with the others. It wasn't what he wanted, but he would take it.

The food was as delicious as it had smelled, and Alex made sure to let Rebecca know he appreciated the effort she had put into the meal for his family and friends. As he watched her talk with Tyler, Ryan, and Melanie, he found himself more curious about the woman she was today.

From the moment he'd gotten the nerve up to ask the cute blonde with big blue-green eyes for a date, she'd been more than happy to let him take care of the details with regards to their dating and even their wedding. He'd made the arrangements for getting the license and then the marriage at the courthouse along with the motel they'd stayed at afterward. He'd been willing to do whatever he had to in order to have forever with the young woman who'd captured his heart.

It was obvious now, however, that she was more than capable of taking care of herself and Jordan. She really didn't need anything from him anymore. What Alex couldn't figure out was why that bothered him. He should have been happy that she wasn't asking him for anything. He should've been relieved that she wasn't trying to get her hands on the money he had earned through his hard work growing BlackThorpe into the company it was today.

Instead, it was as if he was just a casual acquaintance who had no impact on her life one way or another. In his head, Alex knew that there was no future for them. The people they'd been fifteen years ago were not who they were now. The woman he had loved then was not the Rebecca he saw before him today. Gone was the girl who wanted him to take care of her. In her place was a confident, mature woman, who not only didn't want him to take care of her but didn't need him for anything.

Questions came to him as he sat there across the table from Rebecca. Why hadn't he sought her out when he'd returned from the Middle East? Surely he would've been able to find some information on her once he left the military. At the very least, he should've pursued getting a divorce from her once he realized that she had no intention of maintaining their marriage. Why hadn't he done that?

Instead, he had allowed those ties to continue to exist. Though they might have been fragile — nearly nonexistent — he had allowed them to remain in place, even though choosing not to divorce Rebecca had limited his options for relationships in the future. But what was he supposed to do about it now? It was apparent that she had no interest in resurrecting the past between them. So why then did the idea of divorce still not sit well with Alex?

"Earth to Alex," Melanie said as she jostled his elbow.

He glanced over at her before returning his attention to the food on his plate. "Sorry. What did I miss?"

"We were just discussing what size tree we should get tomorrow," Melanie informed him. "What are your thoughts on the matter?"

Alex returned his gaze to her, lifting an eyebrow. "Seriously? With the size of this house, I would say the bigger, the better. That's usually what we do, right?" He glanced around the table. "Was anyone really suggesting that we get a teeny tiny tree?"

"I just hope we can figure out how to get the beast home once we've chosen it," Tyler said before tearing off a chunk of garlic bread.

"I'm pretty sure my truck can handle it," Alex assured him. "Are Mom and Dad coming with us to the tree lot?"

"That's the plan." Melanie leaned back in her chair. "I think Dad mentioned something about picking up their tree at the same time."

"Do we get to chop the tree?" Jordan asked. "Or are we just choosing it?"

"I think where we were planning to go, the trees are already chopped," Alex said. "But if you want the experience of chopping down the Christmas tree, I'm sure we can find someplace that does that."

Jordan appeared to mull it over before giving a shrug. "Probably better to just pick one."

"Good choice," Rebecca said. "I'm not sure I'm comfortable with the idea of you wielding an ax to chop down a huge tree."

"Ah, Mom." Jordan shifted in his seat. "Guys my age are doing stuff like that. Even shooting guns."

"You interested in learning to shoot?" Tyler asked.

"Yes!"

"No!"

The answers from Jordan and Rebecca were given simultaneously with equal amounts of emphasis. Alex couldn't help but smile.

Rebecca turned to Jordan. "You are not shooting a gun." Then she looked at Tyler, Ryan, and Alex in turn. "And you're not to encourage him."

"Mom!" This time, Jordan's reaction was tinged with embarrassment.

Rebecca waved a hand in the air. "Yeah, I know. Guys your age shoot guns. That's all well and good, but you're *my* guy and you're *not* shooting guns."

Alex cleared his throat. "Not wanting to barge into this discussion, but just wondering if your objection is a political one or from a safety standpoint."

Rebecca glared at him, but Alex didn't look away. This might just possibly be something he could offer Jordan. A chance for the two of them to do something together.

"I just don't understand why it would even be necessary for a boy his age to know how to shoot a gun." Rebecca pushed her plate away and leaned her arms on the table.

"I'm not saying that if I had known how to shoot that

things would have turned out differently for me as a teen," Melanie said. "But I do know that having that knowledge now gives me confidence."

Rebecca stared at Melanie. "Are you saying that you know how to shoot?"

"Yes." Melanie gestured to the rest of them at the table. "We all do, actually."

"It's a part of what BlackThorpe provides for its employees. The opportunity to learn how to protect themselves," Alex explained. "If you're really not comfortable with Jordan being around guns, then we'll just let the subject drop. However, if you'd like, both of you could come out to the BlackThorpe training center where we have a gun range. You could learn about guns and then practice shooting them. If it's something you want to do." He turned his attention to Jordan. "I know this is something that interests you, but your mom has the final say, okay?"

Jordan's shoulders slumped, and Alex found himself feeling a similar sense of disappointment. It seemed they both figured that Rebecca would be putting her foot down.

"I'm not saying yes. I'm not saying no. Just let me think about it."

The conversation moved away from the subject of guns, but Alex found himself sending up a silent prayer that Rebecca would agree to this. And not just for him and Jordan, but he found himself wanting her to be there too.

10

As THE MEAL wound down, Alex found that Jordan seemed to be casting more glances his way. Was it possible that this was something the two of them could bond over? Or would Rebecca squash it before it had a chance to take hold?

Once dinner was over, everyone chipped in to clear the table and to put away the leftovers and clean the kitchen. They ended up downstairs in the game room where there was a pool table along with several different gaming systems. It had been a while since Alex had been down there for anything other than watching some television, but he was happy to join the group tonight.

While Melanie and Rebecca talked—Adrianne had already excused herself—the guys settled on an NBA game for one of the consoles. Alex wasn't up on the game the way that Tyler and Ryan were so he found himself the butt of several jokes when he couldn't get the hang of the game.

Even Jordan got in on the teasing when it became apparent that Alex had no idea what he was doing. In spite of that, it was a nice way to spend a Friday evening.

But when ten o'clock rolled around, Alex set down his controller. "I'm afraid I'm going to have to call it quits. I signed up for eleven to midnight on the twenty-four-hour prayer chain for Alana."

Tyler glanced up at him, controller still in hand. "Maybe I'll go now too. I had signed up to be there from midnight to one. There's probably no harm in being there for two hours instead of just one."

"I'll go with you too," said Melanie, stretching as she got up off the couch.

It didn't take long to get the controllers put away before saying good night to Rebecca and Jordan then leaving for the church. Melanie rode with Tyler while Alex went alone in his truck. It wasn't a long drive to get to the church that Justin and Alana attended. Alex parked his truck and waited for Melanie and Tyler to join him. Looking around, he was surprised by the number of cars in the parking lot, but also thankful that Justin had this type of support.

The three of them walked to the church doors, and Alex was grateful for the warmth as they stepped into the foyer. A man stepped forward to meet them, a welcoming smile on his face.

"Are you here for the prayer time for Alana?" he asked.

Alex nodded. "Yes. We've volunteered to be here for a couple hours."

"We had originally planned to do this in the basement, but so many people have shown up that we decided to move it to the sanctuary." The man led the way to a set of large doors then he reached out to grip the handle. "The prayer is ongoing though they do take the time to break for words of encouragement. We just ask that you enter quietly and take a seat as close to the front as possible."

When he finished talking, the man pulled the door open and gestured for them to enter. The sanctuary looked much like any sanctuary in a church. A long aisle to the front divided two sections of pews. Alex was one to usually take a seat as close to the back as possible, but following the man's instructions, he trailed Tyler and Melanie down the aisle to the first empty pew behind the group already gathered there. He sat on the outside edge of the pew with Melanie beside him. Someone was already praying, so he bent his head and closed his eyes. As he listened to the prayer, he also heard soft instrumental hymns.

The person finished praying and silence fell over the group, interrupted only by the faint strains of the music playing in the background. He sat there, fingers intertwined, hands hanging between his knees, head bent. He had prayed so much for Alana over the past few weeks. It seemed she was never truly far from his thoughts, and he had taken the *pray without ceasing* command in the Bible to heart. But even though he prayed silently to himself, Alex found it difficult to think about praying aloud among people he didn't know.

They sat there in silence for a few minutes before he heard movement and Tyler began to pray. Glancing over, he saw the man standing, his hands gripping the pew in front of him, his head bent.

"Heavenly Father, we come to you tonight lifting Alana before you. We know that you are with her wherever she is. In Your word, you tell us that you will never leave us or forsake us. We claim that promise now and pray that You will allow her to feel the touch of Your hand. That she will know that she is not alone. We ask for wisdom for those of us who have a role in seeking out where she might be. We pray You will bring to light the information that we need in order to move forward to find her and bring her home to Justin and Caden. We know that this did not take You by surprise even though it did the rest of us. So we ask for Your peace to accept the situation and to allow You to work through it.

"We pray for Justin and Caden." Tyler's voice cracked on Caden's name and he paused. Alex looked over, his own throat tight with emotion, and saw Melanie reach out to cover Tyler's hand with her own. "Heavenly Father, please give them peace in the midst of all of this. Give them hope and let them know that they are not alone. You are there for them just like You are there for Alana. And we are there for them too. We look forward to seeing how this situation will bring honor and glory to Your name. We pray that good will prevail. That joy will come in the morning. We commit this whole situation into Your hands. In Jesus' name, Amen."

Alex kept his head bent even after he heard Tyler sit back down on the pew. He continued to pray silently, specifically naming each person involved in the investigation to find her. A couple minutes later, a man spoke from the front.

"I think we will take a little bit of a break here. I know some of you have committed to the full twenty-four hours, but if you wish to speak with Justin or take advantage of the opportunity to change position, please do so now. We'll continue with the prayer time in about ten minutes or so."

As people got to their feet, Alex did as well and made his way to the front pew where he saw Justin sitting with his brother-in-law, Dan. Justin looked up as Alex approached and smiled. There was a peacefulness about Justin now, one that hadn't been present until Alana had come into his life. Even though Alex knew that this whole situation must be tearing him up inside, Justin seemed to be filled with a peace that Alex truly didn't understand, so he knew it had to be a God thing.

He sat down next to Justin, slipping an arm around his shoulder to give him a one-armed hug. "It's good to see you, man."

Justin shifted on the pew so he could face Alex. "Thank you for coming, Alex. It means a lot to me that you're here." He looked up, beyond Alex, and smiled again. "And you too, Tyler and Melanie. It means so much that you guys are here to pray for Alana."

"We've been praying for her every day," Tyler said. "But it's a blessing to be able to gather with others to pray for her as a group."

Justin nodded. "I don't know what I would've done without the support of you guys at BlackThorpe and the people here at the church. They have been so wonderful to Caden and me."

"I feel really good about this prayer time," Tyler said. "I really think that things are going to change soon."

Alex looked at Tyler in surprise. He seemed so confident in his words and in the belief of what he said. Was it possible that this time of prayer would be the game changer? There was really nothing else left. Every avenue they had gone down had been a dead end. Every clue, every lead, every bit of information seemed to lead nowhere. They were at the end of their rope, but maybe now it was time for God to step in and reveal His plan to them. It sure seemed like that was what Tyler expected to happen.

Justin nodded. "I, too, believe that God is just beginning to work in the situation. You guys have all worked so hard to help bring her home, but I know how frustrating it's been to not be able to resolve this. I'm trusting that in God's time and in His will, this will come to an end. And like Tyler, I feel like it will happen soon."

Other people came up to talk to Justin then, so after giving Justin's shoulder a squeeze, Alex returned to his seat with Melanie and Tyler. None of them spoke as they sat there, watching as people approached Justin and spoke with him. Alex couldn't help feeling a rush of guilt. He and Marcus both believed that the person responsible for the attacks was someone from their past. And yet he had targeted those who had nothing to do with what had gone on between them all those years ago. If it hadn't been for what had happened, Alana would still be safe with Justin, planning her wedding.

When things had gone south early on when they tried to set up a company with the two other guys, Alex had never imagined that this would be the outcome of their disagreement. One of the guys had gone on to lead a normal life, by all accounts. A police officer with a family living in California. Unfortunately, the same could not be said for the other man. There had been enough sketchy behavior from him to help Alex and Marcus come to their conclusion. The question now was, where was he?

The man at the front called them back to their seats and the prayer time started again. This time, Alex silently prayed for those involved in the kidnapping of Alana. That their hearts would be softened towards her and that they would do her no harm. He prayed for protection for the employees at BlackThorpe and their loved ones. He prayed that the man would no longer be able to reach anyone to cause them harm. But if he did, Alex prayed that he would make a mistake. Something that would allow them to find him and bring him to justice. There would be no peace until he was caught, even if Alana was safely returned home.

Alex ended up staying the additional hour with Melanie and Tyler. When their time was up, they quietly stood and left the sanctuary. Outside in the cold night air, Alex looked up at the sky, drinking in the beauty of the stars. He waited as Melanie said good night to Tyler and then the two of them climbed into Alex's truck and headed for home.

"I'm ready, Mom, so I'm going to head over to the house," Jordan called from the living room.

Rebecca pulled on a pair of thick socks. "Be sure you have your hat, your mitts, and a scarf. It's windy today so it's going to be cold."

"I've got them all. I'll see you in a few minutes."

Rebecca heard the door shut, and silence filled the apartment as she finished getting dressed in the warmest clothes she had with her. She hadn't planned on participating in something like this when she packed frantically in Chicago, so the jacket she'd brought wasn't warm enough for the activities of the day. Thankfully, Melanie had offered her a jacket the night before. Rebecca pulled it on now and did up the zipper. It was a little snug since Melanie was a size or so smaller than Rebecca, but it would keep her warm and that was all that mattered.

When she got to the house, everyone was there including Tyler and Ryan. Though Rebecca understood Tyler's presence since he was Melanie's boyfriend, she hadn't expected Ryan to show up as well. It seemed he was Tyler's best friend and had been welcomed by the Thorpe family as readily as Tyler had been.

She spotted Jordan talking with his grandparents. Rebecca was glad to see how well they interacted together. Any fears she'd had that the relationship would be like the one he had with her parents were put to rest as she watched them together. It was a relief, and she was glad for Jordan. At least this set of grandparents would be closer than his other ones. A couple hours flight from Chicago to Minneapolis was much more doable than the longer flight to Germany. Not that Jordan had ever expressed any interest in traveling over there to see his grandma and grandpa.

Alex's parents came to greet her as soon as they saw her, welcoming smiles on their faces.

"It's good to see you again, Rebecca. I'm so glad you and Jordan have decided to join us today for this little expedition," Alex's mom said, her blue eyes—so like her son's—sparkled with excitement.

Rebecca couldn't help but return her smile. As she looked at Alex's father, standing beside his wife, his arm around her waist, Rebecca could see so much of Alex. This would be what he would look like in another thirty or so years. The man had Alex's height and build, though his hair had thinned and grayed with age. But like his wife, his eyes shone with excitement.

"I think we can leave now that we're all here," Melanie announced from where she stood near the front door, Tyler at her side.

It took a while to figure out where everyone was going to ride, but soon they were on their way to the Christmas tree farm. Somehow Rebecca had ended up in Alex's truck with Ryan and Adrianne. Jordan had joined his grandparents in their truck, which they had brought along since they were also getting a tree. Melanie and Tyler were in Melanie's truck because apparently Tyler was also getting one for his place.

It felt odd to be sitting in the front seat with Alex, but

when they'd approached the truck, Ryan and Adrianne had climbed into the back. Not wanting to make a scene, Rebecca had climbed into the front and buckled herself in. Ryan and Alex kept up the conversation for most of the half hour drive out of the city to the tree farm. Occasionally Adrianne would add a comment, but for the most part, Alex's twin remained silent.

One day we'll have a home of our own, and we'll go to a place to cut down a tree that will fit just perfectly," Alex said, his arms around her as she sat in front of him on the bed.

The memory flashed into Rebecca's mind completely out of the blue. She immediately jerked her head to the side, staring out the window and trying her best to focus on something else in order to keep the rest of it at bay. But she knew it was a lost cause and pressed her fingers to her lips as more of that day played on in her mind.

They were curled up on a bed in the motel where they had gone after their wedding at the courthouse. This was their first Christmas together, and it was spent in a room devoid of all decorations. The holiday was just a few days away and then Alex would be gone again. His family didn't even know that he'd gotten leave to come home for just over a week. Thankfully, her parents had made the last minute decision to go on a cruise with their best friends, and they'd taken her sister with them since the other couple was taking their daughter of the same age. Connor was already deployed, so there had been no questions when she'd said she would be fine to stay behind because she had to work.

Christmas had never been a holiday her family really got into, but it was one that Rebecca loved. It pained her each year that the most her family did was decorate a small tree and maybe hang a wreath. And presents? They each got one—usually something practical—and that was it. Her parents claimed it was just a commercialized holiday designed to make people spend money. They felt the same way about Valentine's Day and Easter. The only holidays they really went out of their way to celebrate were the Fourth of July and Thanksgiving. Maybe it was because those holidays didn't involve giving gifts.

"I promise, baby, we'll get a home where you can decorate to your heart's content," Alex said as he nuzzled her neck. "We'll buy the biggest tree there is. One you'll have to climb a ladder to decorate the top of. And you can hang stockings and wreaths and play Christmas music starting as early as you want. It will be a huge deal in our family. We'll make our own traditions. Okay?"

She looked over her shoulder at him. His warm gaze did funny things to her stomach as she nodded and smiled when he leaned forward to press a kiss to her lips. It was so nice to be able to be this way with each other now that they were officially married. They belonged to each other now. And this week together would just be the beginning. The next time he came home, they'd announce their marriage to their families and finally begin to live the life they wanted. Together.

Only that wasn't what had happened at all. She'd been trying to keep her mind from focusing on the day that loomed large in the not-so-distant future. It had taken several years for her to not focus on it each December. Their anniversary date. In recent years, she didn't even think about it until at some point during the day she'd write the date or look at the calendar and realize what it was. This year that wasn't possible. The date had been in the back of her mind since she'd stepped off that airplane and seen Alex again.

And now they were off to get the biggest tree they could find. Was the memory in Alex's mind the way it was in hers? Or had he succeeded in cutting out all memories of their brief time together? The Christmas thing had been more important to her than it had been to him. His family had celebrated like everyone else. But Alex's promise that day had meant so much to her. The promise of a future where he would give her the opportunity to have something she wanted so much.

Later that night as she'd laid there listening to Alex's breathing, her head on his chest, she'd pictured that future he'd promised her. Only it was never to be. Rebecca recalled that first Christmas after everything had fallen apart when she'd decorated a tiny tree in the bedroom she shared with Jordan. Her heart ached as it hadn't in years as she remembered sitting on the floor with all the lights off but the ones on the small tree in front of her. She'd cradled three-month-old Jordan in her arms and rocked him, tears streaming down her face as she sang one Christmas carol after another to him.

Rebecca swallowed hard and blinked back the tears that had suddenly flooded her eyes. Along with the pain came a rush of frustration. Those memories shouldn't have this sort of impact on her any longer. She'd worked past all of that years ago. Okay, so maybe shoving them down deep and never thinking about them wasn't really working past them all, but still...

The vehicle came to a stop, drawing Rebecca's attention from her thoughts. *Not now. Not now.* Rebecca kept repeating it to herself as she slid from the truck, snow crunching beneath her boots. A gust of wind lifted strands of her hair making her tighten the scarf she wore more snuggly around her neck.

"Well, trust us to choose the coldest day so far this winter to do an outdoor activity," Adrianne said as she came to stand next to Rebecca.

She looked over at Alex's sister who stood with her shoulders hunched up and hands in the pockets of her jacket. Rebecca noticed that she wasn't wearing her glasses and wondered if they were for effect or just not something she needed when she wasn't working.

"Yeah, that wind is something fierce."

As the group huddled together, Alex's mom said, "I think they sell hot chocolate and coffee around here somewhere. Why don't we go get some before searching out the perfect trees?"

No one objected to the idea of having a warm drink while they walked around and quickly moved to find where they were served. Once they all had hot beverages in hand, Alex and his dad led the way to where the trees were.

Melanie and Jordan seemed to be of the same mind, dismissing any tree that didn't meet whatever height requirement they had apparently decided on at some point. Alex's parents found their tree rather quickly, and a helpful young man wearing a Santa hat offered to take it to the entrance and get it ready for them. Tyler and Ryan also found a tree quickly which just left the one for Alex's house.

With her hot chocolate gone and the wind biting through her jeans, Rebecca was almost to the point of telling Jordan that he was allowed one more objection and that was it. Thankfully, excited conversation between aunt and nephew indicated that perhaps the trip was near its conclusion.

"Are you two kidding me?" Alex asked.

Rebecca glanced over to where he stood, hands on his hips as he surveyed the tree Melanie and Jordan had chosen. It was a big one, but the house could handle it since it had high ceilings.

"It's perfect, Alex," Melanie said, a wide smile on her face. "The best tree we've ever had."

Rebecca moved to stand next to Jordan just as Tyler stepped up to wrap his arms around Melanie.

"It is a beautiful tree," Tyler said. "But you're gonna need a ladder to decorate the top half of it."

Before she could stop herself, Rebecca looked at Alex and when her gaze collided with his, she knew...she just knew...that he remembered too. It seemed like an eternity passed—but in all likelihood, it had been just seconds since no one was clamoring for their attention—before Rebecca had the strength to look away.

"You're right," Alex said, his voice gruff. "It's perfect. We'll take it."

Rebecca spent the rest of the time at the tree place trying to avoid Alex. It had been bad enough to have that memory herself, but it was even harder now that she knew that Alex remembered as well. What she *needed* to keep remembering was what came *after* that time in the motel. But mostly she needed to remember that the memories were their past. They weren't anything they could use now.

The people they'd been back then weren't who they were now. The girl she'd been was not the woman she was now. She was stronger. She was more confident. She no longer needed anyone. She was more than capable of taking care of herself and Jordan. Memories had no place in her world now.

Though she didn't want to be near Alex, Rebecca also didn't want him to think the memories could affect her in any way. So when they loaded up to head for home, she climbed back in the front seat of Alex's truck.

Once they were back at the house, they were talking about setting the tree up and bringing the decorations out of storage. That likely meant they wouldn't be decorating for a little while, so Rebecca decided to take advantage of that and take a little break.

"Jordan, I'm going to go to the apartment for a bit. I have a few things I want to check on," Rebecca said as they stood in the snow watching the men finagle the tree off the back of the truck. "Come get me when it's time to decorate."

Jordan nodded his agreement then went to help the others as they carried the tree from the truck into the house. When Rebecca entered the apartment, she closed the door and leaned back against it, letting out a long sigh. The warmth of the room felt good as she straightened and began to pull off her scarf and hat. She worked her boots off and hung her coat on a hook.

Moving slowly, she went to the kitchen and made herself a cup of coffee then headed into the bedroom to her laptop. She settled into her chair and took a sip of coffee as she brought her laptop to life. Over the next few minutes, she spent time checking the ranking of her new release then moved on to her social media. She sent out a few tweets before replying to a couple of comments on her Facebook page.

The actions helped her feel more centered. More in the present, less of the past. This was her life now. Jordan. Her writing. His homeschool work. Those were the things that were important to her right now. She didn't want or need Alex to be part of her life in any way except for whatever role Jordan allowed him to have.

Alex had given no indication that he wanted to revisit the past with her. But he also hadn't made any mention of the fact that they were still married or what they should do about it. Her lawyer had emailed back with information on filing for divorce when they lived in two separate states. It should be a relatively straightforward process. He would keep what was his. She would keep what was hers. There would be no alimony or child support. The most complex part of the whole thing would likely be the situation with Jordan. They'd have to come to some agreement on how custody would work.

Of course, she would want to maintain full physical custody of Jordan while granting Alex visitation rights. If that was what Jordan wanted. The upside to all of this seemed to be that Alex wasn't pressing Jordan for a relationship. For Jordan's sake, however, she was glad that Alex had decided to put in an appearance when they were all together. His absence had been noticeable since they told Jordan about what had happened in the past. She didn't know what had changed to bring him around, but she hoped for Jordan's sake that he would continue to be there, willing to have a relationship with Jordan if he should ever decide that was what he wanted.

After she had hit all her usual sites, Rebecca pushed back from the desk and went to stand at one of the windows that framed the bed. She brushed aside the curtain and stood with her coffee cup in hand. The snow that had fallen over the past few days hadn't been heavy, but there was enough to have blanketed the ground and changed what had been a fall landscape into winter. Rebecca enjoyed the view, looking out over the barren trees.

Would this have been how their life would've turned out if they'd stayed together?

Rebecca tightened her grip on the mug as she lifted it to

take another sip. She didn't want to think about the 'what if's', but they wouldn't leave her thoughts. What if Alex had been happy to hear that she was pregnant? Excited to welcome a new life into theirs? What if they'd raised Jordan together? Would they have had other children?

But what good were 'what if's'? They would change absolutely nothing in the present. Early on, after she'd fled to Chicago with her family, Rebecca had constantly thought about how things would be different if Alex had taken the news in a better way. There were times when it had consumed her and she'd spent way too much time crying over the situation she found herself in instead of the one she dreamed of. It had taken Jordan's birth to pull her from that mindset.

The 'what if's' didn't matter.

The reality.

The present.

They were what mattered. And Jordan was both of those to her. When she'd held him in her arms for the first time, Rebecca had realized that she could no longer focus on what might have been. Jordan was her future, and she'd known then that regrets had no place in her life. Her future would be different than what she dreamed, but that didn't mean it couldn't be as good, if not better, than what she'd hoped for.

Now fifteen years later, she could truly say that her life was fulfilling. Her career. Her family. Her friends. Her church. They fulfilled her in a way that she could never have foreseen at the tender age of nineteen.

And Alex wasn't going to change any of that. He had his own life now. A company that he founded and seemed to be totally committed to. His family. In just the little time they'd spent together, Rebecca had seen how much he cared for his sisters and his parents. There was no reason that working together for Jordan's sake all these years later should disrupt the lives they built for themselves. The memories needed to stay in the past. Rebecca was determined to move forward as she'd always done.

11

ALEX GRIPPED the trunk of the tree and held it in place while Tyler and Ryan tightened the base that Melanie had provided. This was the biggest one they'd ever had, and Tyler had been right. They were going to need a ladder to hang any decorations on the upper part of this tree. Even with three of them there who were six feet or taller, there was no way they'd be able to reach the top branches.

Christmas music played in the background as Adrianne and Melanie brought the decorations out of the storage room under the staircase. Alex was trying to keep his attention on what they were doing, but his thoughts kept going to that moment when that memory had struck him out of the blue. And when he looked at Rebecca, he'd known that she was remembering too.

It wasn't the best place to come to the realization, but Alex couldn't help but acknowledge that there was a big part of him that was still drawn to Rebecca. She was the first girl he'd ever kissed. The first and only woman he'd made love to. Now that the door had opened on those memories, it was hard for him to dismiss the attraction as easily.

He remembered their closeness—it had been more than physical—but at their young age, the physical part had been overwhelming. All-consuming. That week they had together before he'd returned to his base, they'd spent most of their time in that motel room, leaving only to grab food to eat. With him leaving for his first tour, they had tried to cram in as much together time as they could.

The motel room had been cold and drafty. He had tried to shove towels along the window to keep the wind from coming in, but soon they'd just decided it was best to cuddle up under the blankets on the bed. So they'd spent time just touching, holding hands, cuddling...all the things they wouldn't be able to do when he returned to his base and left for his first tour. And it was hard to not remember that time and want that closeness again.

Over the years, there had been plenty of women interested in him. He was a catch, apparently. A man with his own company. Wealth. Security. He had what some women wanted in a man. There had been perfectly nice women who had expressed an interest in dating. Women from his church. But he had rebuffed them all, knowing that any type of relationship was impossible while he was still legally married. But truth be told, it was just an excuse. Though he had craved the intimacy — both physical and emotional —of a relationship at times, he had smothered over that need with his work at BlackThorpe.

Rebecca's reappearance in his life, however, had stirred things to life within him once again. Unfortunately, it appeared that he did not have the same effect on her. And he knew that he had no business pursuing a relationship with her when he needed to be focusing on Jordan.

"Do we even have a ladder here?" Melanie asked as she stood surveying the height of the tree which somehow seemed a whole lot taller in the house than it had when they'd looked at it on the tree lot.

"We do have a ladder," Alex said. "But are you sure we have enough lights and decorations for this thing? It's not like you can only just decorate the front half of the tree since you had us put it in front of the window."

"We have enough decorations. Jordan and I picked some more up the last time we went to the store."

Alex looked around the room, spotting his mom and dad sitting on a couch watching them. Adrianne had curled up in one of the armchairs, leaving Alex to wonder if she planned to participate in the decorating. Rebecca's absence was noticeable, at least, to him. He wanted her to have the experience of decorating this huge tree just the way he promised her all those years ago. He knew it wasn't in their home —one they shared together — but he hoped that she would enjoy decorating this tree all the same.

As Melanie began to unpack boxes of lights and decorations, Alex turned to Jordan. "Why don't you go get your mom so we can get this tree decorated?"

Jordan nodded eagerly and dashed out of the room. Alex watched him go, wondering if he'd ever been so energetic and excited over decorating a Christmas tree. It made him happy to see Jordan like this. To see his eagerness to participate in doing something with his family. It gave him hope that one day Jordan would forgive him and accept him into his life as his father.

When Jordan returned a short time later, he had his mother in tow, and soon she was caught up in the decorating spirit and helped Melanie sort out the decorations. The men began to string the lights on the tree, checking first to make sure each strand worked.

Once the lights — hundreds of them — were strung to Melanie's satisfaction, Alex stepped back to allow the others to begin to hang the decorations on the tree. His mom helped, and Adrianne also got out of her chair to hang a few. Alex found the ladder and set it up so that Jordan could climb up and hang the decorations that were handed to him by his mom and aunts. Alex settled onto the couch next to his dad, feeling strangely contented. Like this was the life he and Rebecca had been meant to live.

As he sat there watching, Alex found himself praying for a Christmas miracle. That Rebecca would let him discover who she was now. He could tell she was different from the girl he fell in love with fifteen years ago, but the woman that stood at the tree, a smile on her face as she handed decorations to Jordan, was someone who fascinated him. He wanted to learn all about her and the life she'd led over the last fifteen years that had turned her into the woman she was now.

Would she give him that opportunity?

As he watched his family all together for the first time, Alex found his thoughts going to Justin and Caden. Would they have Alana back in time for them to be together for Christmas? That was another Christmas miracle that Alex found himself praying for as he sat there listening to the Christmas music and the conversation of his family and friends.

Rebecca handed ornament after ornament to Jordan, who was perched at the top of the ladder, hanging the decorations as Melanie directed him. The atmosphere in the room was so much like what she had dreamed of during those early years. The music. The tree. The lights. The decorations. Being with family.

Except they weren't her family. They were Jordan's.

She had to remember that. She had to keep that in mind so that she didn't allow herself to get trapped in the emotions of the moment. But being surrounded with all of this made it a huge struggle.

She and Alex would need to have a talk soon. It would be common courtesy to let him know that she planned to file for divorce. She couldn't imagine that he'd object to that since there was no way that they had anything even close to resembling a marriage between the two of them. It was time to close the door on that part of her past and move on.

Rebecca took a step back and crossed her arms. Why did the thought of moving on from Alex and a marriage that was basically nonexistent make her feel unsteady? Apprehensive? She supposed in some way there had been a certain amount of security in being married. She had known that she could never get involved with another man as long as she was married to Alex, which meant she hadn't risked getting hurt again.

"Jordan is doing a great job decorating the high part of that tree," Alex's mom said as she came to stand next to her. "Thank you so much for allowing us to get to know him and to spend time with him."

Rebecca was grateful they hadn't been upset with her about keeping Jordan from them. She knew it was different to be introduced to a grandchild at birth than it was to be introduced to one at the age of fourteen. Thankfully, Alex's parents had been accepting and tolerant of what had happened. Their focus, like hers and Alex's, was on Jordan and what was best for him. She appreciated that about them.

"He has always loved to decorate the Christmas tree," Rebecca said, her gaze on Jordan as he reached to hang another ball on a tree branch. "Jordan has enjoyed getting to know you as well. I'm afraid he hasn't been able to spend much time with my parents, so he's really enjoying the time he's able to spend with the both of you."

"Are your parents not living there with you in Chicago?"

Rebecca hesitated to bring up too much about her family, but she had opened the door so she felt obliged to answer the question. "Though my parents have a home in Chicago, they spend a good chunk of their time with my younger sister and her family. I haven't seen them since July when they left for Germany to visit her. As far as I know, their plans to return haven't been decided on yet."

Alex's mom glanced at her. "Will they be home for Christmas? Because if not, we would really love for you to spend Christmas here so that we can celebrate with Jordan."

Rebecca stared at the tree, mulling over the request Alex's mom had just made. She'd be lying if she said that the idea hadn't crossed her mind. There really was no need for them to return to Chicago to celebrate Christmas there. Her folks wouldn't be there, and she still hadn't heard anything definite from Connor either. If he did decide he wanted to spend Christmas with them, he could come to Minneapolis as easily as Chicago.

"I've been thinking about it. At this point, I'll have to see what it is that Jordan wants to do. This is all very new to him, so I want to do what he's most comfortable with. Right now, it does appear that he would be happy to stay here for Christmas, but we'll need to talk about it a little bit more."

"Well, thank you for at least considering the option," Alex's mom said with a smile. "I know all of this is very confusing and new, for you as well as for us. I'd like to think that if we work together, we can figure out what's best for Jordan."

Rebecca nodded. Jordan had always been the center of her world even though she tried not to spoil him, but in this situation he had become the center of it all. She was grateful that neither Alex nor his parents seemed too set on showering Jordan with gifts. It was clear that Alex could afford to do that, but for some reason, he decided not to go that route. Rebecca thought it was for the best. Otherwise it might seem as if Alex was trying to buy Jordan's love. Of course, with Christmas coming, there would probably be no shortage of presents for Jordan under this massive tree.

Once the tree was decorated to the satisfaction of Melanie and Jordan, attention turned to the supper that they planned to have. Rebecca and Melanie had put together a stew in a couple of crockpots earlier that day. The aroma of it drifted through the house and made Rebecca's stomach rumble. With many people to help, it didn't take long to get the meal on the table. The familiarity of sitting at the table with these people wasn't something Rebecca wanted to get used to but it was hard not to. Her and Jordan's presence at the table with this group of people seemed natural. Even normal. And the thought crossed her mind that this was how it should be.

But the only way it could ever be that way was if things changed between her and Alex. Unfortunately, it wasn't as simple as picking up where they left off. Too much had changed since they were first married. Alex was a stranger to her, even though she was getting to know him a little bit more just by virtue of having to spend time with him. But at the very bottom of it all was a need that could not be ignored. And that was her need to be able to trust him.

Unfortunately, his response to the news that she was pregnant was deeply embedded in her mind. At a time when she had needed him the most, he hadn't been there for her. He should've known that abortion was not an option for her, and it shouldn't have been an option for him. The moment he had presented that to her, Rebecca had felt like she hadn't known him at all. Though they hadn't talked at length about having a family, it was something that they had agreed on. So his reaction to her news had taken her completely off guard.

Hearing him explain to Jordan why he had said what he did had been an eye-opening experience. It brought clarity to her now, but Rebecca wasn't sure that it would've made any difference back then. Over the years, as she'd matured, she'd come to understand that things were rarely black or white. That experiences could influence people in ways she never imagined. Back then, even if Alex had tried to explain to her his reasoning, Rebecca was sure that all she would've seen was that Alex was rejecting their baby.

Unfortunately, understanding what had been in Alex's mind back then really had no relevance now. He was a different man than he had been fifteen years ago. No doubt faced with the same scenario now, Alex's reaction would be much different. She sensed that he had somehow developed the ability to separate his work from his personal life.

Thinking of his personal life, Rebecca wondered if he'd had any relationships over the years. Obviously, he couldn't get married, but that didn't mean he couldn't get involved with someone. She glanced across the table to where he sat between Ryan and Adrianne. He was attractive in a more mature way than he had been at nineteen. His hair was more styled. His face was leaner with lines that he hadn't had back then. All in all, however, he was still an attractive man.

Rebecca steered her thoughts away from that direction. Thankfully, Alex's mother was happy to engage her in conversation about her books. It was just the distraction she needed. A good reminder that she had a life that she needed to get back to sooner rather than later.

After dinner was finished and the dining room cleaned up, they returned to the living room where the tree was. They each had a cup of coffee or hot chocolate, and Adrianne also carried a plate of Christmas baking that her mom had brought over. They hadn't turned on the lights of the tree earlier, wanting to wait until it was dark to get the full effect of it. Rebecca sat down on one end of the loveseat, tucking her feet up under her, and gripped her mug of coffee tightly in her hands. She took a sip, watching as once again Melanie and Jordan surveyed their work.

She was a bit perplexed by how involved Melanie was in the decorating and yet Adrianne didn't seem as interested in it. Alex's twin had been present for everything, but she hadn't participated in the way everyone else had.

Movement to her right grabbed her attention and she looked over to see Alex settling onto the loveseat beside her. She didn't let her gaze linger and hoped it appeared natural when she looked back to where Melanie and Jordan were. Alex leaned forward resting his elbows on his thighs as he held his own mug of coffee. It shouldn't have felt as right as it did. To have him sitting there beside her like it was the most normal thing in the world. But she couldn't allow herself to think that way. Not with the way things were between them.

"They did a good job, don't you think?" Alex asked as he glanced over his shoulder at her.

Rebecca nodded, not sure what sort of conversation Alex was looking for. "I'm glad Jordan was able to be here for this. He had a really good time today."

Alex's head bobbed once, his gaze still on the tree. They sat in silence for a few minutes then Alex straightened and leaned back. He took a sip from his mug and shifted slightly in her direction. His knee brushed against hers and she fought the urge to pull back.

"I know that I don't have the right to ask, but I'm wondering if you would be willing to consider staying on here through the New Year. There is still cause for concern on the safety side of things, but to be honest, I just want you and Jordan to stay to see if we can work this out somehow."

Her heart thudded in her chest. Was he asking for something more than just the opportunity to get to know Jordan? The idea both frightened and excited Rebecca. But she knew that this could never work. Their life was in Chicago. And there was just no way to erase fifteen years and try to make a marriage out of what was left.

"I've already been thinking about when we should return to Chicago." Rebecca looked over at Jordan, watching as he laughed and joked with Tyler and Ryan. "I think Jordan will want to stay at least through Christmas. At this point, I would probably be willing to commit to that, but beyond that, I don't know. We do need to get back to our lives in Chicago. That's where our home is."

Alex nodded. "I understand that. I just want the chance to get to know you again." He paused and cleared his throat. "To get to know you and Jordan. If I'm going to be part of Jordan's life, it's important that you and I also get along. I know we've both changed a lot over the years, so I'd like to get to know the person you are now a little bit better before you go back to Chicago."

Rebecca knew that Alex was right, but the prospect of getting to know him better scared her. She didn't want to find herself falling for this man again. Not when she was in the midst of trying to untangle their lives. The past just made her more susceptible to Alex. If she allowed herself to, she could still feel the emotions she'd had back then for him. She thought the years had dulled the memory of it, but after spending even just a few days with Alex, everything was back in full force. It wouldn't do her any good to put herself in a situation where those emotions and feelings would compromise her ability to make the best decisions for her and for Jordan.

"I also want you to know that I am very thankful for the

opportunity you're giving me to get to know Jordan. You didn't need to do that given the circumstances, so I just want you to know that I appreciate it." He glanced one more time in her direction then pushed to his feet, leaving her alone to mull over his words.

Rebecca took another sip of her coffee and tried to remember all the reasons why letting Alex close again was a bad idea. It was too easy to see all the ways their lives could mesh together even now. With her writing and Jordan being homeschooled, the only things they'd really be leaving behind in Chicago of any value were their church family and friendships.

But she would basically be starting over again if they moved even though this was where she had grown up. After leaving with her parents, she had made no effort to keep up the friendships she'd had in high school.

The cushion beside her dipped and she glanced over to see Adrianne in the spot Alex had vacated. She held the plate with the cookies and other Christmas dainties on it.

"Do you want one?" Adrianne asked as she held the plate toward Rebecca. "My mom makes the best Christmas stuff. Unfortunately, I can never eat as much as I want or I'll pay for it later."

"Everything does look very delicious," Rebecca said as she took two different dainties from the plate. "I'm just going to have to hope the calories eaten at Christmas don't count."

Adrianne rolled her eyes with a laugh. "If only!"

It was the first time Rebecca had seen Alex's sister relaxed with her. When the woman set the tray on her lap and leaned back in the loveseat, she wondered if Adrianne had something to say to her about Alex.

Rebecca decided she might as well head off any conversation about Alex with a question of her own. "So you live here with Melanie and Alex too?"

"Yes. I had an apartment of my own, but when Alex offered to build this place, I thought it would be fun to live with them." Adrianne wrinkled her nose. "It hasn't been all fun and games. We eventually had to set up some ground rules, especially when it came to our social lives. It was sort of like living with my parents all over again. I figured I was too old to be asked where I was going and what time I'd be home. Of course, at the time, I was the only one with any sort of social life."

Rebecca looked to where Melanie stood with Tyler and asked, "Do you have a boyfriend?"

Adrianne didn't answer right away. And when Rebecca looked at her, she saw that Adrianne was also watching her sister and Tyler. "No, not at the moment. I have been getting lots of pressure from my mom to find a man and settle down to have a family." She glanced at Rebecca and smiled. "Having Jordan show up has helped take the focus off me. Now that they have a grandchild to dote on, I hope they'll be willing to leave me alone."

Rebecca was surprised at her level of empathy for the woman. Although it had not been grandchildren, she had understood the pressure that parents could put on someone. It was a difficult life to live when you constantly felt like you didn't measure up. "I'm glad Jordan's presence has helped alleviate that pressure on you."

"But it's only temporary, eh?" Adrianne glanced over to where her parents were. Jordan was now seated on the floor in front of his grandparents, talking to them. "You guys are going to go back home at some point, right?"

Rebecca couldn't tell from Adrianne's tone if that was a good or bad thing in her estimation. The woman had never really warmed up to her or Jordan the way that Melanie and their parents had.

"Yes, at some point, we will have to return to Chicago. That's where our life is now."

Adrianne's expression gave nothing away as she said, "Well, at least I got a break for the holidays."

The conversation with Alex's sister left Rebecca a little confused. Did the woman want them to go or to stay? It was pretty clear even without asking them that Melanie and her parents would want Rebecca and Jordan to stay in the Twin Cities. They had each developed a relationship with Jordan rather quickly. The affection they held for her son was very obvious, and they had even been welcoming and friendly with her. That was not the case with Adrianne. The woman had been aloof from the moment they'd first met. This brief conversation had held the most warmth so far and even that had been precious little.

It left Rebecca to wonder if there was something in the past that made Adrianne act this way towards her and Jordan. Or was it just that she was close to her brother and wasn't happy with the way things had changed between him and Jordan these last few days? Without coming right out and asking, Rebecca supposed that there was no way to know for sure. And given that there were enough complexities in the current situation, she didn't feel the need to add any more.

It would be different if they were going to be moving there. Then it would be important to develop some kind of relationship with the members of Alex's family, but since that wasn't the case, Rebecca would let it go. She would continue to be friendly to Adrianne, but she would not try to delve further into why the woman was rather standoffish when it came to her and Jordan.

Alex stared blankly at the stage at the front of the sanctuary the next morning. He had thought about offering to bring Rebecca and Jordan with him, but then Tyler had extended an invitation to the church he, Melanie, and Ryan attended. Jordan had jumped at that, so Alex had kept quiet. It briefly crossed his mind to consider going to their church as well, but then he didn't want Rebecca to think that he was trying to force his presence on them.

So here he was at his own church. It was the same church that Than Miller attended along with his fiancée Lindsay Hamilton and her brother Lucas and his wife, Brooke. It was a large church that he had been attending for the last five years. He felt comfortable there and was involved in the men's ministry. Even though on the whole he enjoyed the church and appreciated the ministry it had in his life, it was hard being perceived as a single man. The first couple years had been especially difficult, trying to dodge the interest of the single women of the church. By this point, everyone knew that he didn't date so they basically left him alone.

Usually, he came alone to the service, but today he'd been surprised to find Adrianne waiting for him in the kitchen when he'd come downstairs. She attended church sporadically with him, but it had been several weeks since she'd last gone. Seated with her now, Alex quickly glanced through the bulletin then set it on the pew beside him.

The service began as most every service did. They didn't change much when it came to the format of their service each Sunday. They had two services available, one at nine-thirty which catered to a more traditional style of worship and then another at eleven o'clock which was more of a contemporary service. Alex preferred the earlier service, but today he'd been running late and ended up there for the eleven o'clock. But he had a feeling that for the month of December there wasn't going to be much difference between the two services.

As Alex watched, a young child made her way carefully to the front holding a lit candle in her hands. As the piano played *O Come, O Come Emmanuel*, she lit two of the candles on the Advent wreath that sat on a table at the front of the church. When she had blown out her candle and returned to her seat, an older child walked to the podium.

In a slightly wobbly voice, the boy began to read, "Today we light the candle of preparation or, as it's also known, the candle of Bethlehem. In Luke three verses four to six it says: "As it is written in the book of the words of Isaiah the prophet, saying:

"The voice of one crying in the wilderness:
'Prepare the way of the Lord;
Make His paths straight.
Every valley shall be filled
And every mountain and hill brought low;
The crooked places shall be made straight
And the rough ways smooth;

And all flesh shall see the salvation of God.'"

As they'd stood to sing the carol the pianist had been playing, Alex realized that his outlook on Christmas was a bit different this year. Having Jordan there, he found himself thinking of gifts and things to do to celebrate the season with his son. Normally, they wouldn't have made such a big deal out of setting up the Christmas tree. Melanie would have just taken care of it herself with Adrianne's help if she was around. But setting it up and decorating it the previous day had been more enjoyable than Alex had thought it would be.

But watching the children also brought a melancholy ache to Alex's heart. How many times had Jordan been involved in something like the candle lighting and he'd not been there to see it? Regret and guilt swept through him again. His impulsive words had cost him so much and might still cost him even more.

Once they finished the song, the pastor got up to preach. Alex knew from the previous Sunday that he was tying his sermons to the meaning of the Advent candle. So he listened as the pastor expounded on the candle of preparation.

"This is a time of year when everyone is focused on preparation. It starts with Thanksgiving and all the preparations that are needed for the special meal that you're going to have with your friends or family. There might even be preparations made for Black Friday. How you plan to tackle the stores to get the best deals. And then the preparation kicks in for Christmas. The gifts. The wrapping of the presents. Christmas baking. Concerts. Gathering together as a family. And finally, it culminates on Christmas Eve and Christmas Day when hopefully you have prepared everything you needed to so that you can have a happy and joyous day with your family.

"Nothing is wrong with all those preparations. Nothing is wrong with preparing for anything in our lives. Whether it be a move. A new job. A wedding. The birth of a child. There so many things in our lives that we prepare for, sometimes we forget to prepare for the most important thing of all. We forget to prepare ourselves for God's will. We become so mired in our day-to-day lives, in the preparations that we need just to get through them that we forget to prepare our hearts and our minds for what God's will might be for us.

"We must prepare our hearts to be obedient to God. And part of that preparation is an understanding and an acceptance that God's will might be different from what we see for ourselves. God may open doors that we had never imagined or He may close doors that we very badly want to be opened. But if we have prepared our hearts to seek God and to seek His will regardless of the door that opens or the door that closes, we're prepared for God to lead us in the right direction. His direction.

"Even as you look at the story of Mary and Joseph. The preparations they had made for their future did not involve Mary getting pregnant. They had likely not prepared for a trip to Bethlehem only to find that there was no room for them. It wasn't like calling ahead and making reservations and using your credit card to secure a room. They *had* to go, and so they went, trusting that God would take care of them, preparing in their hearts for what lay ahead. The unknowns to Mary and Joseph in their journey were not unknown to God.

"Are you facing unknowns today? Are there things in your life that you would like to prepare for a certain way? It is easy to believe that we know what's best for ourselves and to prepare accordingly. Some of us prepare in great detail, organizing everything. Others are more likely to just go with the flow. But regardless of which type you are, you need to prepare your heart for God's direction. So that when the time comes and His will becomes clear to you, you are prepared to go the way He has planned for you."

Alex stared down at his hands as he listened to the pastor. He was definitely facing a lot of unknowns. Between the situation with Jordan and Rebecca and the one with Alana, he felt like everything was an unknown. All the security BlackThorpe had prepared for its employees had meant nothing in the end for Alana. And nothing in the world could have prepared him for becoming the father of a fourteen-year-old boy.

12

HE WAS SCARED, Alex realized, that maybe God's will didn't involve Rebecca and Jordan staying in the Twin Cities with him. Maybe God knew just as Alex did, that he didn't deserve to be Jordan's father. That he didn't deserve the type of relationship he wanted to have with his son.

Alex didn't want to accept—or prepare himself for—Rebecca and Jordan's return to Chicago. His heart wanted them to stay. He wanted to keep them close, not just to keep them safe, but because he wanted them in his life. But was it really possible that that might not be God's will? And was he prepared to accept that if that ended up being the case?

As the service drew to a close and they sang the final him, Alex was at war with himself. The sermon had shone a light on the fact that he really wasn't prepared to accept anything but what he wanted in his life. He wasn't willing to accept anything but the best possible outcome for Alana. Until listening to the pastor today, he had been absolutely certain that the outcome of Alana's situation would be her return to Justin. He had been less certain, although still hopeful, that the situation with Jordan and Rebecca would also resolve itself the way he wanted it. He had just felt that he needed a little time to convince Rebecca that it really was the best thing for her and Jordan to move to the Twin Cities.

He now realized how selfish that was. And yet he couldn't stop from hoping that that was still the way things would work out. Did that mean he was not preparing his heart for God's will? Alex sighed and rubbed a hand against his chest. The ache there had been constant, starting the day he'd seen Justin and Caden in the gym, and intensifying with the discovery that he had a son.

Adrianne followed him from the sanctuary into the foyer. "Did they finally decide on a restaurant to meet up at after church?"

"Not the last I heard." Alex held Adrianne's coat for her and then shrugged into his own. He pulled his phone from his pocket and sent a quick text to Melanie.

Without waiting for a reply from her, he and Adrianne left the church and climbed in his truck. Once he had it running, he checked his phone again and saw that Melanie had replied. "Looks like we're heading to the buffet."

Adrianne groaned. "Like we're not eating enough already, with it being Christmas and everything."

Alex was actually quite happy at the thought of a buffet, but he did understand why his sister wasn't nearly as thrilled. "I could drop you off at home. If that's what you'd prefer."

"No. It'll be a good exercise in self-control," Adrianne said, resignation clear in her tone.

Lunch at the restaurant unfolded much like Alex had anticipated. Jordan happily engaged with everyone except him. Rebecca also kept her distance, seating herself at the other end of their table between Melanie and Adrianne. It was a struggle to stick to the decision that Melanie had encouraged him to make to be there for Jordan. He wasn't used to being in a place where he wasn't wanted. And clearly Rebecca and Jordan would've preferred him to be anywhere but there at the restaurant with them.

Alex talked with Tyler and Ryan, mainly about work-related things. Though they did touch briefly on some sports. Jordan joined the conversation then but made it clear that his attention was on Tyler and Ryan. Apparently, at some point, plans had been made for Jordan to join Tyler at a basketball game. Alex tried not to resent the relationship his son was building up with the other man. He told himself he should be happy that Jordan had chosen a good man like Tyler to befriend.

Between the sermon that morning and the discomfort he was feeling now, Alex wondered if perhaps it was time to rethink his strategy. He wanted to be important to Jordan and, if he were honest, to Rebecca as well. But the next best thing was to have Jordan develop a good relationship with his family. Hopefully, that would at least guarantee he wouldn't completely vanish from their lives once they returned to Chicago.

Though he was discouraged, Alex tried to shift his mindset from what he thought was the best for him, Rebecca, and Jordan. God might have other plans for Rebecca and Jordan that didn't include him. And he needed to accept that. It wouldn't be easy, but he could only hope that as things developed over the next few weeks that God would give him the wisdom to deal with it and the grace to accept it.

Rebecca stared at the email on her laptop screen. Her lawyer had gotten back to her with the information that was needed to file for divorce. She propped her elbow on the desk and rested her chin on her closed fist. The words on the screen blurred as her mind went back to the conversation she had with Alex.

She really wasn't sure what Alex expected. It had almost seemed as if he wanted them to be a real family. But how could they do that when they didn't know each other? And what if, after getting to know each other as he suggested, they found that they just weren't compatible? What if they didn't fall in love? There was absolutely no guarantee that they could come together in the way that she was beginning to think Alex wanted.

Rebecca straightened and clicked the touchpad to reply to her lawyer. She was positive that filing for divorce was a right option. After all, it had been fifteen years since they'd last been together. Surely God wouldn't expect them to stay married when they were virtually strangers. Even as she tried to convince herself that it was the best thing to do, Rebecca just couldn't type out the email giving her lawyer the go-ahead to file.

When her phone rang, she let out a sigh of relief and picked it up. Seeing it was Maureen, Rebecca didn't hesitate to tap the screen and answer. She'd met Maureen when she'd gone to a mom and baby playtime at Maureen's church which hadn't been far from where Rebecca lived with her family. Being a couple of years older than Rebecca but with a baby the same age, Maureen had taken her under her wing and soon Rebecca started going to the church regularly. She had told Maureen a bit about her situation early on in their friendship. When Maureen had asked about Jordan's father, she had just told her that his father hadn't wanted him. Which at the time had not been far from the truth.

"Hey, Becs. How's it going there?" Maureen asked when she answered the phone.

With the phone pressed to her ear, Rebecca got to her feet and moved away from the laptop and the email waiting for her. She settled in the chair in the corner, propping her feet on the ottoman. "About as well as could be expected."

"Can you tell me about it yet? Last time we talked you didn't seem too keen to give up information."

Rebecca sighed. "Yeah. I can tell you about it. I just feel kinda weird about the whole situation."

At Maureen's prompting, Rebecca shared the whole story starting from the first time she and Alex had met in high school. Maureen understood when she talked about how they dated secretly because of her parents' strict rules. That was one thing they had in common. As she talked about them getting married and the time they'd spent together on his break before he left for his first tour, Rebecca felt warmth envelope her at the memory.

She closed her eyes as she found herself giving the details of their wedding. She'd saved up money to buy a white dress because they had waited, and she wanted to be able to wear it as a sign of her purity. Alex had worn a pair of black pants and a white shirt. He'd bought her burgundy and white flowers and told her, with color high in his cheeks, that he had chosen his tie to match the color of her bouquet.

Then he had held her trembling hand in his firm grip as he slipped on the ring they had purchased online. It was a simple stainless steel band, and then she had slipped a matching one on his finger. Later, after they were officially man and wife, Alex had lifted her hand to his lips and kissed the band and promised her that someday he would buy her a ring made of gold with diamonds.

Rebecca thought of the ring, tucked away in the top drawer of her dresser. She hadn't looked at it in a long time, but she knew exactly where it was and how it felt on her finger.

After Rebecca had told Maureen about her plans to file for divorce, her friend asked, "Did you think it was God's will for you to marry Alex all those years ago?"

Rebecca thought over Maureen's question, not sure how to respond. Had she prayed to ask God if it was His will that she marry Alex? She didn't recall asking if it was God's will, but she certainly remembered praying hard that it would all work out. That they'd be able to get married in secret. That he'd come back one day and they would tell their families. That eventually they would have a home together. She had prayed for her *happily ever after*.

"I don't think I knew how to pray regarding God's will when I was eighteen," she murmured.

"But you're sure now that it's God's will that you divorce Alex?" Maureen was certainly not pulling any punches with her questions. "Have you prayed to see which way God would have you go with this? I know you have your reasons for having waited and not filing for divorce sooner, but I think you owe it to yourself—and to Alex—to really make sure divorce is the right option here."

"I don't understand how it could possibly be the right option to stay married." Rebecca rubbed a hand across her forehead, frustration growing with her friend. "We are two completely different people than we were fifteen years ago. It would be like being married to a stranger. Surely, God wouldn't expect that of us."

Maureen chuckled. "I think you've lost your focus here. I'm not saying that God *is* expecting that of you. What I am saying, however, is that He certainly *could*. There are so many examples in the Bible of God expecting people to do difficult things. I mean we're celebrating Christmas, right? The best example of God expecting something difficult of someone is the story of Mary. So is God expecting you to stay married to Alex? I have no idea. But could He expect that of you? Oh yes, I think He could."

Rebecca leaned her head back against the chair. What was she supposed to do now? How was she supposed to approach this? Having just relived her past with Alex through sharing her memories with Maureen, Rebecca felt raw, her emotions so near the surface. "How will I even know what His will is in this situation?"

"Well, for starters, I think we need to pray about it. And then I think you need to be open and prepared for what might happen. You have the time and the ability to stay there and see what God might want for you, Alex, and Jordan."

"I'm not sure I want to stay here." Rebecca swallowed hard. "After all, this isn't where my best friend is."

She heard Maureen give a weak laugh. "I know, and that's what makes it hard for me to encourage you to consider staying there. But we'll work it out."

There was silence between them for a little bit. It was a comfortable silence of friends who knew each other well. It was hard to consider doing what Maureen had suggested. It would mean giving up her whole life in Chicago because she knew there would be no way for Alex to relocate since his business was firmly established in the Twin Cities.

"Let me pray for you," Maureen said softly.

Rebecca let the tears she'd been blinking back finally fall as she listened to her friend pray. She was scared. Scared to love the man who had hurt her so much. She didn't want to give him access to her heart again. And that, more than anything, filled her with apprehension about seeking God's will. What if He really did want her to become vulnerable to Alex again?

When Maureen finished praying, Rebecca thanked her. "I could really, really use a hug from you right now."

"I could use one too. If you do end up living there, we will make sure to have regular chats and regular visits for both the boys and us. You will still be my best friend ever."

"Yeah. We are BFFs."

They laughed together and then changed the subject to what was going on in Maureen's life. When they finally hung up, Rebecca felt more at peace. She stood up and walked to the laptop. Without even sitting down, she clicked to close the reply window that she had opened. This was a decision she needed to pray about some more.

Rebecca decided that while she was praying about what to do, she would give Alex the opportunity to get to know her and Jordan better, as he had requested. Which was why on Tuesday afternoon, they found themselves at the BlackThorpe compound preparing to shoot at targets.

"Am I really going to be able to shoot?" Jordan asked as they watched Alex take some guns out of a locked cabinet.

"Yes. I thought about it and decided that in a controlled environment like this, it would be okay for you to learn how to safely handle a gun."

Alex approached them with the weapons and ear protectors then directed them to a table nearby. She had anticipated that they would just walk in, get some guns, and shoot at targets. But Alex took the time to explain each part of the gun to them and then showed them how to load and unload the weapon. She noticed that Alex took particular care to show Jordan how to safely handle the weapon he'd chosen for him. As she stood there watching them, their heads bent together over the gun, Rebecca knew that coming here to the range had been the right decision.

When she'd suggested to Alex that they would like to go shooting, he had initially offered to have one of his men teach them. She sensed that he felt that was what she wanted, and he had seemed surprised when she had asked if he could be the one to take them instead. And now that Jordan was willingly interacting with Alex, Rebecca knew that this was an important time for the two of them.

It wasn't much longer before Alex took them through a set of doors that led to the shooting range. There were a couple of people already there, but he found them side-by-side spots so that he could help them both. She waited patiently while he worked with Jordan, both of them watching as their son shot at the target for the first time.

His excitement at having hit the paper showed as he spun around to high-five them both. "That was so cool."

"Take a few deep breaths to calm yourself before you shoot again," Alex told him. "Just keep it steady and you'll hit the target."

Rebecca watched as Jordan did as his father had told him. Taking his time paid off when he finally hit the shoulder of the figure on the target. Instead of turning around to high-five them, Jordan remained focused on the target and shot again. She and Alex both watched until he had emptied the clip on the gun. His aim had improved with each shot.

"You're a natural at this," Alex said when Jordan turned from the target. "You just needed to settle yourself and focus and you hit that target every time."

"Can I shoot some more?" Jordan asked.

Alex nodded and together they reloaded the gun for him. With Jordan focused on the target once again, Alex turned toward her. "And now it's your turn."

Rebecca had no real desire to learn to shoot. She was there more for Jordan than for herself, but she nodded and turned toward the target at the end of her spot.

"I chose a lighter weapon for you. Hopefully, you'll be able to manage it."

She felt Alex move in behind her and nerves fluttered in her stomach at his nearness. She lifted the weapon, preparing to shoot, but his hand touched her shoulder.

"Let me help you line that up a little bit," Alex said as his hand moved down her arm to where she gripped the gun.

He was so close that she could see the stubble on his cheeks when she glanced up at him. And the scent of his cologne surrounded her. His fingers were warm and steady as he adjusted her grip on the gun.

How on earth was she supposed to focus on the target with Alex standing so close? She hadn't anticipated having this type of reaction to him, but seeing him patiently work with Jordan had moved something in her. Even though he no doubt had plenty of work to do at his office, he had willingly dropped it all to spend time with them. And he didn't seem to be in any hurry to finish this and get back to work. She appreciated his patience.

"Okay. Give it a try," Alex said as he stepped back from her.

Rebecca took a moment to try to calm herself down. Several deep breaths later she focused and then fired. She looked in dismay at the target to see that, unlike Jordan, she hadn't even hit the paper, never mind the figure that was printed on it.

With a huff of frustration, she lowered the gun and looked over at Alex. "What did I do wrong?"

Alex stepped to her side again. "You didn't do anything wrong. Sometimes it takes a bit to get used to pulling the trigger and not pulling the gun at the same time."

Rebecca turned back towards the target and lifted her gun. Once again, Alex's hands were on hers adjusting her grip and lining it up with her shoulders. "That was your first shot so you didn't know what to expect. This time, you have a better idea of what's coming, so focus, aim, and pull the trigger."

Hoping Alex was right, Rebecca tried to let go of the

frustration of totally missing the target the first time. She took a couple of breaths, focused in on the target at the end of the range, pulled the trigger and...missed the target for the second time. She glared at the gun as she lowered her arms.

"I think there's something wrong with this gun," she said as she turned to face Alex. Jordan had now joined him, and the two of them looked at her with raised eyebrows. She held the gun out, muzzle to the floor and said, "You try and shoot with it."

Alex hesitated a moment but then reached out and took the gun from her. She stepped back to stand by Jordan so Alex had room to shoot. He took his position exactly where she had, lifted his arms and fired the gun. Rebecca was so enamored with his smooth, quick motions as he shot at the target that it took her a moment to realize that the bullet had gone right through the heart of the figure on the paper.

"Well, Mom, I do believe that this is what they would call user error," Jordan said with a smirk on his face.

Rebecca gave him a light smack on his shoulder. "Okay, so maybe shooting isn't really my thing."

"Don't you write about shooting in those cozy mysteries of yours?" Alex asked.

"Sure. But clearly my characters have better aim than I do." Rebecca crossed her arms. "I guess I do better at writing about shooting than actually shooting itself."

Alex handed the gun back to her. "Sometimes it just takes a little more practice. Not everybody gets it on the first go around. It took Adrianne a little while to get the hang of it."

"What about Melanie?" Jordan asked.

With a smile, Alex said, "You don't want to mess with Melanie. That girl knows her weapons and took to shooting like a duck to water. She's actually a better shot than a lot of the guys around here. But like I said, not everybody takes to it like she does."

"Well, I'll finish off this clip," Rebecca said. "But I'm going to go out on a limb here and say that I don't really think shooting is something I'll be doing very much of."

Alex didn't say anything as he helped her get into position again. Out of the remaining shots, she managed to hit the paper of the target twice but nowhere near the figure.

When she was done, she handed the gun back to Alex and then told them that she would wait for them in the area where they'd first come in. The large glass wall would allow her to continue to observe them. She left as much for Jordan's sake as for her own. This would give Alex a chance to interact with Jordan one on one. And it would get her away from having to humiliate herself any longer.

Alex stood a few feet behind Jordan, watching as the teen shot round after round at the target. A swell of pride filled Alex at how well Jordan was doing. It seemed to come naturally to him, and Alex was glad that this was something they had in common. For the first time in a week, he felt a bit of hope for his relationship with Jordan.

He'd been surprised when Rebecca called to ask about going to the shooting range with him. After their last discussion regarding guns, Alex had figured that it was a closed subject. So when she called, he'd been more than willing to clear his afternoon to spend it with them. And he wasn't just glad to be spending the time with Jordan, he'd been grateful to be able to spend it with Rebecca as well.

More than anything, he hoped that this time spent together would be a turning point for all of them. Alex didn't expect miracles. He certainly didn't expect Rebecca to suddenly decide to move to the Twin Cities after spending just a little bit of time with him, but at least, it was a step in the right direction. But still he was trying his best to be prepared for whatever God may have planned for him. With or without Rebecca and Jordan.

He glanced through the glass to see where Rebecca had gone. She sat at a table, her ear protection in front of her, watching them. When their gazes met, she gave him a small smile then looked past him to where Jordan stood. He turned back just as Jordan finished another clip. It didn't take him long to reload and soon he was shooting again. He was doing a much better job of hitting the figure on the target and seemed to actually be aiming for certain parts of the body outline.

Alex wondered if perhaps Jordan might be interested in working with the company when he got older. Though the company was large, he still thought of it as a family-run operation. Although not related by blood, he and Marcus were as close as brothers could be.

"How much longer can I shoot?" Jordan asked after he'd finished another clip.

"You can shoot until your mother says we need to leave. You're doing a great job with hitting the target." Alex pressed the button to bring the target sheet toward them. "Why don't we set up a new one for you? Are you trying to aim for specific spots?"

Jordan nodded. "Yeah. I thought it might be good to help my aim instead of just randomly shooting at the target."

After the target was back in place, Alex stepped back. "There you go. See what you can do with this one. I'm going to go talk to your mom so if you need me just tap on the glass. And remember what we talked about for safety and using the weapon."

"I remember. I'll be careful."

Alex waited for him to get the first couple shots off then he turned and headed for the exit. Once back in the other room, Alex pulled off his ear protection and walked to the table where Rebecca sat. She looked up and gave him another small smile, but he could see the wariness in her eyes as she watched him sit down. At some point, they would need to discuss their marriage. But for now, he would be content to have discussions centered around Jordan.

"He's doing really well," Alex said as he set his ear protection on the table next to hers. "Thank you for agreeing to let him do this. I know you aren't exactly keen on it."

"I wasn't," Rebecca agreed. "But when I realized it was more than just handing him a weapon and showing him where to shoot, I felt a lot better about it."

"We take gun safety very seriously around here." Alex

shifted, his leg bumping hers under the table. "We encourage our employees to learn how to shoot as well as take self-defense classes. Given the work we do, it's important that people know how to take care of themselves. Of course, some require more training for their jobs than others."

"What exactly do you do at BlackThorpe?" Rebecca asked.

As Alex laid out what all the company was involved with, he could see that Rebecca's interest wasn't faked. She asked knowledgeable questions, so he knew her interest was genuine. For some reason, that pleased him. He liked that she was interested in something that was important to him. In a way, BlackThorpe was like his child, and just like he wanted to get to know about Jordan, she seemed to want to get to know about his company.

"So Justin was in charge of this center?" Rebecca's glance went quickly to Jordan and then back to Alex.

Alex nodded. "He still is in charge, but of course, right now it's in a greatly reduced role. The other guys working under him have done a great job of stepping up during this time."

Rebecca regarded him for a moment, her eyes intent. "Do you think Alana is still alive?"

Alex's gaze dropped as his fingers ran along the smooth edges of the ear protection in front of him. He sighed then looked back up at Rebecca. "The length of time that she's been missing doesn't bode well under normal circumstances. But because we are almost one hundred percent certain that she was taken by her ex-husband, I have hope. I know that sounds strange, especially since her husband was abusive to her, but I've just been praying that the man would be bombarded by happy memories they shared. I understand that it's entirely possible that Alana won't come home to Justin, but for now, it feels right to hope."

Rebecca nodded. "I can't imagine what they're both going through. I mean, I've worried about Connor a few times over the years when he's dropped out of communication." She hesitated, her gaze dipped away briefly. "But I think it would be different with someone you love like that in danger."

"Yes. I think it would be very different." Alex sat for a moment, searching for another safe topic, but before he could say anything further, Rebecca spoke.

"Do you think there might be other things that Jordan would enjoy doing with you?" Rebecca asked. "For what it's worth, I don't think he's totally rejected the idea of having a relationship with you."

Hope surged through Alex, stronger than what he'd felt earlier. "I don't want to push him."

"He might need a little enticement, more than a push." Rebecca's lips curved up into a small smile as she tucked a strand of hair behind her ear. "That's what I've learned as his parent. Sometimes he needs a push, but I think in this situation he needs enticement. And by that, I don't mean buying him expensive toys or the latest electronic gadget. I mean finding the things he enjoys doing and offering to do them with him."

"Well, we can continue to come out here to the gun range to shoot. I know he likes basketball, and Tyler might be willing to sacrifice his tickets so the two of us can go to a game sometime. What else does he enjoy?"

"He enjoys gaming. I know you have several systems, so it's just a matter of finding out which games he likes. He likes to skateboard, but I realize that's more of a summer sport. I think he might enjoy seeing more of what you do at BlackThorpe."

"Okay. Thank you for the info." He sensed someone coming up behind him and glanced back to see that Jordan was headed their way. He held the gun as Alex had directed him and had a pleased smile on his face.

13

DID YOU KILL all the bad guys?" Rebecca asked as Jordan sat down in the chair across from Alex.

"That was a blast." His cheeks were flushed and his eyes sparkled. "I can't wait to tell Robby all about it."

"So you think you've had your fill for today?" Alex asked, pleased to see the excitement on Jordan's face.

"I think so." Jordan met his gaze for what felt like the first time since their discussion a week earlier. "Will I be able to do this again?"

"I think we can arrange that," Alex said. He gestured to the gun that Jordan had set on the table in front of him. "You ready to get that cleaned and put away?"

Jordan nodded and, over the next few minutes, they cleaned both guns and put them and the ear protection away.

Once they were done, Alex asked, "Would you like a quick tour of the compound?"

Rebecca glanced at the time on her cell phone then nodded. It didn't take too long to show them the gym area where Jordan was impressed with the workout machines they had available there. After checking out the gym, they headed to the basement and the passage that led to the living quarters in the adjacent building. There were a handful of people around, a few who recognized Alex and stopped to chat.

"There is more to the compound, but it's best seen in summer since it's out on the acreage the company owns," Alex said as he gestured to the windows of the cafeteria that faced the back part of the compound.

"Do they train out there in winter?" Jordan asked.

Alex glanced down at him. "Yep. We have a lot of people who come here specifically to do winter training. The people we work with need to be able to function in all kinds of weather."

"Melanie doesn't work here, does she?" Rebecca asked.

"No. She's at a different location not far from here. I can show it to you on our way out. Maybe Melanie can arrange a tour for you one day. She's done a great job making the BlackThorpe Wellness Center what it is today." Having completed the tour, Alex said, "It's getting late. Did Melanie mention anything about dinner?"

Rebecca shook her head. "I think she and Tyler had something planned for this evening. But I'm not sure about Adrianne."

"Well, would you like to grab a bite to eat since it's nearly time for supper?" Alex asked the question, knowing there was a good chance that Rebecca would decline. But he was at that point where he was willing to take any chance to try to move things forward.

"Yeah, I'm starving, Mom. Can we go out to get something to eat?"

Though Alex was glad for Jordan's support, he didn't want Rebecca to feel as if she was being ganged up on.

Thankfully, she just smiled and nodded, and soon they were on their way out of the building to his truck. They only had the one vehicle since Alex had decided it would just be easier to swing by the house to pick them up when Rebecca had called to ask about going to the range. After they had climbed into his truck, they had a short discussion on where to eat then he pulled through the gates of the compound and turned toward the highway.

When they got to the booth in the restaurant of Jordan's choice, Alex settled on one side while Jordan and Rebecca sat across from him. It didn't take too long to order or to get their food. Thankfully, Jordan seemed to be in a mood to talk which meant Alex was able to learn a little more about his son. Even Rebecca chimed in with a few things that gave Alex additional insight into their life in Chicago.

"So have you managed to talk with Connor lately?" Alex asked after she mentioned a bit more about what her brother was currently up to.

"I called him the other day, and it went right to voicemail." Rebecca shrugged. "That's not an unusual occurrence with him. But I'm hoping he'll get back to me soon since he had mentioned at one time coming to Chicago for Christmas. If we're going to be here instead, I'm not sure what he will do."

Alex leaned forward, his arms braced on either side of his plate. "You know that he's welcome to come here as well. The more, the merrier."

Rebecca smiled, and Alex suddenly remembered how much he had loved to coax smiles from her. She had always been a bit shy. It had been that shy smile with her big blue-green eyes that had first captured his attention. She'd asked him a question about something in a class they had together even though she was a junior and he was a senior. He'd had to ask her to repeat the question because he'd been so captivated by her smile. When he finally got up the nerve to ask her out on a date, he'd gotten another shy smile that had, unfortunately, slipped away too quickly as she'd explained that her parents would not allow her to date in high school.

After that, he had tried to find ways to spend time with her at school until she finally caved, and they'd started to date in secret.

He'd gotten to know her brother a little bit when Connor had hung out with Alex and his group of friends on occasion. But his main focus had been on Rebecca. And now here he was, almost seventeen years later, trying to get Rebecca to smile for him again. It seemed to be as important to him now as it had been back then.

"Well, if or when he gets hold of me, I'll pass on the invitation," Rebecca said. "I really would like him to be home for Christmas, but his schedule doesn't always allow for that."

"When was the last time you saw him?" Alex asked.

It was Jordan who answered with a wide grin. "He flew us to Hawaii last winter to spend some time with him."

"Yeah, it's been almost a year since that trip." Alex saw the sadness in Rebecca's eyes and realized how fortunate he was to have his family so close.

"I'll certainly be praying that he gets hold of you in time to join us here for Christmas," Alex said, wishing he could do something to bring the smile back to Rebecca's face.

Once they were finished their meal, they left the restaurant and headed back to the house. When they got there, Rebecca and Jordan said good night and went upstairs to their apartment. Alex wished he could have prolonged their time together, but he was thankful for the time they did have. Besides, with him having cut out of work early, he no doubt had emails and messages he needed to follow up on.

But as he climbed the stairs to his suite, all Alex could think of was what he could plan that would include all three of them again.

The next morning, Alex was at the office early. After grabbing a cup of coffee, he settled behind his desk. He stared out the large glass window next to him and once again wondered where Alana might be. Then, strangely enough, the thought popped into his head that Connor was also out there somewhere. Though they weren't connected, Alex prayed that both of them would soon be in contact with those that loved them.

A knock on the door drew his attention. He looked over to see Eric standing there with a file in his hand.

"Do you have a minute?" Eric asked as he stepped into the office.

Alex nodded then took a sip of his coffee. "What's up?"

"Would it be possible to have a meeting with everyone first thing this morning?" Eric asked, tapping the file against his leg. "I have come across a very faint lead for Alana. I'd like to share it with the team to get their thoughts on it."

Alex set his mug down with a thump. The hot liquid splashed onto his hand, but he ignored it. "A lead? What kind of lead?"

"Is it possible you could wait till we gather everyone? It would be easier to just present this once."

Though Alex wanted to know all the details right then, he nodded and proceeded to send out an urgent message through their intra-office messaging system. He wanted to be excited about the lead Eric had, but there was apprehension on the man's face which caused the pit in Alex's stomach to grow. Abandoning the coffee mess on his desk, Alex walked with Eric to the board room and waited for the others to arrive.

It didn't take long for the rest of the team to show up, their faces reflecting different levels of anticipation. Marcus, as usual, showed very little emotion at all, while Than's excitement was clear in the smile on his face. Alex hoped the lead didn't end up in disappointment once again. The only one not present for this meeting was Justin. There was no sense in getting his hopes up until they had a better idea of what Eric had found.

Once the others were all seated, Alex stood beside his chair and repeated what Eric had told him earlier. Then he turned the meeting over to the man and sat down, hoping that they were at the beginning of the end of the situation with Alana.

"I've been looking for even the smallest connection to Alana's ex." Eric opened the file he held in his hand. "As I combed through these connections I found one that held some promise. What we needed was to find potential places where Alana could be held. Her ex has several properties in his name which we have investigated to no avail. I then moved to properties his father owned. Again, we were able to rule them out as places where Alana might be. While investigating his mother's past, however, I discovered that her parents divorced when she was young. Her mother remarried and her husband's parents had a property in rural Tennessee. That property had been left to Craig's mother by her stepfather."

Eric pulled several pieces of paper from his file and handed them to Trent. He took one sheet and passed the rest to Alex. Soon everyone in the room had a copy. Alex stared down at it, taking in the familiar angle of a satellite photo of the property.

"Not even going to touch the convoluted familial relationships involved in this," Marcus began. "What exactly are we looking at here? What makes you think that this may be where Alana is being held?"

"I realized it was a long shot, but at this point, I figured that we needed to be grasping at straws. I did a little research on the address and discovered that the electricity to that property had been turned on just days after Alana was taken."

"Just electricity?" Than asked. "Wouldn't they have needed water as well?"

Eric shook his head. "With a rural property like this, it's likely that they have a well on the grounds. Any water they needed would be pulled from that. I know it seems like a stretch, but I'd really like to send a team of guys down to watch the property for a few days."

"Were you able to find out who requested that the power be turned back on for that house?" Alex asked. He was trying very hard not to allow his hopes to rise, but he wasn't very successful.

"I had Trent uh...tap into their system to see if he could see who was billed for usage at that address. It came back to a corporation that is owned by Craig. It's possible that it's a vacation cottage and someone was planning to use it over the holidays, but I just can't shake the feeling that it's something more significant for us."

"I agree," Than said. "It's the best lead we've had in way too long."

"The question is, do we take this lead to the FBI or do we check to see if there is any substance to it first?" Eric asked.

"We send our guys down there first." There was no room for argument in Marcus's tone. "We have the resources, and this case means more to us that it does to them. We will sort out the mess afterward if this does end up leading us to Alana."

"Okay. Eric, pick five guys to go down there with you," Alex said, glad that they were finally moving in a positive direction. "I want coverage of the house tied into us here. We'll have someone monitoring on this end twenty-four hours a day."

Eric nodded. "I know who I want to have with me. Are we going to tell Justin?"

"No." Once again Marcus was firm with his answer. "Until we know more, we don't tell anyone that doesn't need to know."

Marcus got to his feet, which signaled the meeting was dismissed. Though he was confident that Eric knew what he was doing, Alex found himself walking with him to his office. Trent and Than were there with them.

For the next hour, they worked over the plan for surveillance. A call was made to prepare the BlackThorpe jet for immediate departure, and the men who were going to be accompanying Eric were notified to prepare and meet at the airport.

When everything was in place, the four men stood together in Eric's office and prayed for the success of the mission. And then it was out of his hands. From this point on, all Alex could do was watch and pray as events unfolded several states away. He hoped that there would be a quick and positive resolution to the situation. More than anything he wanted to bring Alana home to Justin.

Rebecca told herself that the disappointment she felt when Alex texted to say he wouldn't be at the house for dinner was solely for Jordan. She did feel bad that Jordan wouldn't have the opportunity to spend more time with Alex. But try as she might, Rebecca couldn't escape the knowledge that some of that disappointment was on a personal level.

As she put together the ingredients for chicken and dumplings, Rebecca knew that she had brought this on herself. Allowing the memories of their past to take up residence not just in her mind, but in her emotions, had opened her up to feeling more for Alex now. Add to that her decision to put off the divorce and give the situation a chance, and her disappointment was as much for herself as it was for Jordan.

When suppertime finally rolled around, Adrianne, Melanie, Tyler, and Ryan were there to share the meal with her and Jordan. As usual, Adrianne was fairly quiet, but the other three and Jordan made up for it. Midway through the meal, Rebecca's phone rang. She recognized the ringtone as the one she'd given Connor and quickly jumped up to grab the phone off the counter.

"Excuse me," she said to the group at the table. "I've got to take this."

She hurried into the living room where the Christmas tree glowed in the darkness. Without bothering to turn on any other lights, Rebecca tapped her phone to accept the call as she sank down into an easy chair.

"Connor! It's about time you called me back."

"Sorry, sis. I was on a job that took me out of contact for a while. How are you doing?"

Rebecca sat for a second, staring at the Christmas tree, and wondered where to start. She supposed the beginning was the best place. "I'm doing okay. But there's been a few changes since we last talked."

"You get a boyfriend? Get married? Get pregnant?"

Rebecca chuckled. "None of the above. Well, sort of none of the above."

There was a beat of silence before Connor growled, "What's that supposed to mean?"

"Well, remember how I've never identified who Jordan's father is?"

"Uh, yeah. Best kept secret of the century. So what's happened? Somebody spilled the beans?"

Rebecca sighed. "Sort of. Someone took it upon themselves to tell Jordan."

"I don't understand. Who else knew who his father was? I mean you told everyone that it was just some random guy. That you didn't remember his name. Or how to contact him. Oh, and just for the record, I never bought that. So are you going to tell me who it is and how Jordan found out?"

Tucking her feet up under her, Rebecca relaxed back into the chair. "My best guess is that the person who told Jordan found the marriage certificate."

"Say what? A marriage certificate?" Connor gave an audible huff. "You can stop dropping these bombs anytime you want."

"There's just one more bomb. Alex Thorpe is Jordan's father. And my husband."

The silence on the other end of the line seemed to drag on forever before Connor spoke again. "You married Alex Thorpe and then had his baby? I don't get it. If you're married, why wasn't he around when you had Jordan?"

This was a part of the explanation that Rebecca really didn't want to share, but Connor was her brother and he deserved to know. Speaking slowly, Rebecca relayed all that had happened back when she'd found out she was pregnant. She found herself adding in the information she had just learned during the conversation she and Alex had had with Jordan. Alex's reasons for why he'd asked her to do what he had.

When she was done talking, she waited for Connor to

respond. Uncertain how he would take the news that one of his friends from high school was actually the father of his nephew.

"First of all, I can't believe that you were able to hide the fact that you were dating Alex from all of us. Never figured you for a rebel... Well, until you turned up pregnant, claiming no knowledge of who the father was." Connor sighed. "Seriously, though, I kind of understand where Alex was coming from."

Rebecca was shocked that Connor would take Alex's side. "You do understand what I said, right? He wanted me to abort Jordan."

"I am in no way saying that he was right in asking you to do what he did. What I'm saying is that I understand his mindset. We see a lot of things, traveling into different parts of the world exposes us to evils that the average person living in their comfortable home with their jobs and kids will never be able to comprehend. It's scary to think of bringing a defenseless baby into a world that has the capacity for such evil. And yes, I'm sure the situation with his sister being kidnapped only added to the mess that was in his mind." Connor paused. "I can almost guarantee you that once he had some time to think about it, Alex changed his mind."

"What?" Rebecca didn't even want to consider that that might have been a possibility. Alex hadn't said that during the conversation with Jordan, so maybe Connor was wrong in his supposition.

"Becca, he was young, no doubt scared, and worried about bringing a child into a world that he knew was not all sunshine and roses. I'm sure his response to what you told him was in the heat of the moment. I bet if you asked him now if he had changed his mind, he would say yes. Because the Alex I knew cared deeply for his family. Once he had time to think about it, I'm sure Alex would have told you that he was wrong and that he wanted you to keep the baby. Did he try to get hold of you again after that conversation?"

Rebecca pressed the heel of her hand against her eye. She had a sudden pulsing pain in her head.

"I don't know," she said in a ragged whisper. "I deleted our chat program, changed my phone number and shut down the email address he had for me. And then we moved to Chicago."

"So you never had any more conversations after he told you to abort the baby?" Connor asked.

Rebecca was grateful for the darkness of the room as a tear trickled down her cheek. "I was so young, Connor. That wasn't how he was supposed to react to the news that I was carrying our baby. I didn't think for a minute that he would change his mind. He had seemed so determined. It was like he was totally different from the man I married, and it scared me."

"Ah, Becca. I'm so sorry, sweetheart. I wish you'd told me sooner."

Rebecca sniffled as she nodded even though she knew Connor couldn't see her. "We are here with him now. After Jordan discovered who he was and where he lived, he came to find him. Things are a bit tense."

"I can imagine that's a bit of an understatement," Connor said. "How did Alex take the news?"

"The way Jordan found out about him has been concerning, but Alex has taken it in stride. The tension mainly comes from telling Jordan the truth about what happened. About why Alex hasn't been in his life up until now." Rebecca sighed. "He didn't take the news that Alex had asked me to abort the baby too well."

"I can imagine that's true, knowing Jordan like I do. However, I do think that he'll come around in time. But how are you doing?"

"I'm doing okay. I didn't think this day would ever come, to be honest, but now that it has, it's a bit of a relief. Everything is still up in the air, though. I think Alex would like me to consider moving back to the Twin Cities so that he's closer to Jordan, but I'm not willing to make that big of a decision just yet."

"Yeah, that is a pretty big decision to make, though at least with your career and Jordan being homeschooled the transition wouldn't be too bad."

"Yes, you're right about that," Rebecca agreed. "But we both have friends in Chicago and it has been our home for the last fifteen years. And there's still the matter of the marriage that needs to be cleared up."

"The marriage? Are you telling me that you never divorced Alex?"

"Yep. At the time, I was too scared that he would find me and discover that I kept the baby. And to be honest, in my mind back then, he'd suddenly become a very different person than the man I'd married. And that person scared me. If he could so easily dismiss our child's life, what else might he do? So, at the time, fear and just not knowing what to do kept me from filing for divorce."

"Well, that was your excuse then. What's been your excuse for the past few years?"

Rebecca sat for a moment, trying to gather her thoughts. "Still fear, I would imagine. If I were to file for divorce, I figured I'd have to reveal Jordan's presence. And if I did that, I didn't know if he would then file for custody. Or worse yet, he'd reject Jordan...again."

"I guess the reason you're such a good writer, is that your imagination is really crazy. You certainly managed to imagine scenarios where Jordan was at risk. Do you still feel that way now?"

Rebecca shook her head, then remembering Connor wasn't there with her, she said, "No, I don't feel that way at all. Alex hasn't made any demands where Jordan is concerned. He has asked if I'll allow him to be a part of Jordan's life, and of course, he asked about us moving here, but he's made no outright demands on either of us."

"That sounds about right. Alex always was a pretty standup guy."

Not wanting the conversation to turn toward all of Alex's positive qualities, Rebecca endeavored to steer it in a different direction. "Well, enough about my soap opera of a life. What's been going on with you?"

Connor chuckled. "Nice try, Sis. You know I can't talk

about a lot of what I do. However, there is something that I can share."

"Are you going to be able to make it home for Christmas?" Rebecca asked excitedly.

"Well, I don't know. It doesn't sound like you're going to be *home* for Christmas."

"Oh." Realizing what she'd said, Rebecca sat speechless for a moment. "You know how it is. Anywhere Jordan is, is home to me. Alex told me that you're more than welcome to join us here for Christmas. In fact, he seemed rather excited at the idea. Would you be able to come here?"

"I most definitely would," Connor agreed readily. "And not to put any pressure on you, but it would be really helpful if you would decide where you're actually going to end up."

"End up?"

"Yep. I don't really want to try and land a job in Chicago if you're planning to pull up roots and move to the Twin Cities."

Rebecca gave a squeal of excitement. "You're coming home for good?"

"That's the plan. I finished my last job, and now I'm just going through debriefing and preparing to leave the company. I should be finished all of it before Christmas. I'll be packing up my stuff here and shipping it home. I suppose for now I'll have it shipped to Chicago, but if things change, I can always ship it on from there."

The idea of having her brother close by again after so many years was a huge answer to prayer for Rebecca. Of all of their family, he was the one she'd always felt closest to. To think that he'd be home now and not off risking his life was a relief. "I honestly don't know where we'll end up, but if we do move here, you can just ship all your stuff along with ours."

"Well, now that we've both shared the big news of our lives, I'd better scoot. I just got back a few hours ago and got your message. Now I need to go take care of some paperwork and a few other things before I call it a night. I'll call you again soon. I love you, Becca."

"I love you too. Your news has made me the happiest girl in the world. I can't wait to see you and hug you again."

Rebecca stayed in the chair for a few more minutes, shivering against a bit of a draft. Her emotions were all over the place. Once again. For someone who tried to not let their emotions rule them too often, Rebecca had certainly been fighting with hers ever since she'd called Jordan to find out where he was. As her conversation with Connor replayed in her mind, Rebecca realized there were a few things that she would need to rethink over the next few days.

It sounded like Connor thought it might be a good plan for her and Jordan to move to the Twin Cities. Knowing that he would most likely come with them, the idea suddenly held a lot more appeal. Rebecca realized that she hadn't wanted to be on her own in an unfamiliar city. If Connor made the move as well, it would make the adjustment a whole lot easier.

With a smile on her face, Rebecca left the living room and returned to where the others were still gathered around the dining table. No one questioned her about the call as she slid back into her seat and finished up her now cold dinner. She'd talk to Jordan about it when they got back to their apartment. He was no doubt going to be as thrilled as she was at the prospect of Connor finally putting down roots close by.

14

As SOON AS Alex made it to his room, he quickly set up his laptop on his desk and logged in to see the images that were being fed to them through the cameras worn by the surveillance team. He'd hung around the office long enough to hear that the team had reached their location. It had been difficult to set up since it was a rural property with no buildings around. In the end, the guys had had settled within a grove of trees. They would take turns moving to the edge of the grove to maintain a constant surveillance of the property.

With winter upon them, the days were shorter so the sun was already setting by the time they'd arrived. Surveillance now was done using night vision goggles and cameras. Alex had taken the time to drive home as they were setting up camp, but now they were feeding live images back to the command center. He made sure the sound was turned up and walked to his bedroom to change out of his suit.

While he was glad to be home, Alex could've done without hearing Rebecca tell somebody she loved them and couldn't wait to hug them as soon as he'd walked in the door. It was the one question that he had so far not been able to bring himself to ask her. Just because he'd chosen to remain uninvolved over all these years didn't mean that she had done the same. While it gave him a bit of a sick feeling to think that might be the case, right then there was nothing he could do about it. If, in fact, she was involved with someone else, moping around wouldn't change anything.

Right then, he needed to focus on the situation with Alana. He would deal with things with Rebecca once they determined whether this was a valid lead or not.

After pulling on a pair of jeans and a sweatshirt, Alex sat down in the chair at his desk and stared at the images on his laptop screen. He'd looked through enough night vision goggles over the years to be able to determine what he was looking at. Unfortunately, the house appeared deserted from where they sat. There was no movement in or out of the building. He tried not to feel discouraged, knowing things could change in an instant.

Conversation between the surveillance team members flowed from his speakers. Most of it had to do with the setup of their camp and the logistics of the surveillance. Each of them was miked and would remain so for the duration of their time in Tennessee.

On occasion, Alex missed the adrenaline rush of being part of something like this. He participated in training events at the compound that would often involve working alongside the BlackThorpe team against another visiting team. Those scenarios would sometimes involve surveillance and searching for the enemy. But this situation with Alana was the most high-stakes surveillance they'd conducted in a while.

Hearing a tap on his door, Alex pushed back from his desk and walked over to open it. When he saw it was Adrianne, Alex stepped back to let her into the room. He shut the door behind her and motioned for her to follow him to his desk. The meeting earlier that day hadn't involved her and Melanie, mainly because this wasn't something that fell under their responsibilities at the company. Also, the fewer people that knew, the better. Not that he didn't trust his sisters, but at the time, seeking them out to update them hadn't fit into his day.

Adrianne gestured to his laptop. "What's going on?"

Alex pulled another chair around to face the laptop then sat back down on his own. Adrianne sat in the one next to him, her brow furrowed as she stared at the monitor.

She shot him a quick look. "Is that an active mission? Did one of them get into some trouble? You don't usually monitor these things, especially from home."

"Yes, it's a surveillance mission." Alex debated telling her the details. If this turned out to be nothing, the fewer people that knew about it, the better. But she was his sister, and she knew how much Alana's disappearance had affected him. "Eric found a potential lead on Alana. The team is down there now checking it out."

Adrianne's eyes widened as her gaze went back to the screen. "When did this all happen?"

"Eric came to me this morning with a possible lead. We met with Marcus and the others who would be involved in the surveillance after that. Once we determined it was worth pursuing, Eric and a team of guys headed down there."

"Where exactly is down there?" Adrianne asked, wincing as a particularly colorful phrase came through the laptop speakers.

Alex reached out and turned down the volume a bit before answering her. "They're in Tennessee at a property that is owned by Craig's mother's family."

Adrianne listened, her gaze locked on the flickering images on the screen, as Alex laid out all the details of the mission.

"Tyler and Melanie didn't mention anything about this at supper. Do they know what's going on?"

Alex shook his head. "We kept the information limited to

PROOF OF LIFE   173

those who would be directly involved. If we need more help,
we'll let others know."

They sat in silence for a couple of minutes, both of them
listening and watching. Alex sensed that like him, Adrianne
struggled with allowing herself to become too hopeful.

"Did you grab something to eat on the way home?"
Adrianne asked.

"No. I came straight here. I wanted to be here when they
started actively surveilling the house."

"We had chicken and dumplings for supper. It was pretty
good." Adrianne got to her feet. "I'll go grab you something
from the kitchen."

Before he could say anything more, she'd exited his room,
leaving the door open a small crack. Alex turned his
attention back to the screen, recognizing Eric's voice as he
spoke with a couple of the men. It appeared that they were
going to try approaching the house to use infrared goggles.
That might give them a better idea if someone was in the
house.

The fact that the building remained dark even after the
sun had set didn't mean too much. Someone determined to
stay hidden would most likely cover windows so that no light
escaped. Infrared, however, would reveal heat sources that
they couldn't otherwise see with the naked eye.

This could be a turning point in the investigation if it
revealed one or more heat sources within the house. Alex felt
his muscles tense as the men began to make their move. He
almost wished that he'd stayed at the command center, but
he had also felt the pull of being with Rebecca and Jordan.
He could always go back to the office, but since he was
already set up here and things were beginning to unfold, he
figured he might as well just stay put.

It didn't take long for the men to come back with the
information that there appeared to be no heat signatures
within the house. That included light fixtures or anything
that could have given off heat.

"I still think we have a valid lead here, guys," Eric said,
his voice strong and steady. "It's entirely possible that this

house has a basement or some sort of crawl space underneath it. If that's where Alana is being held, we wouldn't be able to pick up the heat signature for her since the ground would block us. I'd like to wait at least another day or two to see if there is any activity around the house. Craig could be staying elsewhere, but he'd need to come back here at least every couple of days."

Alex sighed. All of that was assuming that Alana was still alive. And that Craig actually cared enough to still take care of her. He leaned back in the chair and rubbed a hand across his eyes. And as he'd been doing throughout most the day, he once again prayed. For Alana wherever she was. For the safety of his men. For wisdom for Eric to know what moves to make.

The door pushed open and Alex glanced over to see that Adrianne had returned with a tray. He moved his laptop over slightly so that she could set it on the edge of his desk. When his stomach rumbled at the enticing warm aroma, Alex realized it had been a long time since lunch. And even then it had been a quick sandwich eaten while they continued to discuss the mission. Eric and his crew had already been on their way at that point, but Trent had continued to dig into the property and its surroundings.

"I'm going to head to my room," Adrianne said. "Let me know if something comes up. No matter what the time."

Alex nodded as he lifted a spoonful of food from the bowl. Once she disappeared, he began to eat in earnest. He was pretty sure that he'd have his laptop set up on the bed beside him when he decided to finally go to sleep. No doubt the excitement of something happening would come through the speakers and wake him up.

Once he'd finished the bowl of chicken and dumplings and eaten the brownie Adrianne had added to the tray, Alex felt marginally better. Since nothing was happening with the men aside from the surveillance, Alex decided to take a quick trip down to the kitchen with his dirty dishes.

He was surprised to find Rebecca and Jordan still there, seated in the breakfast nook with Melanie and Tyler.

"I didn't even know you were home until Adrianne came looking for food for you," Melanie said as she slipped out of the booth. "What are you doing holed up in your room?"

"I'm just monitoring a mission that we have going on right now." Alex looked over the table and met Rebecca's gaze. "I assume you are responsible for the supper?" When she nodded, he said, "It was very good. Thank you."

"You're welcome."

"Rebecca has just been telling us that she finally heard from her brother Connor and that he is planning to join us here for Christmas," Melanie said with a smile.

Realizing that was probably who he'd heard her talking to, Alex felt a little chagrined. Thankfully, he hadn't made a big deal out of it. "That's good news. The more, the merrier."

"Also, Mom and Dad want us to go to their place for supper sometime this week," Melanie said as she began to take the dishes off his tray. "I told her I'd check with you guys and let them know."

Alex leaned against the counter, crossing his arms over his chest. "A lot depends on the status of this mission. I would like to monitor it until it's finished, but at this point, we don't have a definite end date."

"Okay," Melanie said without argument. "I'll let Mom know. Chances are she'll be happy with whoever comes as long as Jordan's there."

Alex glanced at his son and saw a grin spread across his face. "That is no doubt true."

Realizing he was probably going to be up for a few more hours, Alex turned to grab a mug from the cupboard. He poured himself a cup of coffee from the still warm carafe and took a sip.

"Well as long as this mission doesn't run over Christmas, I think Mom will be okay if you miss one meal," Melanie said.

"I certainly hope that it's over well before then." He took a few more sips of his coffee then turned to top up his mug.

"And on that note, I need to get back upstairs. Have a good night."

Back in his room, Alex took his seat once again. The minute seemed to tick slowly by as he sipped on his cup of coffee and listened to the conversation that flowed through the laptop speakers. Finally around midnight, he moved his laptop onto one side of his queen-size bed. He was tired enough that the off-and-on conversation between the guys didn't keep him awake, and he fell asleep praying that he would be woken in the night with good news.

Rebecca heard the alarm on the security panel on the wall in the kitchen beep, signifying someone had walked into the house. She looked up from the casserole she was making, expecting to see Tyler and Melanie. When Alex appeared in the entrance to the kitchen, Rebecca looked at him in surprise. Based on what he'd said the night before, she'd figured he'd be late getting home again that night.

"Everything okay?" she asked as he walked into the kitchen.

Alex went to one of the cupboards and pulled out a mug. "Yeah. As well as can be expected."

He set the mug under the spout of the single cup coffee maker and slid a pod into place before starting it up.

Rebecca could sense the tension in him as he stood there waiting for his coffee. She wanted to ask him more about what was going on, but that really wasn't her right. Though, technically, she *was* still his wife. "Are you going to be here for supper?"

Alex nodded, his gaze on the stream of coffee pouring into his cup. When it was done, he picked up the mug and took a sip. The look of satisfaction on Alex's face after he took a couple more sips almost made her want a cup for herself. Maybe once she was done the casserole.

Rebecca was surprised that he didn't leave the kitchen immediately upon filling his mug. She picked up the large glass pan she'd used for the casserole and carried it to the oven. After she slid it inside and set the timer, she turned around to look at Alex. She could see the strain on his face and the circles under his eyes made it seem like he hadn't slept well in days.

"What's Jordan up to?" Alex asked as he continued to lean back against the counter and sip his coffee.

"I left him upstairs working on a project with his friend Robby. They're both doing the same homeschool units so Robby's mom and I set up a project for them to do. He'll be going with Tyler a little bit later to a basketball game." She wondered how Alex might feel about Jordan continuing to spend time with Tyler.

"I hope he has fun. Tyler's a great guy. I wish I had been able to go with him too, but this mission came up unexpectedly and I need to be available at a moment's notice. I'd hate to drag Jordan out in the middle of the game because something came up."

"I explained to Jordan after you talked to us last night that you might be tied up for a few days. He said he understood, but that he hoped you'd be able to take him to the shooting range again soon."

Alex nodded. "As soon as this situation is resolved, one way or another, I will make sure that Jordan gets to go back to do some more shooting."

"I didn't really get a chance to talk to you last night, but I just want to make sure that it's still okay with you that Connor comes to join us here for Christmas."

"That's fine. I know that you are looking forward to seeing him, so I would never deny you that." Alex took another sip of his coffee then looked at her. "Did you talk to him at all about what's going on here with you, Jordan and me?"

Rebecca nodded then busied herself making her own cup of coffee. "I never told him that you were Jordan's father, so he was pretty shocked. Pretty surprised that we managed to date without our parents or him ever finding out."

"I really thought he knew something was going on. But then he wasn't really one to talk since I'm pretty sure he was dating while in high school too."

Rebecca looked at him in surprise. "Connor was dating in high school?"

"Pretty sure he was. Although I can't tell you who. I was kind of wrapped up in keeping our own dates secret. I didn't want to delve too deeply into what he was doing for fear that he'd want to do the same with me."

Rebecca laughed. "I guess I'm as surprised to hear that he was dating as he was to hear that I was."

Alex regarded her over the edge of his mug. "So how did he take the news?"

"That you're Jordan's dad?" Rebecca asked. She cupped her mug in both hands and took a sip, grateful for the warmth.

Alex nodded, but he didn't say anything further.

"He was surprised of course, but he wasn't upset." Rebecca wasn't about to go into detail regarding their conversation. At some point, she'd need to address it with Alex, but she only planned to do that if and when it became apparent that there was something more there between them. "I think he's looking forward to touching base with you again."

"I am too." Alex seemed to be about to say something more but then he just took another sip of his coffee. "I want to thank you for the cooking and baking you've been doing around here. I certainly didn't expect that of you."

"It's no trouble at all. Jordan and I are kind of keeping the same schedule here that we keep when we are home in Chicago."

Alex tipped his head back and emptied his mug. As he leaned to put it in the dishwasher, he said, "All the same, I appreciate what you've done for us. I can't lie, it's nice coming home to find supper on the table. Between all of our schedules, we usually have to make supper after we get home or if it's too late, we get takeout."

"I enjoy cooking, and it gives me something to do while I'm here."

Alex nodded then said, "Well, I need to head up to my office for a bit. I'll see you in a little while."

As Rebecca watched Alex walk away, she acknowledged the warmth that had filled her when he'd voiced his appreciation for her cooking. It had been one of those things that she dreamed of during those couple of months between their wedding and her discovering that she was pregnant. She'd longed to create a home with Alex where she could do the things she enjoyed like cooking, baking and decorating.

Alone with her thoughts as she cleaned up the kitchen, Rebecca once again pondered the whole situation with Alex. The emotions she was experiencing the most, stemmed from the memories of when she and Alex had been together. She knew that that was not what she should base any of her decisions on now. She had loved the Alex she thought he was all those years ago. Could she trust Alex enough now to open her heart to him again?

By all appearances, Alex seemed to be a man of integrity now. She could see he cared for his family. He worked hard at his company. And she'd seen the respect the BlackThorpe employees had for him. She knew he was a man of faith. But was all of that enough? There were glimpses of the man she thought him to be. Thinking back to the time before their separation, Rebecca could see hints of the man Alex would become before fear had clouded both their judgements. Was there still love in her heart for him?

Rebecca stared down at the cloth she clenched in her hands. That was a question she wasn't sure she was prepared to answer. In her mind right then, the bigger question was if there was still love in Alex's heart for her? When he looked at her, did he see glimpses of the woman he once loved? Over the years, Rebecca had often wondered if Alex had really loved her. Back then, represented their love. At the time, it had felt like he was dismissing their love as easily as he dismissed their baby.

But now, between the conversations she'd had with Alex and then with Connor, Rebecca realized that she'd had it all wrong. Though she could never accept what Alex had asked her to do, she understood now what had brought him to the point of asking her to do it. And if Connor was right when he said that Alex would've changed his mind, Rebecca wondered if her hasty actions had killed any love Alex might have had for her.

Though he treated her with the utmost respect now, there were few indications that Alex was experiencing any of the emotions that she was. And it wasn't just the emotional memories. She struggled with the physical ones as well. When they'd gotten married, she'd never felt as safe in her life up to that point as she had in Alex's arms. She'd loved the feel of his arms around her, holding her as if she were the most precious thing in the world to him. They'd only had a few short days together but it had been enough to leave her with memories for a lifetime.

During the time between when he had to leave to return to his base and when she let him know she was pregnant, their communication had been somewhat sporadic. She had hoped that they'd be able to chat online on a regular basis, but their schedules and the time difference seemed to constantly defeat their efforts. In the end, they'd relied more on email communication than anything else. That, in and of itself, had been a huge challenge.

While her emails to him had always been full of news and updates, his emails in return had been much sparser. It had also become pretty clear that she was much more comfortable expressing her love and affection for him in emails than he was. Maybe that was why she had been so easily convinced that Alex had been rejecting her along with the baby.

The noise of the door opening pulled Rebecca from her thoughts. Pasting a smile on her face, she turned to greet Melanie and Tyler as they walked into the kitchen together. She barely had time to greet them before the door opened again and Jordan appeared.

While they all discussed their plan for the evening, Rebecca finished setting the table and by the time Adrianne arrived about fifteen minutes later, the casserole was ready to come out of the oven.

"Alex came home earlier," Rebecca said as she finished making a salad. "Does someone want to see if he wants to come down for dinner?"

"I'll go and let him know," Adrianne said. "I want to change before eating anyway."

By the time Adrianne returned with Alex, all the food was on the table and waiting for them. After Alex had said grace, they all dug in. Throughout the meal, Rebecca noticed Alex frequently checking his phone. Once again she was thankful for Melanie and Tyler's presence. If it had just been her, Jordan, Adrianne, and Alex, it would've been a very quiet meal.

They didn't linger over the meal like they had on previous nights. Melanie, Tyler, and Jordan had to leave for the basketball game, and Rebecca could see that Alex was eager to return to his office. Adrianne stayed around long enough to help her clean up the dishes from the meal, but then she too disappeared upstairs.

Though she knew that she could always use the extra time to work on her book, Rebecca decided to give Maureen a call and have another girl chat. This time, maybe they could video chat because Rebecca found herself really missing the visual interaction with her best friend. So, after getting herself a cup of coffee, Rebecca grabbed her phone and made her way into the living room where the Christmas tree was. She supposed that she should've returned to the apartment, but for some reason, it felt better to stay in the house where Alex was.

she hadn't been able to believe that Alex could love her and ask her to do something so horrible. That he would want her to get rid of the baby that

Alex rested his arms on the desk and leaned forward to watch the movement on the screen. It was the end of day two, and still they had no definite proof that Alana was being held in the house they were surveilling. He wasn't sure how long they were going to let this mission run without something more concrete. He knew that Eric felt, in his gut, that this house was of some importance to the case. Something told him that even if they didn't see any other signs of life, Eric would want to investigate the interior of the house before finally pulling out. Alex wouldn't have a problem agreeing to that. And he didn't think Marcus would either.

He'd been sitting in front of the laptop for a couple hours now and needed a break. Pushing his chair back, Alex got to his feet and lifted his arms above his head to stretch out the kinks in his back. He twisted side to side and then, with one last look at the laptop, he grabbed his phone and left his room. The house was quiet as he made his way down the stairs. Although, as he got closer to the bottom of the staircase, he could hear conversation coming from the living room. Not wanting to interrupt anything, he veered off towards the kitchen in search of a cup of strong black coffee.

As he waited for the coffee to fill his mug, Alex investigated a few of the containers on the counter. He struck jackpot when he opened the third container and found a batch of chocolate chip oatmeal cookies. At least, he hoped they were chocolate chip. He inspected them a little more closely before snagging three of them. He wasn't normally such a pig, but then it wasn't a terribly common occurrence to find homemade cookies in the house. Periodically, his mom would bring some over, but that was more sporadic than he would've liked.

Taking his cookies and mug of coffee, Alex settled into the breakfast nook, phone close at hand in case anything should come up. He knew he didn't need to be monitoring the situation as closely as he was but he just couldn't seem to help himself. All of them had a lot of emotional investment in what had happened with Justin and Alana. It was hard to keep an objective outlook when it was someone they cared about who was in danger.

Alex broke off a piece of cookie and popped it in his mouth. He stared out the windows beside the breakfast nook as he took a sip of coffee to wash it down. Sitting there in the quiet, Alex allowed his thoughts to go to Rebecca and Jordan. He would've liked to have been the one taking Jordan to the basketball game, but with things the way they were with the mission, it was better that he stayed at the house.

But had it really been more important that he be there to monitor his laptop? He would've had his phone if something had come up. They would've been able to contact him immediately if he were needed. As he sat there now, having spent the evening watching nothing happen, he realized that he'd wasted an opportunity. He'd put his work before his son. Maybe he really didn't know how to be a father. Especially in these beginning stages when it was even more important that they spend time together.

Alex sighed and bent his head forward. Once again doubts filled him and made him question whether he was worthy to be a father. He'd heard all the sayings over the years about how contributing biologically to a child didn't necessarily make a man a dad. That a dad was the one who was there with the child as they grew up. Who made the child feel loved and cherished and safe. And he had done none of those things. And now that he had a chance to spend time with Jordan, he was brushing it aside in favor of work.

Maybe Rebecca saw the inadequacies in him and that was why she was unwilling to commit to the move to the Twin Cities. He didn't want to lose contact with Jordan, but there was a part of him that kept popping up to remind him how woefully inadequate he was for the job of father. Dad. It hadn't escaped his notice that Jordan didn't call him father or dad. In fact, Jordan seemed to go out of his way to call him nothing at all. Not even Alex.

After the time at the shooting range, Alex had hoped that it was the start of rebuilding the relationship he'd had with Rebecca and also the one he'd started having with Jordan before the revelations had ruined it all. But now it felt like, for that one step forward, he had taken two steps back. How many times could he falter in this process and expect Rebecca and Jordan to give him another chance?

"Alex?"

15

ALEX JERKED HIS head around to see Rebecca standing next to the counter in the kitchen. "Oh, hey. I didn't realize that you were still here."

Rebecca came over to the breakfast knock and slid in across from him. "Yeah. I decided to hang out and wait for Jordan to get home. I called my friend in Chicago and had a video chat with her to pass the time."

Her words reminded Alex that Rebecca had a whole life in Chicago. "Do you have a lot of friends there?"

Rebecca reached across the table and snagged one of the cookies sitting in front of him. She took a bite of it before responding. "I don't have a huge circle of friends, but I do have a couple of good friends and then Maureen, the woman I was speaking with tonight, is my best friend. She has a son the same age as Jordan and they're best friends too."

Was it even fair of him to ask her to give up those friendships in order to move to be closer to him? Surely, if put on a scale of importance in her life, everything about Chicago would outweigh him. "I'm beginning to realize how unfair it is of me to expect you to give up your whole life in Chicago and move here. I just want you to know, I won't pressure you about that anymore. I do hope that you might be willing to work with me on some sort of visitation schedule with Jordan. I could come to Chicago or maybe he could fly here, and I'd cover all expenses if that was what turned out to work best."

Rebecca stared at him for a minute, and Alex wished he could read her mind because he certainly couldn't read her expression. Unfortunately, before she could react to his offer, the front door opened and he heard Jordan's excited voice as he and Tyler exchanged thoughts on the game.

"Hey, Mom," Jordan said with a wide grin on his face. "They won!"

"That's great, sweetheart. I'm glad you had a good time."

Alex sat silently as Jordan plopped down in the seat next to his mom, listening to his excited recap of his evening with Melanie and Tyler. Would Jordan have been nearly as excited to spend the evening with him? Even if the Timberwolves had won?

Of course, it made sense that Jordan had enjoyed his evening with Tyler and Melanie. Tyler was an outgoing man, and Melanie had really come out of her shell in recent weeks, thanks in no small part to Tyler. As part of his job, Alex had learned early on to never let his emotions show. Unfortunately, it carried over into his personal life and now to his interactions with Rebecca and Jordan.

Adrianne was usually more engaged and outgoing then she had been recently. Alex still thought that something was wrong there, but his sister was keeping whatever was bothering her to herself. Usually, he would've tried harder to get to the bottom of what was bothering his twin, but with everything else going on at the moment—all the balls that he was trying to keep in the air—Adrianne was a ball that had gotten dropped. Except he was pretty sure he'd also dropped the Jordan and Rebecca balls. The only thing that had his complete attention lately was work.

What was it that kept him from being able to rearrange his priorities to what they needed to be?

"So you're still not sure about making dinner tomorrow night at Mom's?" Melanie asked as she stood next to the breakfast nook, Tyler's arm around her waist.

Alex thought for a minute. Here was another opportunity and this time he needed to make the right choice. "Go ahead and tell her that I'll be there as well."

Melanie's brow furrowed. "But what about the mission that you're monitoring?"

"I'll make time for the dinner. If something happens with the mission, they know how to get hold of me."

He saw Tyler give a slight nod of his head. The man had been briefed along with Ryan on the mission earlier that day. Though the two men weren't technically part of the management team of BlackThorpe, Alex saw potential in both of them to one day move up into those positions if they wanted to.

"Mom will be happy to hear that. Now if I can just get Adrianne to agree, it will be a great evening."

"Make sure to extend the invitation to Ryan as well, if you'd like him to be there," Alex said as he lifted his mug to his lips. He knew that Ryan had no family in the city, and as Tyler's best friend, it had only been natural to start including him in their get-togethers once Tyler and Melanie were dating.

"I'll make sure to let him know," Tyler said.

"I'm not sure if any of you would be interested, but our church is having their Christmas program this Sunday night," Melanie said. "I'm going to see if Mom and Dad want to come too."

As Melanie talked a little bit more about the program, Alex realized that this was the first Christmas season where he was getting more involved than usual. Between the decorating of the tree and going to the Christmas programs, this was definitely one of the more active Christmas seasons he'd been a part of. If only the situation with Alana was resolved. It was hard to truly get into the spirit of Christmas with something like that hanging over their heads. While this may be one of his better Christmases, he had a feeling it was one of the worst for Justin and Caden.

He had just finished off his coffee and the last cookie when Tyler announced that he was leaving. Jordan jumped up and gave him a hug, thanking him once again for taking him to the game. Melanie walked with Tyler to the door, leaving Alex alone with Rebecca and Jordan. There was no awkward silence, however, as Jordan continued to talk about the game and how much he wished his friend Robby could've gone with him.

Melanie returned a few minutes later but only stayed long enough to say good night. Alex figured that Rebecca and Jordan would be next to leave, but to his surprise Rebecca told Jordan to go to the apartment and that she'd be there in a few minutes. Jordan's gaze darted between the two of them before giving a nod and leaving them alone.

"I just want to make sure I understood what you said correctly." Rebecca leaned forward, bracing her elbows on the table. Her brow furrowed over her blue-green eyes. "Are you saying now that you don't want us to move here?"

Alex fought the urge to look away, afraid she would see too much in his eyes. "No. I'm just acknowledging the fact that you have a whole life in Chicago and that it was wrong of me to pressure you to move here. If you decide that you want to move here, I want it to be your decision only. No pressure from me. And if you do decide to stay in Chicago, I will do my best to work with you to arrange some sort of schedule for me to see Jordan."

Rebecca sat back in her seat and stared at him. "What brought on this change of heart? You seemed quite determined that us moving here was the best decision."

Alex shifted in his seat, his feet bumping into hers. He drew his legs back and sat forward. "I just realized that I'm asking you and Jordan to give up an awful lot and I don't have much to offer you in return."

"What about the opportunity for Jordan to get to know his father?" Rebecca asked, an edge to her tone.

"Well, if you're open to working with me, I think we can make sure that that still happens."

Rebecca pressed her lips together and crossed her arms as she stared at him. "You have been all over the place when it comes to dealing with Jordan and me. One day you seem determined to make things work between you and Jordan, and now you're telling me that you'd be happy if he ended up back in Chicago." She got to her feet and then turned to look at him. "You know, for a little while there I thought that you were going to make the effort to see where things could go for us three. But it seems like maybe that's just a bit too much work for you. What with everything else you have going on in your life right now, I'm just glad you showed your true colors before I wasted any more time contemplating a move here."

Before Alex could say anything in reply, Rebecca walked away, leaving him sitting in stunned silence. Her words shouldn't hurt so much. Had she really been seriously contemplating moving to the Twin Cities? Had his own doubts about his ability to be a father just dashed any chance at a real future with Rebecca and Jordan? He hadn't even realized that she was thinking along those lines.

But now what did he do? It just seemed that whether he was nineteen or thirty-five, he didn't know how to deal with Rebecca. As Alex sat there, anger and frustration began to burn within him. Where on earth did Rebecca get off saying that he was the one all over the place? She hadn't come out and told him that she was seriously considering a move to the Twin Cities. Everything he'd gotten from her had pointed to her wanting to return to the home she shared with Jordan in Chicago.

Alex shoved back from the table, grabbing his empty mug as he stood. True, he hadn't exactly been clear about what he was thinking, but they'd both been at fault here. Not just him. He didn't know about Rebecca's motivation, but for him, underlying it all, was the fact that they were still married. She was his wife. He knew at this point it was merely a technicality, but there was a small part of him—or maybe not so small really—that had wondered if perhaps this was their chance to become a family. The three of them.

After getting himself one more cup of coffee, Alex headed for the stairs. To say he was confused about the whole situation was putting it mildly. And if there was one thing that Alex hated, it was confusion. He liked things well planned out. Well thought out. And under his control. That was absolutely not the case when it came to Rebecca and Jordan. And he had tried to keep control even when he gave it back to her but clearly that had backfired.

So now he was left angry and frustrated, wondering what it was going to take to figure out how to make things work with Jordan, even if things weren't going to work out with Rebecca.

Rebecca tried to get her temper to cool between the time when she stepped out of the house and stepped into the apartment, but one look at Jordan's face as she peeled off her jacket told her that she hadn't been too successful. He remained silent as she hung up her jacket and slipped out of her shoes, but when she turned back around, he said, "What's going on with the two of you?"

Uncertain how Jordan would take the news that Alex was basically suggesting they go back to Chicago, Rebecca took her time answering his question. She went into the kitchen found a mug and made herself a cup of tea. Jordan knew her well enough to understand that she would answer his question, even if she wasn't doing it right away.

When she finally had a cup of hot tea in her hands, Rebecca settled at the table and looked at Jordan. He was seated on the sofa bed reclining against the back of it with his feet flat on the mattress. He held his phone in his hands and had no doubt been texting with Robby, telling him all about the game that he'd been to with Tyler and Melanie.

"Alex wanted to let me know that he was no longer going to pressure me to leave Chicago and move us here."

Jordan swung his feet over the edge of the bed and got up. He walked over to the table and sat down in the chair across from her. "Is that his way of saying that he doesn't want us here?"

Rebecca sighed. "To be honest, sweetie, I really have no idea. I'm not sure what has prompted him to back off from his original desire to have us move here."

With his eyes on the cell phone in his hands, Jordan chewed on his lower lip. He shot her a quick glance. "Do you think it's because of me? Because I was kinda mad at him about what he said last week?"

"Honestly, I kinda get the feeling that Alex is struggling to know how to be a dad. The times he's been most comfortable with you have been when they've involved something from his job. I think BlackThorpe has been his life for so long, he doesn't know how to deal with a situation like he has with us."

"Was he always like that?"

Rebecca realized that this was the first time that Jordan had really asked for any details about what it had been like back then. Before everything had fallen apart. "He's always been a very focused man. He always seemed to know what he wanted in life and was determined to get it."

"And I guess he wanted you, but he didn't want me." Jordan's thumb slid back and forth over the darkened screen of his phone. "Maybe he still doesn't."

Rebecca wished she could say with one hundred percent certainty that that wasn't the case, but she couldn't. Clearly she and Alex needed to sit down and hash all of this out. They just needed to get it all out on the table. The marriage. Jordan. Whether or not she wanted to move from Chicago. Somehow she had to get Alex to open up and put it all out there because the uncertainty was hurting her boy. And if Alex cared anything for him at all, he was going to have to man up and work with her to get this all figured out.

Maureen had asked her once again, about renewing her

relationship with Alex. Up until the moment he'd ticked her off in the kitchen, Rebecca had found herself more strongly considering that option. But now, she wasn't so sure. Which wasn't really fair. Relationships had their ups and downs and if she was ready to bail on Alex the first time she got upset with something he said, then she was as bad as he was for backing down from what had seemed initially to be his desire to work things out.

In all honesty, they were probably both really out of practice when it came to a personal relationship. From everything she'd seen and heard, there seemed to be no indication that he'd ever had a relationship since they had been together. The relationship with friends, family, or children was different from that of a relationship with a spouse or significant other. She needed to remember that as she tried to work this through with Alex. She just really hoped he would listen to her and be willing to knock down a few of the walls that he seemed intent on keeping in place. She wondered if he was actually aware of the fact that he had built those walls around him.

Reaching out, she laid her hand on Jordan's. "I'm going to talk with him to see if we can't just get this figured out. Right now we're all just kind of operating under the assumption of what we think each other is thinking and what the other wants. We need to put it all on the table. I need you to also understand that when you chose to take it upon yourself to come see Alex without telling me, you opened yourself up to the consequences of that decision. And part of those consequences was hearing something that you didn't want to hear. You're blowing hot and cold with Alex as much as he is with us.

"So I need you to really think, Jordan. I haven't pressured you to spend time with Alex, nor have I pressured you to consider a relationship with him. But I think we're at the point now, where you need to put some serious thought into what you want and let me know."

Jordan kept his gaze lowered and didn't say anything, but then he swallowed hard and looked up at her, his eyes damp. "I want him to want me. I want him to love me."

Rebecca's heart squeezed painfully as she took in her son's emotional response. She slid off her chair and moved to his side, wrapping an arm around his shoulders. Pressing her cheek against his head, Rebecca said, "He does want you, Jordan, but I think he's scared that you don't want him." She moved back a little and tipped his head back with the press of her fingers beneath his chin. "And that's why we need to be totally honest with each other. Even if it might hurt, we need to know where each of us stands before we can move forward."

Jordan rubbed a finger underneath his eye. "So do I have to tell him that?"

"I think it would be best if I talk with him first, but then after that — yes, I think you should tell him that. And hopefully, he'll have something to tell you in return. Then we'll have something to work with."

"And if he decides that he doesn't want us, then what?"

"We'll just have to pray that that is not how it turns out. I wish I could give you more of a guarantee — I would love one for myself too — but right now, all I can offer you is that we're going to try and figure this out."

Rebecca returned to her seat and took another sip of her rapidly cooling tea. Jordan sat there with her, clearly mulling things over in his mind.

He looked over at her, the tears and emotions from earlier gone. "Do you think if we do move here, Robby could come to visit and maybe we could go to another game with Tyler?"

Rebecca smiled, glad for the resiliency of her son. "I'm pretty sure that that could be arranged."

After a restless night of sleep, Alex was in his office early the next morning. The sun hadn't even risen in the sky as he stared out the window, coffee cup in hand. So many things were trying to vie for attention in his mind. As he settled into his chair, he wanted to push aside the personal things in order to deal with the work-related ones, but just the thought of doing that made him feel guilty.

And because of that, Alex spent the day in a somewhat distracted mindset. Thankfully, no one really seemed to notice. The things utmost on his mind were Jordan and Rebecca and the mission. They were on day four of the mission with no sign of either Alana or her captor. Alex knew a phone call was coming. It would either be Marcus or Eric and then decisions would have to be made. He knew what Marcus would want, but he just couldn't bring himself to pull the plug on it just yet. So, he came up with a plan in case the call came from Eric before there was news of Alana's release.

He was late leaving the office and traffic didn't cooperate on his way to his folks' house. By the time he pulled into their driveway, he could see that everyone else was already there. No doubt a few figured that he wasn't going to be showing his face.

Alex didn't bother to knock on the large wooden door of his parents' Victorian style home before opening it and stepping into the foyer. He took off his coat and shoes and put them in the closet before heading toward the dining room.

"Alex!" His mother got up from the table and came around to hug him. "I thought something was going to keep you from coming." She patted him on the arm. "Take off your jacket and stay a while."

"I just might do that," Alex said as he slid his suit coat off and hung it on the back of the only vacant chair at the table which, coincidentally, was right next to Rebecca's. He gave her a nod and a smile as he loosened his tie and settled into his chair.

Since it was obvious they'd already started to eat, Alex bowed his head to say grace for his meal before taking the bowls of food his mother handed his way. As he glanced around the table, he was glad to see that Adrianne was there as well. Things had been tense between her and their mom for the past several months, so he was glad to see her there for the family dinner. And hopefully, his mom would lay off the requests for grandchildren now that she had Jordan.

As usual, the meal his mother had prepared was

delicious. Obviously anticipating several hungry mouths, his mother had made plenty of the pot roast and vegetables. Alex noted that he wasn't the only one who went back for seconds. Rebecca, on the other hand, didn't seem to eat as heartily as usual. He wondered if their conversation the night before was still bothering her. It was still bothering him, but there wasn't much that interfered with his appetite when he was hungry.

He had just finished the last of the piece of chocolate cake his mother had given them for dessert when his cell rang. Figuring that it would be a mission related call, Alex pushed back and got to his feet as he pulled the cell from his pocket. He glanced at the display and knew he couldn't put off taking the call.

"Excuse me, I need to take this." His mother gave him a reproving look. "I'm sorry, Mom, but I really do need to get this."

Walking quickly, Alex headed for his parents' living room as the phone rang again. He tapped the screen to accept the call and pressed it to his ear. He ran a hand through his hair as he stared out the bay window that framed the Christmas tree.

"Hey, Eric. How's it going?"

"Sorry it's so late, but I was kind of waiting until the last minute to make this call."

"I understand." Alex sank into a winged leather armchair that sat next to the Christmas tree. "I assume you're calling because there's been no sighting of Alana or Craig."

Eric didn't say anything right away, and Alex could almost feel the man's frustration through their phone connection. "I know I said that I had a good feeling about this, and I still do. But we can't go on indefinitely like this. I'm pretty sure Marcus is getting close to the end of his tolerance for this mission without any concrete evidence."

"You know Marcus wants to find Alana as much as any of us, right?" Alex felt the need to stand up for Marcus. He was aware that most didn't understand the man the way he did.

"Marcus just has a very practical side, so if we're looking for fire, he wants to see some smoke."

Eric sighed. "Here's the thing. I don't want to leave here without looking in that house. If there's a basement or crawl space or something underneath it, we are not able to see it with our infrared. It's a stone that we need to turn over before we leave here. So if you think Marcus is close to pulling the plug, I want permission to go in and search the entire house."

"He hasn't said anything yet about pulling the plug, but I know that this can't go on indefinitely." Alex leaned back in the chair stretching his legs out. "Knowing that this was a likely scenario, I've come up with a possible plan of action."

"One that will involve us getting inside that house before we leave?" Eric asked.

"Yes. It's been four days and there's been no sign of Craig. To me, that says that if Alana is in that house, he has a way to monitor her. We know from our file on the man that he is tech savvy. I wouldn't be surprised if he's monitoring her remotely. So I want you guys to set up something to block the signal of however he might be monitoring her."

Eric was silent for a couple of seconds before he said, "So if his monitoring goes down, he's going to come to find out why."

"Exactly. If he shows up at the house, we'll know that Alana is inside. However, I do not want you to alert him to our presence. If he shows up, I want one of the guys to tag his vehicle. Then once we have Alana, we'll alert the FBI on where he is located."

"Okay. I'll have one of the guys go over to the house in a roundabout way and set up something to block the signal. When he shows up at the house, we'll unblock the signal since he might be more suspicious if he can't figure out what's wrong and if it's not back up again. That way he might just blame it on spotty Wi-Fi or whatever he's using to broadcast. We'll tag the car while he's inside then once he's left and is far enough away from the house, we will have the signal go down again. That's when we'll go into the house to see if we can find her." The excitement in Eric's voice grew as he fleshed out the plan for Alex. "We'll be able to monitor his movements so we can see if he turns around to come back. Hopefully, we'll have enough time to free her and notify the FBI."

"And if, after disrupting the signal, he doesn't show within three days, I'll give you guys the go-ahead to raid the house." Alex knew that if Marcus approached him about pulling the plug on the mission, he'd be more lenient in allowing it to continue if an end date was in sight. This plan seemed to be the only way to resolve this current mission, hopefully, with the end result they all longed for. "Do you have all the supplies that you need to carry out a plan like this?"

Eric gave a huff of laughter. "Did you seriously just ask me that, man?"

Alex chuckled. "Uh... Let's just pretend I didn't."

"Good idea. I'll have one of the guys go over tonight and set up the signal disruptor." Eric paused. "And then I'm gonna pray like crazy that Craig shows up. Because as much as I want Alana back, we also need to get our hands on this guy. I want them both."

"So do I, man. So do I." With the plan in place and Eric ready to set it in motion, Alex said good night and ended the call. He sat for a few minutes in the dark with only the Christmas tree lights for illumination, praying that nothing would go wrong and that they would find Alana.

When Alex got back to the table, Tyler caught his gaze and lifted an eyebrow. Figuring he was asking if there was any news, Alex gave a small shake of his head. Eric would brief the command center and anyone else actively monitoring the mission of their plan. Alex knew that he needed to speak with Marcus, but right now he had to keep his attention on his family. He had to start somewhere with figuring out his priorities, and the dinner was as good a place as any.

It wasn't too long before people began to leave. Adrianne—not surprisingly—was the first. Ryan left shortly after her and then Melanie and Tyler started to get ready to go.

Alex turned to Rebecca. "Would you and Jordan like a ride home with me?"

She hesitated a moment then nodded. "I'm sure Melanie and Tyler wouldn't mind a little couple time."

"Yeah, I never turn down a little alone time with Melanie," Tyler said with a grin.

After Melanie and Tyler had left, Alex pulled his coat along with Rebecca and Jordan's from the front closet. Once their goodbyes had been said, Alex led them out to his truck which he had already started so it was nice and warm when he opened the doors for Rebecca and Jordan.

He anticipated a little awkwardness on the drive home, and he wasn't mistaken. Though they did manage a conversation, it was impersonal and there was an undercurrent of tension beneath it all. When they got to the house, Jordan said a quick goodbye and hopped out of the truck.

When Rebecca didn't get out right away, Alex looked over at her. "Everything okay?"

She turned her head in his direction, but the dark interior of the truck made it impossible to read her expression. "We need to have a talk. Would you have any time in the next few days for that?"

16

ALEX STARED OUT the front window then looked back at her. He didn't know if she was testing him, but it definitely was a test for himself. "Yes. Maybe we could go out for dinner tomorrow night, the three of us."

Rebecca shifted on her seat. "Actually, I was thinking maybe it would be better this time around if it was just the two of us."

Alex's stomach clenched. He had thought that any discussions they had at this point would also include Jordan. Or did his son not want to let him know that he wasn't interested in a relationship with him?

Gripping the bottom of the steering wheel tightly in both hands, Alex nodded. "Will Jordan have something to do if we go out tomorrow night?"

"He'll be fine. Between his games, his phone, and the

television, I think he can entertain himself."

"There is just one thing," Alex began. "There's a potential for things to happen with the mission in the next couple of days. If something comes up, I will need to go to the office right away. I hope you'll understand if we have to postpone our talk until after that situation is taken care of. Normally I wouldn't ask this of you, but this is an extremely sensitive mission."

"Does it have to do with Alana?"

Alex glanced at Rebecca and nodded. They were still trying to keep the mission on the down low, specifically to keep Justin from finding out, but Rebecca knowing wouldn't be an issue. If it all ended up being for nothing, they didn't want Justin to be let down. "Please don't tell anyone. It isn't a very strong lead, but it's the best we've had in a while. We just don't want Justin to know in case we don't find her."

"I understand. And if we have to put off the dinner, I'm okay with that. I just don't want to put it off indefinitely."

Alex nodded. "We'll try for tomorrow night, but if the mission does interfere, as soon as that's resolved, we'll talk."

Rebecca seemed agreeable to that since she nodded then opened her door. Alex also got out, and they said an awkward goodnight at the front of the truck before Rebecca headed for the apartment. As he watched her walk away, Alex hoped that if something was going to happen with the mission, it was after they had a chance to talk. Since the plan was already put in motion, things could change at any time.

Now the anticipation of two things weighed heavily on Alex. He prayed that the resolution for each would be glorifying to God. And he really, really hoped that meant that Alana would be coming home alive and that Rebecca was going to give him a chance...not just with Jordan but with her as well.

As Rebecca looked at her reflection in the mirror, she told herself that it wasn't a date. Even though she'd taken far longer than necessary to decide what to wear and then to do her hair and makeup...it wasn't a date. And who knew if this evening was actually going to come about. Alex had sent her a text around two o'clock saying that he'd be by at six to pick her up. Given that he hadn't texted her again, Rebecca was assuming that the dinner was a go.

Alex hadn't said what sort of restaurant they were going to, so Rebecca hoped that the black pants and soft pink sweater she'd chosen would be appropriate. Even though he had plenty of money, she didn't think he'd frequent the posh restaurants that served fancy food whose name you couldn't pronounce. He just didn't strike her as someone who would enjoy that type of place.

She took the time to put on earrings and had Jordan help her with the matching necklace. When a glance at the clock showed it was almost six, she quickly took one last look at herself as she dabbed on a bit of perfume then pulled on her boots and her jacket. She stood in the kitchen, looking out the window over the sink since it had a direct view of the driveway.

It was just a couple of minutes past six when she saw a sweep of headlights make their way toward her. She grabbed her purse and pulled on her gloves before bending to press a kiss on Jordan's head.

"Be good, sweetie. If you need me, just call."

Jordan looked up from his tablet and nodded. "I'm not a little kid, Mom. I'll be fine."

Rebecca wanted to tell him that in her eyes he would always be her little boy, and she would always want him to be safe. Instead, she gave him a wave as she opened the door and stepped out into the cold night air.

Alex had parked the truck and was coming toward the apartment but stopped when he saw her on the stairs. He waited for her to join him then walked around the side of the truck with her to open her door. When she was inside and buckled, he shut the door then rounded the hood to the driver's side. The warmth inside the truck held a hint of his cologne and surrounded her like an embrace.

"I hope you're okay with a not—so—fancy dining experience," Alex said as he guided the truck around the circular driveway and back toward the gate.

"I'm very okay with that. I was actually hoping that we didn't end up at a place where I'd need to know a second language to understand the menu."

Alex chuckled. "I may be able to afford those places now, but I rarely, if ever, go to them. If I'm going for a meal, I want it to be enough to fill me up."

"So where are we going?" Rebecca asked as the acceleration of the truck when Alex turned onto the highway pressed her back into the leather seat.

"A friend introduced me to a restaurant that's owned by some friends of his. It's great food and great ambiance. Thankfully, they were able to squeeze me in when I phoned for a reservation earlier. It helps to have friends who are connected."

Rebecca looked at him. "I would guess that there are people who appreciate your connections as well."

"No doubt. But not all of them are on the up and up. In this business, you have to be careful about the connections you make."

During the remainder of the trip to the restaurant, Rebecca asked more questions about the business and the people who worked there. She sensed that it was almost more of a family connection then a boss and employee one, especially among those who Alex worked with directly. Given how Tyler and Ryan had both been welcomed into his family without hesitation, Rebecca knew that he trusted the people he worked with. Not just with the job they had to do but also with his family.

Alex pulled the truck into a small parking lot that was nearly full. He managed to find a spot and then came around to open her door for her. *This is not a date.* She had to keep reminding herself of that. A lot was riding on the outcome of the talk that lay ahead. It was so much more than a date would have been.

Delicious smells accompanied the warm air that greeted them as they stepped into the foyer of the restaurant. They hung up their coats then Alex approached the woman who stood behind a small podium. Though there were a couple other groups waiting in the foyer, as soon as he gave his name, the hostess grabbed a couple menus and motioned for them to follow her.

They slowly wound their way among tables that were pretty much all full. Booths lined the outer edges of the room, and the hostess led them to one in the far back corner. Alex waited until Rebecca had slid in one side before he took a seat opposite her, facing the rest of the room. The soft lighting in the restaurant had a somewhat romantic vibe to it, and the low light fixture that hung over their booth gave it a cozy feel. Added to that was the high back of the booth behind her, and Rebecca felt confident their conversation wouldn't be overheard.

There was soft music playing, and the conversation from the tables around them was simply a low murmur. She could see why the restaurant was popular, especially if the food was as good as it smelled.

It didn't take long for a server to approach their table and advise them of the specials for the evening. Over the next several minutes, their conversation centered around the menu and what they wanted to eat.

When that was finally settled, Rebecca relaxed into the soft back of the booth. She waited to see if Alex would pull out his phone to check it and was rather surprised when he leaned forward and said, "Perhaps we should say grace for the food while we wait."

Rebecca nodded and bowed her head, listening with interest as Alex prayed.

"Heavenly Father, we thank you for another day. We pray that You would bless this evening as Rebecca and I talk. Be also with the guys on the mission and give Eric wisdom. Please keep Jordan safe at the house. We thank You for the food that we're going to eat and Your provision of it. In Jesus' name, amen."

Rebecca thought back to the times they spent together and the faith Alex had shown even then. Her family had only attended church sporadically, and it was never something that was carried over into their home. Her own faith had only started to grow when she'd begun attending Maureen's church. Alex's family, however, had attended church regularly and he'd been involved with the youth group there.

She supposed that was part of the reason why she had been so shocked at his response to the pregnancy. It seemed in direct contrast to his faith for him to ask her to abort the baby. That had impacted her own feelings regarding church and the Christian faith. Thankfully, she'd ended up at Maureen's church where her faith and belief in God had flourished. It was a relief to know that they had their faith in common and that wouldn't be something that they would disagree on during their conversations, especially when it came to Jordan and his involvement at church.

"This really is a lovely restaurant," Rebecca said as the silence stretched between them.

Alex nodded as he glanced around. "I've been here a few times. One was for the engagement party of Lindsay Hamilton and Than Miller. You met Than at the office when we went to see Eric. Lindsay's brother, Lucas, is married to Eric's sister, Brooke, and Lucas was the one to introduce me to this place. I've never been disappointed in the food."

They talked a bit more about the restaurant then Alex asked her about her books, his questions showing that he had a true interest in what she did. Rebecca appreciated that and was more than happy to tell him about her career. The conversation shifted once the waitress brought their food and they began to eat.

"So is Jordan enjoying his time here in the Twin Cities?" Alex asked after they'd eaten in silence for a couple of minutes.

"Yes, he is. Even though he hasn't shown it very well, I do think he'd like to spend more time with you. If you're able to free up some time in your schedule."

"I will try to do that." Alex's gaze dropped to his plate for a moment before lifting to meet hers again. "I'm just not sure what to do with him. It seems we don't have a whole lot in common."

Rebecca tilted her head as she regarded him. He still wore the suit he had no doubt worn to work that morning. He seemed perfectly at ease in it, making her think he spent a lot of time dressed in work attire.

"What do you do for fun?" Rebecca asked.

Alex didn't answer her right away as he finished chewing the bite he's just taken. "I guess I don't really do fun if you're talking about stuff like golfing. I do enjoy going to the range to shoot and to the gym to spar or work out. If there's a training exercise going on at the compound, I usually try to participate in those."

"A training exercise?" Rebecca asked. "Is that what you were talking about the other day? The winter training?"

"Yes, we usually have training exercises with groups that come here to work with BlackThorpe. They involve scenarios that we've created to train the groups in various situations. Things like rescuing hostages. Long-range surveillance. It's something I enjoy being a part of."

"But what do you do for fun? Like do you go to basketball games with Tyler? Or bowling? Play video games?"

Rebecca sensed tension in Alex at her question. She didn't mean to stress him, she was just trying to find common ground for him and Jordan. Preferably something that didn't involve weapons.

"I really don't have much time for things like that," Alex said, his voice tight. "It's taken most my time, along with Marcus's, to build BlackThorpe into what it is today. We've worked hard to bring together the best people to work alongside us in our company. It hasn't left us with much time for fun. Probably the only thing I do that might qualify as fun in your books is play chess or backgammon with Marcus once a week."

"You and Marcus are close," Rebecca observed. "More than just co-business owners."

Alex didn't hesitate before nodding. "He's like the brother I never had. He's my best friend. When you go through dark times together, it can be an intensely binding experience. I know that he will always have my back, and I will always have his."

Rebecca wondered about the experiences that bound them together. She wanted to ask him about it, but something told her that was not the time or the place. Instead, she said, "Maybe you and Jordan can work together to find something that you might both enjoy doing. It's not really that unusual for a father and son not to have a lot in common. How about you and your dad? Are there things you and he enjoy doing together?"

Alex seemed to mull that question over for a bit as he ate another bite of his meal. "We don't do much in the winter. In fact, they usually head south to Florida once Christmas is over. But in the summer, we try to make time to go fishing together."

"Jordan's never been fishing before. He might enjoy doing that with you. If you don't mind taking him along."

Alex stared at her for a moment, his gaze intense. "I would never mind taking him along. As long as it is safe for him, I don't mind taking him with me anywhere. It's just that so much of my life is wrapped up in BlackThorpe, and aspects of what we do are dangerous. This is a job that requires Marcus and me to be available twenty-four/seven. I will try my best to be there for Jordan, but there may be times when I just can't."

Rebecca wondered if that was at the root of everything that Alex seemed to be struggling with. The feeling that parenting Jordan had to be all or nothing. She understood about work sometimes needing to take precedence over family. There were times she had to ask Jordan to wait while she worked on something, but then there were times when she set aside work to focus on Jordan. Perhaps Alex felt that because his job was so demanding, he wouldn't be able to give Jordan the attention he deserved.

"Jordan knows that you have a job to do. He knows that I have a job to do. In fact, I didn't come here right away because I needed to finish things up with my latest book. Maybe I should've dropped everything and came, but I knew that he was safe and I would get to him as soon as I could. I didn't raise Jordan to think that he was the center of the world. But when he really truly needs me, I'm there for him. There are times, when it is something less important, that he has to wait. And he does. It doesn't make him doubt my love for him because he knows I'm working to provide for our family. I don't think he'll expect anything different from you as long as he knows that you will make time for him when he needs you. And even more than that, he needs to know that you *want* to make time for him. That you want him in your life."

Alex seemed to be considering what she said, a thoughtful expression on his face. "I appreciate your thoughts on that. You have to understand, after we...split up, I never really had to take another person into consideration. I made decisions based mostly on myself. Yes, I had my parents, Adrianne and Melanie, but I usually didn't have to take them into account when it came to priorities in my life. I had dinner once a week with them, but the rest of my time was devoted to work or sometimes church. I never had to weigh what was more important because my job was the most important thing. Now I have something else in my life that is of even greater importance than BlackThorpe, and that's taking some adjustment for me. But I do want to try."

Rebecca took a sip of water and set the glass down, her gaze slipping away from Alex's. "So in all this time, there was no one else?"

When Alex didn't answer right away, Rebecca looked up to find him watching her, his brows drawn together. "How could there be anyone else? We're still married. I could never date anyone while that commitment was still in place." He paused, his gaze growing even more intense. "Was there someone else for you? *Is* there someone else for you?"

Regretting having even asked the question, Rebecca shook her head. "No. There hasn't been anyone for me."

Before he could respond to her comment, the waitress approached them to see if they were finished. As their conversation had grown more involved, they had stopped eating. At that point, however, Rebecca didn't really feel like finishing her meal. Alex apparently felt the same way since he also nodded when the waitress asked if she could clear their plates.

"Could I interest you in some dessert?" the waitress asked just as Alex pulled his phone from his pocket and stared at the display.

He looked at Rebecca. "I'm sorry we don't have time for dessert. I need to go." He glanced up at the waitress. "Everything has been great, but I have an emergency so we need to leave. Could you just bring me the bill, please?"

They were out of the restaurant and into the truck within five minutes. As he backed out, he glanced over at her. "I really need to get to the office. Can I just get someone to give you a ride home from there?"

"That would be fine," Rebecca said.

The tension coming off Alex was palpable. And clearly his mind had switched gears because there was no conversation between the restaurant and the office. Once they were cleared through the main gate, Alex maneuvered his truck into the basement parking lot. She climbed out of the truck without waiting for him to come to her door, not wanting to slow him down. Rebecca was surprised when he reached for her hand and began walking quickly toward an elevator not far from the truck.

Rebecca wondered if he was even aware that he was holding her hand. He remained silent as the elevator rose to the second floor from the top. Once the doors opened, she tightened her grip on his hand as they walked rapidly down the carpeted hallway. He opened a large door, and suddenly she found herself plunged into chaos.

As his gaze swept the room, Alex registered everyone present. Marcus was there as well as Trent, Than, Tyler, and Ryan. There were a few more of Trent's guys who were there helping to monitor the computer screens. The room was dark except for the light cast from the large screen on the wall facing the door. The screen was divided into six smaller displays. One for each of the men on the team.

The monitors didn't just display what the men were seeing but also their vital signs. Alex looked at each screen, noting who it belonged to. Eric's was in the top left corner, and Alex wasn't surprised to see his increased pulse rate since he was pretty sure his rate was right up there too, thanks to the adrenaline that was pumping through him.

Alex moved to stand next to Marcus, and it was only then that he realized he held Rebecca's hand. Without letting her go, Alex bent his head to her and murmured, "If you can just wait a minute, I'll get someone to take you home."

She lifted her face, her expression only faintly illuminated by the light cast off by the monitor. "Would it be okay if I stayed here?"

Without hesitation, Alex nodded and turned his attention back to the monitor. "What's the status?"

"Eric reported a vehicle that turned onto the road about twenty-five minutes ago," Marcus said. "The car made several passes in front of the house before pulling in and parking. The men have followed the plan as you and Eric decided. They stopped the signal interference as soon as he walked into the house. And Chet took the opportunity while he was inside to plant the tracker on his car. We're waiting now for him to exit the house. We are prepared to track the vehicle when he leaves."

Alex watched the movement on the various screens. Right now the men were in waiting mode. They wouldn't do anything until Craig was a significant distance from the house.

"Have we contacted the FBI?" Alex asked. He knew that they probably should've run this whole mission past their FBI contact, especially since Justin's brother-in-law worked for the agency. But when it came right down to it, Alex refused to trust Alana's life to anyone but his men. The agency could have Craig, but BlackThorpe was going to get Alana.

"Yes, I spoke with them and had a somewhat tense

conversation regarding what we have done," Marcus said, his tone hard. "They're not too happy we moved forward with something like this without informing them of our plans. It didn't seem to matter to them that we were operating on a fairly flimsy lead." Marcus crossed his arms. "Personally, I think they just like to be in control."

"And we wouldn't know anything about liking to be in control ourselves," Than said dryly.

There were a few chuckles around the room, a welcome relief from the tension that still hung in the air.

"Well, I updated them with the latest developments, and they agreed to have a team ready to arrest Craig," Marcus said. "However, I made it very clear that we would be taking responsibility for Alana ourselves. If she requires hospitalization, we will choose the hospital and we will get her there. If she is fit for travel, she will be returned here on our private jet. Once we have her safely home, they are welcome to interview her." Marcus paused. "I believe it is of the utmost importance that we reunite her with her son and Justin as soon as possible."

For some in the room, it was a rare glimpse of a softer side of Marcus. Alex was well aware that that side of the man existed though he knew his friend did his best to keep it under wraps when around anyone but his sister Meredith or Alex.

The tension in the room edged up when the front door of the house opened, and a figure appeared on the porch. The team member closest, the one who had tagged the car, was currently waiting behind the house so as not to be seen by the person they assumed was Craig. So that meant that it was the ones in the field across the road who had eyes on him. Within a minute, the figure had climbed into the car and backed away from the house. The countdown began as the car moved down the road away from the house and, hopefully, away from Alana.

They stood in silence for a few minutes, watching as the GPS put Craig further and further away from the house. Of course, they were assuming it was Craig. Given the darkness of the night, they had not been able to get a visual confirmation. If it did turn out to not be Craig in the car, the person would still be arrested as an accessory to kidnapping. Hopefully, that individual would, in turn, lead them to Craig.

Rebecca shifted next to him but made no effort to tug her hand free of his. Alex knew that the men in the room were curious about her presence. Most knew who she was from their visit to the office, but her presence at his side that night was likely a surprise.

"You still okay with staying here?" Alex asked softly, not feeling the need to have the whole room hear his conversation.

Her cheek brushed his arm as she moved closer and also spoke in a soft voice. "I'm not sure you could drag me away at this point. I really want to see how this works out. I'm just standing here praying that Alana is in that house and that she's fine."

Alex squeezed her hand. "Thank you for praying. There's a lot riding on this."

"Looks like he's making good time," a voice said through the speakers in the room. Alex recognized it as Eric's. "We're going to approach the house now. Move out."

They had decided that for Alana's sake, Eric would be part of the team searching the house while the rest stood guard. She would probably react best to a familiar face.

Alex watched as the camera views on the screens showed the men approaching from different angles. He flicked his gaze to the GPS monitor, relieved to see that the vehicle was still headed away from the house. On the off chance that Craig was monitoring the house as he traveled, they had to wait until the last possible second to turn on the signal interference once again. Hopefully, they would have enough time to find and rescue Alana if he headed back in their direction.

Once the men had formed a perimeter around the house, they paused again. They didn't think there would be any surveillance on the outside of the house, but to be sure they waited to see if their approach prompted any change in his direction. This time, Alex watched the GPS display more closely, but there was no change in speed or direction of the green dot on the screen.

"Okay, team, let's do this," Eric said.

Several things happened at once as two of the team members led by Eric climbed the front porch steps to the door. One other team member moved into surveillance position at the front of the house while another once again activated the signal interference. The remaining member had returned to get their vehicle and bring it closer to the house in case they needed a rapid getaway.

On the monitor, Alex could see the men make quick work of the front door. Once inside, they moved their heads from side to side giving the control center a view of the interior of the home. Without knowing the setup of the home, it took the men several minutes to locate a locked door just off the kitchen.

Alex's heart began to beat rapidly as his gaze kept going between the GPS monitor and the screens of the guys inside the house.

Please God, let us find Alana. Please let her be safe.

There was still no sign of change on the GPS monitor as the guys breached the locked door and began to make their way down a steep wooden staircase into the inky black room below.

"Alana? This is Eric from BlackThorpe. Are you here?"

There was no response, and the room appeared empty. Alex's heart began to sink. Had the lead really been too flimsy? Then what had that person been doing here? Surely they hadn't been wrong.

Eric's camera night vision camera view continued to sweep the room. It moved across a pile of laundry on the floor in the corner and then jerked back. Eric ran toward the pile and dropped to his knees. A band tightened around Alex's chest as he watched on the screen as Eric pulled back a blanket to reveal a figure huddled on the ground. The person didn't move or respond to Eric's presence, and Alex bit his lip to keep from crying out.

Were they too late?

They couldn't be. Alex refused to believe that God would've brought them this far in their search for Alana only for them to find her dead. There was absolutely no sound in the room as they waited for some indication from Eric of her condition.

"Alana?" Eric called her name again as he pulled off his glove and pressed his fingers to the pulse point in her neck. Her head lolled back, the tangled mass of her long hair sliding away, giving them their first view of her face. Suddenly, Eric was moving, shouting out commands as he scooped Alana into his arms and headed for the stairs. "Into the vehicle now."

Rebecca's hand tightened around his, and Alex was suddenly very glad he had her by his side for this moment. She moved closer to him, her shoulder pressed firmly against his upper arm as they watched Eric race up the stairs and through the house to the front door.

By the time Erik and the other two made it to the front porch, the vehicle was already waiting, its engine running.

Once Eric and the two team members were inside with Alana, the vehicle shot towards the highway. A quick glance at the GPS showed that the other vehicle continued to move away from the house.

"She has a pulse, but it's weak," Eric said, tension clear in his voice. "I think he's drugged her."

Best case scenario would've been to find her alive and well. Right then, Alex just hoped she would hang on until they could get her to the hospital. Next to him, he could hear Marcus on the phone alerting someone to an incoming medical emergency. Than was also on the phone with Lucas Hamilton. Since the BlackThorpe jet was in Tennessee with the team, they had made alternate arrangements to get Justin to Alana if she had needed to be hospitalized. These were all the plans that had been put into place since he'd spoken to Eric the night before with the anticipation of finding Alana within the next two days.

Alex let go of Rebecca's hand as he reached for his phone.

With trembling fingers, he scrolled through his contact list for Justin's number. He tapped the screen for speaker mode then reached again for Rebecca's hand.

"Alex?" Justin's voice came through the speaker, confusion evident in his tone.

"You need to get to the airfield, Justin. There's a plane waiting for you, to take you to Alana." Alex knew that his voice had cracked as he shared the news, but he didn't care. Emotion was running high for all of them in the room.

17

Y OU FOUND HER? You really found her?" Justin's voice was tight with emotion. "Is she okay?"

Alex wished with all his heart he could tell him that she was. "When Eric found her she was unconscious. We think she may be drugged. But they're on their way to the hospital now. You need to get on the plane so you can be there when she wakes up."

"Okay. Where is she?" They could hear rustling in the background as Justin prepared himself to leave.

"She's in Tennessee. Eric's there with the team from BlackThorpe as well as the plane, so Lucas Hamilton has arranged to have his jet fly you down there. Than will meet you at the plane and go with you." Alex swallowed hard around the tightness in his throat. "We're continuing to pray for Alana. If you need anything at all, you be sure to let us know."

"I will. And thank you for praying." Justin paused. "Thank you to all of you who were involved in finding her. I don't think I can ever thank you enough for bringing her back to me."

"She's one of ours, Justin. And we always take care of our own." As he hung up the phone, Alex's gaze went back to Eric's monitor. His head was down, so his camera could clearly show Alana's face. Her eyes were closed as she laid there motionless. "Come on, Alana. Hang in there. Your love is coming to you. Just hang on."

He felt a tug on his hand and turned toward Rebecca. There were streaks of tears down her face as she let go of his hand and wrapped her arms around him. Alex froze for a moment then as the emotion he'd been trying to hold back swept over him, he slipped his arms around her and pulled her close.

All the uncertainty of the past few weeks, all the loneliness of the years gone by, all the pain when they had been driven apart by his words. It went from seeming so important to being almost totally irrelevant. In the light of what was happening with Alana and Justin, Alex wanted to hold his family as close as possible.

As he pressed his face into the fragrance of Rebecca's hair, Alex realized that now more than anything, he wanted his wife back and he wanted his son in his life. It was frightening to think about. He still wasn't sure he was going to be any good at being a husband or father. But he had to try. If Rebecca would let him, he had to try.

When Eric's voice came over the speakers again, Alex lifted his head and turned to look at the monitors. He kept one arm loosely around Rebecca as they stood side-by-side. If she stepped away from him, he would've released her immediately, but as long as she stayed there, pressed against him, she was right where he wanted her.

Eric's screen showed their arrival at the hospital. As soon as the vehicle stopped, medical personnel rushed to meet them. Within minutes, Alana had been whisked away, and Eric just stood there looking around. They hadn't really discussed what would happen beyond this point, but Alex was sure that Eric wouldn't leave until Justin had arrived.

"Any word from the FBI?" he asked Marcus.

"It appears they've caught up with the vehicle and are following it now to wherever he's going," Marcus said, his gaze still on the monitor.

The team members that had remained behind were busy packing up their site. Once Justin landed, the team would return on the Hamilton jet, leaving the BlackThorpe one for Justin and Alana. Depending on how things went at the hospital, he or Marcus might need to fly down there as well to run interference with the FBI.

Alex looked down at Rebecca, whose gaze was also on the monitors. "I can get someone to give you a ride home now if you'd like. I'm going to be here for a while yet."

Though she had declined the offer each time before, this time, Rebecca nodded. "I think maybe it would be a good idea for me to head home. I was glad I got to see Alana being rescued. Definitely an answer to prayer."

Alex knew they still needed to talk—now more than ever—but it wasn't the time or the place. Turning, Alex looked for Tyler and found him standing next to the door. His head was bent over his phone. Alex walked over to him.

"Are you planning to go see Melanie?" Alex asked.

"Yes. I thought I'd head over there for a little while. Will you be sending out a message to the staff or are we still keeping this quiet?" Tyler asked.

"Let me talk to Marcus about that, but you can go ahead and tell Melanie about it. And Adrianne too if you see her." Alex glanced over to where Rebecca stood, still watching the monitors. "Would you be able to give Rebecca a ride home as well? I want to stay here for a bit longer to see if we can get an update on Alana."

"Sure. That wouldn't be a problem at all since I'm going there anyway."

Alex thanked him and went back to speak with Rebecca. "Tyler will give you a ride home since he's going to see

Melanie. Will that be okay?"

"That would be great."

Alex hesitated then said, "I'm sorry our evening was interrupted but thank you for understanding."

"Of course. I know how important this was for you and your team. We can talk more later."

He walked with her to the door of the room and then said goodbye. It was a bit awkward given their interactions throughout the evening, or, at least, he felt it was. Rebecca, on the other hand, seemed to take it all in stride as she said goodbye and left with Tyler.

With a sigh, he returned to stand next to Marcus. They stood in silence for a few minutes. Alex could hardly believe that what had started out as such a flimsy lead had resulted in finding Alana. He knew that everyone involved in the rescue had been emotionally invested in bringing her home to Justin. He took a deep breath and let it out. Some of the weight of the past few weeks had eased away, but until they knew exactly what condition Alana was in, he wouldn't be able to totally relax.

Over the next hour, they sent out a notification to the staff to let them know that Alana had been found and to ask for continued prayers for her physical well-being. Eric had remained at the hospital, but so far they had received no update. They likely wouldn't release any information until Justin arrived which could still be an hour or so away.

One by one the screens on the large monitor began to go dark as the team disconnected their cameras. Eric had also turned his off but was currently on his cell phone talking to them over the speakers. The update from the FBI came a short time later to notify them that Craig had been arrested at a hotel about half an hour away from the house where he kept Alana.

Slowly but surely, the pieces of this puzzle were beginning to fall into place, but the most important pieces for this particular situation were held by Craig. They needed to determine if he was in any way connected to the previous attacks on BlackThorpe. They had updated the FBI on the attacks so that Craig could be questioned about any possible involvement.

Alex still had a hard time believing that somehow the situation with Jordan was tied in with everything else that had happened. Why would whoever was behind the attacks decide to do something that was actually good instead of harmful? Or had they hoped that the revelation of his marriage to Rebecca and Jordan's presence would have a negative impact on his life? While finding out he had a son had definitely impacted his life, it wasn't in a negative way. He wouldn't go back in time to where he didn't know about Jordan. Yes, it had been a challenge, but one he was going to try very hard to rise to.

Unfortunately, there was no guarantee that whatever the person had planned next would be as harmless as the situation with Justin. Now that they had Alana back, they would have to be on high alert for any more potential attacks. The stakes were higher than ever for Alex, now that he had Rebecca and Jordan in his life. A small part of him wondered if perhaps the person had given him Jordan only to turn around and take him away.

It was that fear that made him determined to do whatever he had to in order to make sure that both Rebecca and Jordan were safe.

Given the late hour, the traffic back to the Thorpe house was light enough that they made good time. Tyler had been more subdued than Rebecca had ever seen him, which she didn't quite understand given the good news they'd gotten earlier. She toyed with the idea of asking him what was wrong but then realized she really didn't know him well enough for him to spill his guts. No doubt Melanie would be the one who would be able to get him to share what was still bothering him even after they'd receive news that Alana had been rescued.

After thanking him for the ride, Rebecca let herself into the apartment quietly but wasn't surprised to find Jordan still awake. He was tucked into his bed but had his tablet in his hands.

"Say hi to Robby, Mom," Jordan said as he turned the tablet to face her.

The familiar face of her son's best friend filled the screen then blurred as he lifted a hand to quickly wave at her. "Hi, Mrs. MacKenzie."

"Hi, Robby. How are you doing?" she asked as she sank down onto the bed next to Jordan.

"I'm doing good, but I really miss Jordan. When are you guys coming home?"

Rebecca sighed. Wasn't that the question of the hour? "We don't have a definite date yet. But it won't be before Christmas."

She could see the disappointment on Robby's face and decided the next time she talked to Maureen, she would see if they could arrange to have Robby fly out to spend some time with Jordan. It might be a little too close to Christmas to have him come now, but maybe the week between Christmas and New Years might work.

She got up then bent to press a kiss to Jordan's head. "I'm heading to bed. You guys don't stay up too late talking, okay?"

The boys both promised her they'd be going to bed soon and then said good night to her. It wasn't until she was in her bed with the light off that she allowed her thoughts to go back to the embrace that she and Alex had shared. Was it really possible that there was someone special just for her? When Alex had wrapped his arms around her, it had truly felt like coming home. His body had changed some in the years since they had last embraced, but there had still been enough familiarity to it, to the way he held her, that it just felt right. Like she belonged in his arms and no one else's.

Had he felt the same way too? Or had he gotten caught up in the emotion of the moment? Had he recognized the perfume that she wore? He had been the one to give it to her for the first time and she had worn it ever since.

There was still so much they needed to talk about, and Rebecca had been working hard to keep her heart and emotions out of the mix. But after that hug earlier, on top of the time they had spent together before getting called to the office, there was just no way she could keep them separate any longer.

But she needed to know what was in Alex's mind and heart too. Would she be brave enough to come right out and ask him? She was going to have to be because she just didn't have the desire to pussyfoot around it all anymore. So in addition to the things they still needed to discuss from earlier, she now wanted to add a topic that had the potential to be even more loaded and difficult.

Rebecca curled onto her side, her hand reaching out to the empty half of the bed next to her. They had only shared a bed as a married couple for little over a week. And then it had been fifteen years of sleeping alone. Of taking care of a sick child alone. Of cheering on her son's accomplishments alone. Of lying in bed in the dark, wishing for someone to talk to. To pray with. To hold her. Would she get another chance at her marriage or would Alex want to move on?

She closed her eyes and began to pray, asking God to show His will to them and to give her the peace to accept whatever that was.

Despite a late night, Alex was up early the next morning. It was a Saturday, but he had work to do. They had waited for Justin to arrive at the hospital and to get that first update before shutting down the monitoring of the mission. As they had suspected, Alanna had been drugged. She had also been dehydrated, so they'd hooked her up to an IV while they took blood to determine what was in her system.

Alex had heard the worry mixed with happiness in Justin's voice. How he wished that they could have given him back his love completely healthy so there would be none of this worry over her physical health. But apparently God wanted them to continue to trust Him with all of this, so they would.

He'd spoken briefly with Lucas Hamilton the night before and had made arrangements to meet with him in the morning for coffee. It was mainly to thank him for his help the night before, but Alex also wanted to talk to him about how he'd learned to balance fatherhood and his work. Because Brooke had a ten-year-old son already when they met, Lucas had become a father when they'd married. Alex wondered if the man had had as much trouble adjusting as he was having.

Lucas had invited him to their home, and as Alex got closer to the address he'd given him, he was rather surprised at the state of the neighborhood. The Hamilton family was one of the richest ones in the state, and yet Lucas and Brooke lived in a rather modest neighborhood. The driveway he pulled into led to a rather simple looking two-story home. Alex took a minute to confirm the address before he climbed out of the truck and made his way to the front door.

He'd barely pressed the doorbell when he heard barking. The barking quickly stopped, and the door swung open to reveal Lucas standing there in a pair of faded jeans and a University of Minnesota sweatshirt. The man stepped back and motioned for Alex to come inside. A large golden long-haired dog sat next to Lucas, its tail swishing back and forth along the floor.

The warmth of the home was filled with the scent of cinnamon and fruit. Alex's stomach growled in response.

"Sounds like you're hungry," Lucas said as he took his coat and hung it up in the closet. "That's good because Brooke and Danny made way too many muffins for breakfast."

When the dog beside him whined, Lucas ruffled a hand across its ears. "This is Ava, by the way. She likes to be introduced. Ava, shake."

As Alex bent over to scratch the dog's ears, she lifted a paw. Grinning, he shook it and then straightened to greet Lucas.

As Lucas led the way into the house, Alex glanced to his right and saw a large living room with a decorated Christmas tree in front of the window. There was a staircase at the end of the hallway, but Lucas turned to his left and made his way through the dining room into the kitchen.

"Coffee?" Lucas asked as he gestured to the coffee maker on the counter.

"Please. And just black." Alex glanced around the kitchen, once again surprised at the simplicity of it.

Lucas filled two mugs then carried them to a small table under the window that looked out over their backyard. He set them on the table then went to get a container off the counter along with two plates.

"Have a seat."

Alex pulled out a chair and sat down. He picked up the mug Lucas had put at his place and took a sip, grateful for its warmth. "So are Brooke and Danny here?"

Lucas shook his head. "Danny had hockey practice, so Brooke went with him."

"Does she usually take him or do you share that responsibility?" Alex asked, well aware that his question might be a little weird to Lucas.

Apparently, it wasn't too weird for him to answer, though, since the other man responded. "We take turns for the most part. Sometimes all three of us will go, but other times Brooke will have to take him if something's come up that I need to deal with. When it comes to his games, however, I make an extra effort to be there for those if I can."

Alex traced a finger around the thick rim of the coffee mug. "Have you found it difficult adjusting to having a son in your life?"

Lucas arched a brow as he lifted his mug to take a sip of coffee. "It was definitely an adjustment. But I knew it was one I had to make if I wanted to have Brooke and Danny in my life." He regarded Alex thoughtfully for a moment. "So is the rumor true then? You've discovered you have a son?"

Alex nodded, not surprised that Lucas knew. With his connection to Than, it was only natural that he would have found out. Alex hadn't asked anyone to keep it a secret after all. "Yes. Jordan is fourteen years old."

"And you knew nothing about him?"

Alex didn't even hesitate before sharing the whole story with Lucas. If he wanted to ask the man's advice, it only made sense that he should know exactly how Alex, Rebecca, and Jordan had ended up at this point. And even though it painted him in a bad light, Alex didn't even leave out his actions that had led to his and Rebecca's split.

"I'm really struggling to find the balance between being a father and a businessman," Alex said. "BlackThorpe has been my life for so long that I don't know how to give anything higher priority in my life. I don't seem to have anything in common with Jordan, and to be honest, right now, he doesn't seem too interested in spending time with me after finding out how I reacted to hearing about Rebecca's pregnancy with him."

Lucas nodded, his gaze serious. "The situation certainly does seem to be challenging, but that doesn't mean it's impossible." He paused as if contemplating his next words. "Well, starting at the beginning, have you forgiven yourself for how you reacted with Rebecca?"

Alex knew his question was valid, but he didn't really want to dwell on it. The guilt had been there almost from the minute the words had escaped his mouth and then when he'd hoped to take them back, Rebecca had already disappeared. The guilt was no doubt one of the reasons why he'd never sought out Rebecca and filed for divorce. He didn't deserve to be free to find love with another woman when he'd so badly hurt the first one he'd ever loved. It hadn't felt right to think about finding happiness for himself when it came to a relationship, when the memory of how bad he'd messed things up with Rebecca never seemed to leave him.

"I guess I've always felt that the guilt I carried for what I said was justified." Even now it weighed heavily on Alex. "I didn't deserve to be free of it."

"You know that's not true, though, right? God never meant for us to carry guilt when He has offered us forgiveness. He didn't send His son to die on the cross for our sins in order for us to still carry the guilt of them." Lucas leaned forward, bracing his elbows on the table. "I really think that part of the struggle you have with Jordan is that you can't look at him without being reminded of what you said. You look at him and see the life you lost because of your words. But somehow you need to get past that and realize that in spite of your moment of weakness, when you demanded of Rebecca something you normally wouldn't have, God intervened. Rebecca decided not to do as you had asked her to and in doing so brought Jordan into the world. And now Jordan has been brought into your life and you into his. Though the circumstances may seem a bit suspicious, there's no reason why you can't embrace what God has brought into your life. I sincerely doubt that God brought Jordan back to inflict guilt on you, but He may have brought him into your life so you could truly be free from it."

Alex shifted the handle of the mug between his fingers as he thought about Lucas's words. It was true that his guilt was overshadowing his relationship with Jordan. It was the overriding emotion every time he looked at his son. That and the unworthiness he felt to be Jordan's father. Was Lucas right? Had God really brought Jordan back into his life to free him from his guilt?

Lucas reached out and took his cup from him. "Why don't you grab a muffin while I freshen up our coffee?"

18

ALEX LOOKED INSIDE the container at the selection of muffins. A weight on his leg drew his attention down, and he saw Ava sitting with her chin on his leg. She looked up at him with her warm brown eyes, and it almost seemed as if she was there to try and comfort him.

As Lucas came back to the table, he said, "You have a choice between apple cinnamon and blueberry." He reached over to pat Ava on the head. "And Ava doesn't get any because she's already had some this morning. So no matter how cute she looks, resist the urge to feed her more."

Alex chose a blueberry muffin from the container. He peeled the wrapper off and took a bite. "These are really delicious."

Lucas nodded. "The blueberry are Danny's favorite. He's quite a pro at making them. In fact, he'd made them the morning I met him for the first time."

"Did you think twice about being in a relationship with Brooke knowing you'd be an instant father if it got serious?"

"To be honest, in my heart, it was serious from the moment I laid eyes on the two of them. I knew they were a package deal, and I had no problem with that. Danny's a great kid and he's made being a dad easy." Lucas finished off his muffin and took a sip of his coffee. "You're in a unique situation, that's for sure. But don't let that stop you from embracing the role of fatherhood."

"I really want to, but it seems that every time I turn around, there's something to prevent it from happening. First the past and how Jordan reacted to that. And of course, my own issues with what happened. But when I think of trying to connect with Jordan, to make a place for him in my life, I start to feel overwhelmed." Alex frowned and glanced up at Lucas. "And that overwhelmed feeling? Yeah, I'm not so used to it. And I really don't like it. In fact, the last time I felt this overwhelmed by anything was when Rebecca told me she was pregnant. I don't know how to get out from under that feeling and get control of the situation again."

Lucas chuckled as he reached out to clap Alex on the shoulder. "I'm sorry to inform you, my friend, that once you have a family—a wife and a child—you're never really truly in control of the situation ever again."

"And you don't have a problem with that?" Alex asked. Lucas was a businessman like he was. A successful businessman. There's no way that he could achieve any amount of success without being in control of things.

"In my business, I'm still in control," Lucas said, as if reading Alex's mind. "But here at home, they don't need me to be in control all the time. They need me to be present. They need me to be understanding. But most of all, they need me to love them. And I do. With all my heart."

"So does that help with the overwhelmed feeling?" Alex asked as his hand drifted down to touch the soft fur between Ava's ears. It was as if she sensed his emotional distress and was offering comfort in the only way she knew how.

Lucas leaned forward, an intense look on his face. "Here's

the thing about being overwhelmed. There's a saying going around that claims that God will never give us more than we can handle. But I'm here to tell you that's not true."

Alex frowned. He'd heard the saying and in fact, it had come to mind a few times over the past couple of weeks. He tried to find solace in it, but all he'd found was failure since clearly God *had* given him more than he could handle.

"If God only gave us what we could handle, why would we need Him? God, in fact, does give us more than we can handle and then offers us His strength, His wisdom and His peace to deal with it. When we learned that my brother Lincoln might be dead, I definitely felt that God had given us more than we could handle. Definitely more than my mom could handle. But it was then that I learned that God wanted us to trust Him to get through the situation. To not try and do it all on our own. And that applies to your situation as well."

Alex looked at the man sitting across from him, really looking at him for the first time and seeing a man of incredible spiritual depth. They'd been acquaintances for years, but it was only recently as their circles of friends and family began to intertwine that they'd become friends. They attended the same church and were in the same men's Bible study, but it seemed Lucas took his faith much more seriously than Alex had. Sure he prayed and read his Bible, but at the first sign of trouble, his immediate thought wasn't necessarily to pray and ask God for wisdom. He always seemed to try and figure things out for himself until he got overwhelmed by it all. Now Lucas was telling him that God was, in fact, waiting for him to admit his weakness and ask for His help.

"I hope I'm not coming across like I'm preaching a sermon to you, Alex. I just felt that God brought you here for a reason this morning, and I'm feeling even more strongly that way now. I'm glad you felt comfortable enough to share your story with me, and I hope that something of what I've shared with you today might help you in some way. Our journeys may have been different, but we've faced similar situations. I certainly don't pretend to have all the answers, but I know the One who does and that gives me more peace than you can imagine when dealing with things that I feel completely ill-equipped to deal with."

Alex took a sip of his coffee then set the mug down. "I never... I never looked at things the way you presented them here today. I've just always assumed that when facing a difficult situation, I needed to take control of it and not let it overwhelm me. That's why I've struggled so much with the situation with Rebecca and Jordan. I haven't been able to take control of it, and it has certainly overwhelmed me." Ava chuffed softly, and Alex began to rub her fur again.

"Recognizing that is the first step. The next step is turning to God and understanding that He is the only one who can truly help you deal with what's in your heart and then what's happening around you."

When Alex left Lucas's house a short time later, he did so with a sense of peace underlying the overwhelmed feeling he'd been struggling with. Though he hadn't completely escaped the feeling of being overwhelmed, it wasn't as scary as it had been before. He still had no idea what lay ahead with regards to his relationships with Rebecca and Jordan, but he was going to trust God to help him through it.

Throughout the drive home, Alex carried on a conversation with God. He needed to apply what Lucas had said and he did it by asking God for forgiveness for what he'd done and for freedom from the guilt he'd carried for so long. Though he had been willing before to prepare himself for what God's will might be for the three of them, that held a whole new meaning now. Regardless of how all this turned out, he knew that God no longer wanted him living a life filled with guilt. Accepting God's forgiveness would prepare his heart in a way he hadn't realized before.

Uncertain what to expect at the house, Alex let himself in the front door and was greeted by silence. He walked into the kitchen and noticed Jordan sitting at the table with his phone, staring out at the backyard. Alex stood for a moment and looked at his son. He waited for the rush of guilt that usually accompanied being around Jordan, but it didn't come. Instead, he was able to look at his son and truly see him for the remarkable young man he was. Jordan deserved more from him than a relationship mired down in guilt, and Alex hoped that he would give him a chance to create that relationship.

White cords hung from his ears which would explain why he didn't hear Alex's approach. As Alex slid onto the chair across the table from him, Jordan's head turned, his eyes widening in surprise. With slow movements, he pulled the earbuds out and set them on the table.

"Do you have a minute to talk?" Alex asked. He wanted to make the boy listen to what he had to say, but he knew that Jordan would be more receptive if it was his choice.

Jordan nodded as his hand closed around his phone. He shifted on his chair, his gaze dropping briefly to the table before he looked up and said, "Sure. What's up?"

For a moment, Alex began to panic, once again feeling the fluttering of nerves and the feeling of unworthiness as he sat there with Jordan. He swallowed hard and took a breath, remembering Lucas's words as well as the prayer he'd prayed on his way home. Now he was going to trust God to give him the words that Jordan needed to hear in order to heal what was between them.

"Jordan, I know you were hurt when you found out what I said to your mom when she told me she was pregnant with you. And you have every right to feel that way. However, I also want you to know how very sorry I am for what I said and ask your forgiveness for that." Alex stopped and tried to formulate what else he needed to say in his mind. "I've lived the last fifteen years of my life with the guilt of knowing that I had condemned my child to death. It ate at me all those years. When I found out you weren't dead, I thought it would all go away, but it didn't. Every time I looked at you, I was consumed with guilt and the feeling that I wasn't worthy of being your father."

Jordan stared at him, his blue eyes wide and his mouth slightly open as if in shock. Alex wondered if he was going to say anything, but when he didn't, Alex continued on.

"I've also been really worried that I wouldn't be able to be the kind of father you wanted or needed. My whole life has been wrapped up in BlackThorpe. The company has always been my first priority. I want to change that, to give you a higher priority. I want to be able to spend time with you and get to know you better. I want you to know more than anything that I love you." Alex swallowed against the emotions rising within him. "I don't know what you want or need from me, but I hope that you will give us a chance. I'm going to mess up, I know that already, but I'm going to try my best to be the father that you need. Will you let me do that? Will you *help* me do that?"

Having asked him a direct question, Alex waited for Jordan's answer. If his son wanted nothing more to do with him, then he needed Jordan to tell him that face-to-face so that there were no misunderstandings. It wasn't the answer he wanted, but he would accept it until, hopefully, one day Jordan would change his mind.

Jordan gave a shaky nod. "Yes. I would like that."

Relief rush through Alex, wiping out the last of the guilt that had been lingering in his heart. Together, he and Jordan would figure out what worked best for them. Their relationship might be different than boys who had had their father with them since birth, but the one thing that would be the same would be the love Alex had for Jordan.

Silence stretched between them as they sat looking at each other. Grasping for something—anything—to build on what they'd started there, Alex found himself offering to take Jordan shooting at the range that afternoon.

"I need to check in with a couple people before we can go, so why don't we plan on leaving around two or so. And you should probably check with your mom to make sure it's okay with her."

Jordan nodded as he got to his feet then paused. "What if mom wants to come too? Would that be okay?"

"If she wants to come along, she's more than welcome. Even if she doesn't want to shoot."

With a quick grin, Jordan darted from the kitchen,

leaving Alex with more hope in his heart than he'd had in a very long time. As he headed for his room to make a call to Marcus, Alex hoped that the positive result of his conversation with Jordan was just the start of things changing for the better.

19

MOM!"

Rebecca looked over in time to see her son appear in the doorway to the bedroom. She got to her feet as he approached her and caught her up in a tight hug.

When he finally released her, she stepped back and asked, "What's going on?"

She didn't think anything was wrong since his face was lit up with excitement. His grin was even bigger than when he'd heard about going to a basketball game with Tyler, so it was something significant.

"I just talked with...uh... Alex. My dad. He said he wants me to be a part of his life."

Rebecca hadn't seen Alex since he'd said goodnight to her at the BlackThorpe office. She'd popped into the house after breakfast, but there had been nobody around. Obviously, at some point, Alex had returned home and had spoken to Jordan. The huge grin on her son's face warmed her heart.

"That's great, sweetheart. Are you feeling better about things with Alex now?"

"I am." Jordan gave a vigorous nod of his head. "He apologized for what he said to you back then. And he said that it was hard because every time he looked at me he felt guilty for what he said, but he wants us to have a relationship. He wants to be my dad."

Rebecca wished she could've been there for the conversation, but she knew it was something that needed to take place between just Jordan and Alex. It seemed that that relationship now had a firm foundation on which to build, and she was very glad—and relieved—for that. The fear she'd had over Alex's presence in Jordan's life was long gone. She knew now that Alex would try his best to be a good father for Jordan, and she would do what she could to help their relationship flourish.

All that was left now was to figure things out between her and Alex. After coming home the night before, Rebecca had spent time curled up in the chair in her room, thinking over the events of the evening. Their dinner together and the time afterward at BlackThorpe had shown her a different side of Alex. In fact, everything she'd seen of him since arriving in Minneapolis had proven him to be very different from the man she'd imagined he would have become.

For some reason, in her mind, she had imagined him to be a distant, overbearing and controlling man. One without feelings or regard for others. She'd based her assumptions on his reaction to her pregnancy, assuming the man she'd fallen in love with had changed completely. But she saw now that he hadn't. Yes, he was controlling at times and very determined, but then she had also seen the softer side of him. How he indulged his sisters. How emotionally involved he'd been in finding Alana.

She didn't need a man to take care of her like she had when she'd been nineteen, but that didn't stop her from wanting someone at her side. And not just anyone, she knew she wanted Alex. At one time, she would have rejected the thought of sharing the role of parenting Jordan with anyone. But seeing how Alex was with Jordan, how determined he was to try and make things work, Rebecca knew that sharing that role with him would be the best thing for Jordan.

"Mom?" Jordan's voice drew her back to their conversation. "Did you hear me?"

"Sorry, sweetheart. What did you say?"

Jordan gave her a funny look. "Alex said he'd take me shooting this afternoon, and if you wanted to go with us that you could. Even if you didn't want to shoot. Do you want to go?"

While she in no way was interested in shooting, Rebecca wasn't going to turn down the opportunity to spend some time with both Alex and Jordan. "What time are we leaving?"

"Alex said he had to check some things, so we will leave around two." Jordan's body was practically thrumming with anticipation. "Are you going to try shooting again?"

"No way." Rebecca slipped an arm around Jordan's waist and gave him a squeeze. "I'll stick to things I'm good at, like making lunch. Are you hungry?"

A little before two, Rebecca made her way to the house. Jordan had gone over earlier, but she'd taken the time to change into a pair of jeans and a long-sleeved blouse. She didn't even bother denying that the extra effort she took with her appearance was in hopes of pleasing Alex. There was a side of her that was trying to tell her that she was being ridiculous, that she should never dress to please a man, but Rebecca was shutting that voice down. If she wanted to wear something that Alex might think she looked good in, she was going to do it.

Once inside the house, Rebecca heard voices in the kitchen so she headed in that direction. Alex and Jordan stood there talking with Melanie.

"Melanie's coming with us, Mom," Jordan said when he spotted her.

Rebecca felt a twinge of disappointment that it wouldn't just be the three of them, but she tamped it down because she liked Melanie. "Well, I'm going on the record now to say that I won't be shooting."

Jordan and Alex shared a glance and then laughed.

"Practice makes perfect," Alex said. "Not everyone gets it right on the first try."

"I daresay that practice won't help me." Rebecca gave Alex a quick glance with a small smile. "I'm just going along for the company."

Alex stared at her for a moment then said, "Well then, let's get this show on the road."

When they got to the truck, Melanie climbed into the back with Jordan, leaving the front seat open for Rebecca. Alex held the door for her and waited until she was buckled in before closing it. Once he was behind the wheel, they headed around the driveway to the gate and out onto the highway.

"Has there been any more news about Alana?" Rebecca asked as Alex guided the truck through traffic.

"Yes, actually, there is. Justin phoned early this morning to say Alana had regained consciousness. She's still very weak from the drugs and the dehydration, but they say she's going to be just fine."

"*Physically* she'll be just fine," Melanie added from the back seat. "It may take her a little more time to deal with it emotionally and mentally. Did they say if there appeared to be any signs of abuse?"

Alex shook his head. "Justin didn't say anything about that. And I didn't really want to ask. I guess I'm sort of feeling like we've won the war just getting her back, but I know there will be more battles to be fought. We'll make sure that she has access to any sort of help she needs. And not just her, but Justin and Caden too."

"We have plenty of people in–house who can help her. Although, they may wish to deal with people not connected with BlackThorpe. In which case, we have professionals we can refer them to."

"At least you could talk with her, Melanie. Not necessarily as a psychologist, but as a friend who has gone through something similar."

Rebecca recalled the horrible couple of weeks that Alex and his family had suffered through when Melanie had been kidnapped in her teens. Through Alex, she knew more details than most, but they had been careful to shield Melanie from the media once she'd been returned to them. Looking at her now, Rebecca was glad to see her happy and in a relationship with Tyler.

It wasn't long before they were at the gate to the compound. Once inside, Melanie and Jordan led the way from the truck to the building housing the shooting range. Rebecca stayed beside Alex, her hand and arm brushing against his as they walked. She wondered if he'd take her hand again like he had the night before. Or had that just been done in the emotion of the moment? Was he waiting for her to make the first move?

Jordan and Melanie had already disappeared into the building by the time they got there. Alex reached out and opened the door, holding it for her and laying his hand on the small of her back as he ushered her inside.

As they stepped into the long hallway leading to the range, Alex glanced down at her and said, "So you're sure you don't want to shoot?"

"Absolutely positive. Like I told Jordan earlier, I believe my talents lie in other areas."

Alex nodded. "Well, there's no doubt that you are talented at different things. The success of your books proves that, if nothing else. But you're also a pretty good cook."

"Exactly! I'll leave the guns to the people who can actually hit the targets, and I'll do the things I enjoy instead."

When they entered the lobby of the shooting range, Melanie and Jordan were standing near a table talking to a man Rebecca thought looked familiar. As they got closer, Rebecca noticed that there was a woman with them as well. It only took a quick look to realize that the woman had some form of dwarfism.

"Hey, Trent," Alex said as he held out his hand. "And it's good to see you again, Victoria. Are you guys here to do some shooting too?"

Victoria laughed. "Yeah, this is our date for the week."

"I guess you guys have met Jordan already," Alex said as he laid a hand on Jordan's shoulder then reached to lay his other hand on Rebecca's back. "This is his mother, Rebecca."

The lack of surprise on Victoria's face told Rebecca that Trent had already talked to her about the situation. The woman held out her hand, a big smile on her face.

"It's great to meet you, Rebecca," Victoria said. "So do you guys live here in the Twin Cities?"

Rebecca shook her head. "At the moment, we live in Chicago." She glanced at Alex before continuing on. "But we are considering a move in this direction."

"Nice," Victoria exclaimed. "We'll have to get together if you do."

Alex cleared his throat. "Just to make a few connections for you, Rebecca, Trent works for us as our computer guru, and Victoria is Eric's sister. He was the one that helped fingerprint Jordan."

"We like to keep it all in the family. The BlackThorpe family," Victoria said with a smile as she slid her hand into Trent's.

"Well, I came here to shoot," Melanie said, a mischievous grin on her face. "Who wants to try to outshoot me?"

"Not sure I can," Trent replied. "But Victoria might give you a run for your money."

Rebecca looked at the little woman in surprise and saw Victoria nod at Melanie.

"You're on."

Trent, Victoria, and Melanie each had their own weapons, but Alex took Jordan to the weapons case and pulled out a gun for him. It didn't take long before they were ready to tackle the shooting range targets. Rebecca thought Alex would also join them, but instead, he stayed behind when

Melanie grabbed Jordan's arm, and the two of them led the way into the shooting range.

"Why don't we sit down over there?" Alex said as he pointed to a table nearer the glass window. "We'll be able to see them better.

From her seat at the table, Rebecca had a clear view of Jordan and Melanie. They watched in silence for a few minutes then Rebecca looked over and met Alex's gaze. Her cheeks flushed a bit when she realized he'd been watching her.

Clearing her throat, she said, "Jordan told me that the two of you had a talk this morning."

He nodded. "It's taken me a little time, but I think I've finally got a grasp on how to build a relationship with Jordan."

Rebecca tilted her head. "And how's that?"

A smile played at the corners of Alex's mouth. "By admitting that I know absolutely nothing about how to be a dad and trusting God—and Jordan—to help me figure it out."

"Well, that sounds like a pretty good plan." Rebecca smiled as she leaned forward and rested her clasped hands on the table. "None of us really go into parenting knowing exactly how to do it. We can have good examples around us, and yet when it's your child that you're trying to figure out how to raise, it can be pretty daunting."

"I'm just grateful that Jordan's willing to give me a second chance to do right by him."

Rebecca's gaze drifted to Jordan and then to her hands. She shifted in her seat, bits of the conversation she'd had with Connor coming back to her. Did she really want to know? "Did you change your mind?"

When Alex didn't reply, Rebecca lifted her gaze to his. He stared at her for a long moment before responding, as if trying to figure out her question.

"Will knowing one way or the other make a difference to what we are trying to do now?" he finally asked.

Rebecca thought over his words. If he said that he hadn't

changed his mind, would it affect how she looked at him now? But if he *had* changed his mind, would the regret she'd feel over the lost years be too much?

"I don't know. Connor just mentioned when we were talking that he was pretty sure that you would've changed your mind." Rebecca tightened her hands. "It never occurred to me that you might have because I was already wondering if you had changed your mind...about us."

Alex's hand covered hers, his strength and warmth seeping into her. "Why would you have thought that?"

"It just seemed that after you were sent to the Middle East, we were never able to talk with each other. And even when we emailed, I would write you all about the stuff going on in my life, but you never shared anything like that. Your emails were always really short, and sometimes you didn't even say you loved me at the end of them." The rush of emotion at the memories caught Rebecca off-guard, and she had to take a deep breath to regain control. "I thought you were regretting getting married like we did."

The hand covering hers tightened, and Rebecca looked up to see anguish on Alex's face.

"I thought I was protecting you. The life I was living over there was not something I wanted to share with you. Parts of it I wish I could forget. I refused to reenlist after my first term was up, and it took a lot of counseling to get me to the point where I could live with those memories. That's why I didn't share stuff like that in the emails I sent you." Alex's head dipped for a moment then he looked back up at her. "I can't remember why I didn't tell you I loved you in those emails. I just remember being really frustrated with our schedules and the Wi-Fi I had access to. It just never seemed to work out for us to live chat, and I missed that. Emails were never my thing, but I guess I should've made a little more effort."

"Did you change your mind?" Rebecca just couldn't seem to let the question go. Even if he told her he hadn't, she could see now the regret he lived with and the type of man he had become. It wouldn't matter.

She unclasped her hands and turned one face up on the table. As his palm touched hers, their fingers intertwined, and she rested her other hand on top of his. She glanced over at him and saw that he was focused on their hands.

It seemed to take forever before Alex lifted his gaze to hers. "Yes. Yes, I did change my mind."

Rebecca felt a rush of tears and blinked rapidly to keep them from spilling over. Her grip tightened on his hand as if to anchor herself against the pain rushing over her. If only she'd waited.

"Don't think about it," Alex said in a low voice rough with emotion. "It's in the past now. We have to leave it there."

"I'm sorry," Rebecca said, her words barely more than a ragged whisper. "I'm so sorry."

This time, Alex took her hands in his. "I shouldn't have asked of you what I did. If I hadn't, there would've been no need for me to change my mind. I hope you can forgive me for what I said."

"I should have trusted you," Rebecca said, seeing her own pain reflected in Alex's eyes.

"As soon as I sent my email in response to yours, I got tied up in a mission that took me out of contact for a couple of days. By the time I got back, you didn't answer any more of my emails." Alex gently rubbed the back of her hands with his thumbs. "I bear the responsibility for what happened. And I need to beg you for your forgiveness for what I asked you to do."

Fresh tears sprung to Rebecca's eyes, and this time, they spilled over. Alex reached up and brushed them away with his fingertips.

"I do forgive you." Rebecca took a shuddering breath. "Do you forgive me for not trusting you?"

"Yes, I do." Alex leaned closer, his hand cupping her cheek. "I don't know why God allowed everything to happen the way it did, but in my heart, it doesn't matter that fifteen years have passed. I look at you and see a confident, beautiful woman, different from the young woman I fell in love with, and yet, the woman you have become, calls to the man I am today. If I had to say what attracted me to a woman now, it would be everything that you are." Alex paused. "Do you think maybe we might have a shot at a second chance?"

As Rebecca listened to Alex's words, she knew that they were echoed in her own heart. "Yes. I think we might."

A smile broke across Alex's face and his blue eyes lit with joy. He lowered his hand from her face and grasped her hand again. "In that case, Rebecca MacKenzie, would you go out on a date with me?"

Rebecca returned Alex's smile. A date sounded perfect. And this time, there would be no sneaking around. "I would love to."

Movement out of the corner of her eye caught her attention, and Rebecca glanced over to see Melanie and Jordan pressed to the glass watching them. Looking back at Alex, she tipped her head toward the window. As he turned his head to look, Rebecca also returned her gaze to her son and sister-in-law. Both of them were grinning and giving them a thumbs up.

"I'd kiss you," Alex said with a grin. "But I never kiss before the first date. And this time, I'm going to do it right."

Rebecca found herself filled with anticipation and excitement about what lay ahead. She already knew in her heart that she loved Alex and though he hadn't said the words to her, she knew that he loved her too. He wouldn't be asking her for a second chance—and she wouldn't be giving him one—if love wasn't already present in their hearts.

She couldn't wait to see how Alex planned to do it right this time.

EPILOGUE

REBECCA RAN HER HANDS down her sides, enjoying the feel of satin beneath her fingertips. Alex had told her to dress up a bit more for their date that night, so she'd had to go shopping. It had taken a bit of time, but she'd finally settled on a forest green top that had a sweetheart neckline and a fitted bodice. It ended just at her hips, flaring slightly. Her black skirt was straight and stopped just above her knees. Knee-high boots with the heel finished off the look. She taken a bit more time to do her hair and makeup but had to settle for the few pieces of jewelry she'd brought with her, never imagining she'd be dressing up to go out on a date.

After their conversation at the shooting range, Rebecca had been uncertain about what to expect. True to his word, Alex had taken her out on a date the very next night. They'd gone to an early movie and a late dinner that they had lingered over until the restaurant shut down around midnight. He held her hand through the movie and anytime they walked somewhere, but that had been the extent of the physical contact.

Their next date had included Jordan and they'd gone bowling together. As they'd watched Jordan bowl, Alex had kept his arm around her shoulders. They'd laugh together at their son's antics, not really caring who ended up winning the game. Jordan had seemed to enjoy himself as well and had asked when they might be able to do it again. But as the night before, their evening ended without a kiss, although they had hugged briefly.

Rebecca had appreciated that Alex didn't dive right into the physical side of things. They did need to get to know each other once again, to get reacquainted. Each subsequent date over the next week had ended much the same. They had gone out together on a date every night except one. On that night, Alex had gone to see Justin and Alana. He had invited her along, but she had declined. The woman had no doubt been bombarded with strangers since she'd been found. Rebecca was confident that she would still be there to meet her when things had settled down.

Her anticipation for the date that night only grew as she watched the clock. Jordan had gone off with Tyler and Ryan for another basketball game, so she was alone in the apartment. Though Alex hadn't mentioned the significance of the date—the calendar date—Rebecca was sure he was aware of it. December 22. Their anniversary. For the first time since they were married, Rebecca had actually been looking forward to the day.

She saw headlights moving along the driveway and went to gather her things. Unlike the first non-date they had gone on, Rebecca waited for Alex to come to the apartment. He told her that he liked to come to the door to walk her to the truck. She had no problem with that and enjoyed the anticipation of waiting for him to knock on the door.

When the knock came, she pulled the door open and greeted Alex with a smile. She hadn't put her coat on yet, so Alex was able to get a look at her outfit.

He reached out and took her coat, holding it for her so

she could slide her arms into it. "You look very beautiful tonight."

She felt the warmth of his fingers as he lifted her hair out from underneath the coat's collar. As she began to button her coat, she turned around, her cheeks flushed from his compliment. "Thank you."

After she was dressed to face the cold, Alex took her arm and slid it into the crook of his elbow. She closed the door behind them, and together they made their way down the stairs to the truck. He had left it running so it was nice and warm when she climbed in.

"How was your day today?" Rebecca asked as he guided the truck away from the house.

"It was fairly quiet. With Christmas right around the corner, we are not usually too busy with meetings or assignments. We'll enjoy the lull while we can because things will pick up again in the New Year." Once Alex turned the truck onto the highway, he reached out and took her hand. "Now that Alana is back, the Christmas atmosphere at work has definitely improved. It seems each day this week one of the floors has been having a party. Marcus and I try to make it to each one, so we've had a lot of food this week."

"Since I've mostly worked out of the home, I've never really had a company Christmas party to attend. Of course, our church always had something for the entire congregation each year."

"We don't tend to have a companywide Christmas party, but we have a fundraiser at the end of November that employees are welcome to attend. It's usually pretty swanky, so not everyone comes. We do encourage each floor to do something as a department, and we cover the cost for that. This year we had a big company family day and that seemed to go over really well."

They talked a little bit more about Christmas traditions as Alex drove them to wherever he planned for them to spend the evening. When they finally arrived, Rebecca immediately fell in love with the look of the restaurant even from just the outside. It had a stone façade and multi-pane windows with rounded awnings above them. Soft light glowed from the windows and spilled out onto the sidewalk in front of the building.

The inside was just as beautiful with rich burgundy drapes hanging between the windows. All the furniture and fixings were a dark wood. In the centre of the room was a fireplace open on all four sides with stone corners.

She was so captivated by the ambience that Rebecca didn't even hear Alex give his name to the hostess. But he must have because as soon as they had removed their coats, she was leading them to their table.

The restaurant reminded her in some ways of the one they had gone to before. On their non-date. The subtle elegance. The hushed sounds. It was absolutely beautiful.

Their table ended up being tucked away in a corner, separated from other tables by several feet. Alex held the chair for her as she sat down then settled in across from her. The hostess handed them their menus that left them alone to peruse them.

"So does another friend of a friend own this place?" Rebecca asked, her gaze taking in the candles on the table and the lovely way it was all set.

Alex chuckled. "No, not this one. I actually phoned around to a few of the guys for some recommendations, because I really had no idea where to bring you. I'd already taken you to the one nice restaurant that I knew about."

"Well, if the food tastes as good as the restaurant looks, you've picked a winner."

It wasn't long until Rebecca discovered that the food was, in fact, delicious. Since she didn't date, her eating out usually consisted of places Jordan would like. Sometimes she and Maureen would go out, but even then it was usually to a place they knew serve their favorite desserts. She hoped that in the future, she and Alex would have frequent dates to places like this.

After their meal was over, they didn't linger long. Rebecca would've liked to, but Alex seemed to have more planned for the evening. Once they were in the truck, he fiddled with the radio until he found the station playing Christmas music. He made a stop to get them each a cup of coffee, and then he just drove them around looking at Christmas lights.

Their conversation included topics such as Connor's arrival the next day, plans for Christmas, and gifts that still needed to be bought and wrapped. Rebecca wasn't paying too much attention to where exactly they were driving until Alex swung into the parking lot of a darkened building.

Rebecca stared out the front window at the motel—now clearly abandoned--where they had stayed after their wedding ceremony. Tears sprung to her eyes as she thought back to that time and the girl that she had been.

She reached for Alex's hand and gripped it tight as she turned to look at him.

Alex stared at her for a moment then said, "I made a lot of promises to you as we lay together in that bed in our motel room. I broke a lot of those promises, but if you give me another chance, I'd like to see if I can do better this time around."

Rebecca hadn't realized how much she wanted to let that young girl inside of her dream again. She was here, back where it all started. The place may have been run down, but it hadn't mattered to her because she'd been with the man she loved.

Alex reached into his pocket and pulled out a small box. He let go of her hand for a moment so that he could open it and then he turned on the overhead light in the truck. "One of the promises I made to you was that one day I would replace that stainless steel ring you had with one made from gold and diamonds."

Rebecca watched as Alex freed the ring from the box and gripped it between his fingers. Rebecca pressed her hand to her mouth and prayed that if this was a dream, she would never wake up. Alex held out his hand, palm up and waited. Her hand was shaking as she laid it on his.

"Rebecca, I have committed myself to doing what I could to make our marriage work now. Spending this past week with you has reinforced my feelings for you, how very much I love you."

"I love you too," Rebecca said, her words barely a whisper as she tried to speak through the tightness in her throat. Tears blurred Alex's face for a moment, but she blinked them rapidly away.

"I know legally we're already married, but I need to ask the woman you are today if you will marry the man I've become."

"Yes." Rebecca wrapped her fingers around his hand, holding tight to his strength. "Yes, I will marry you."

Rebecca's gaze dropped to their hands as Alex slid the sparkling ring onto the ring finger of her left hand. He lifted their hands and pressed a kiss to the back of hers then he reached out to lay his other hand on her cheek. He leaned toward her as Rebecca laid her hand on top of his, pressing it tightly to her face. As the distance close between them and their lips touched for the first time in fifteen years, Rebecca couldn't stop her tears.

She had missed this man.

The lost years still filled her with regret, but Rebecca planned to make the most out of each day they had together from this moment on.

Alex stood at the large window that faced the frozen lake and watch snowflakes drift down from the sky. It was hard to believe that he was there on his honeymoon with Rebecca. He glanced over his shoulder to the large bed where she lay sleeping.

After asking her to marry him again on the anniversary of their previous wedding, they decided together that they wanted to have a renewal of their vows in front of their family and friends. So on the first day of the New Year, those who loved and cared about them gathered at Alex's church for their service. Rebecca's best friend, Maureen had come with her family which had thrilled Jordan since it meant his best friend was there too.

Though Rebecca had phoned to let her parents know about the wedding, they hadn't been able to attend because of the short notice. Alex knew it had disappointed Rebecca, but at least, Connor had been there for her and had walked her down the aisle with Jordan. After fifteen years, they had finally gotten their church wedding.

After the wedding, they'd had a dinner with those closest to them and then they'd left to come to this cabin on the lake. For the next week, it was going to be just the two of them. Jordan had flown back to Chicago with Connor and Robby's family. And when their week-long honeymoon was up, they were going to join them there. Plans were underway for Rebecca, Jordan, and Connor to move back to the Twin Cities.

Alex would be glad when everything was settled. Even the house was undergoing some renovations while they were gone. They were building a new bedroom and bathroom in the basement for Jordan. Rebecca would move in with Alex and Connor would take over the apartment. There were a lot of changes going on, but Alex was looking forward to every one.

He heard movement behind him and turned to see Rebecca sitting up. Rather than have her leave the warmth of the bed, Alex joined her. Once under the covers, he drew her close and she tucked her head in the crook of his neck.

"What were you thinking about?" she asked as her hand settled over his heart.

Alex covered her hand with one of his, holding it closely. "I was just thinking about all the changes that have come about in my life in the last little while. And how very grateful I am for each and every one."

"You think you're ready for me and Jordan to take your life by storm?"

Alex chuckled and pressed a kiss to the top of her head. "You've already taken my life by storm, babe, and I wouldn't have it any other way." They lay in silence for a few minutes and Alex's thoughts continued to wander. "I'm so very grateful that you were strong enough to walk away from what

I asked you to do. Looking at Jordan used to fill me with guilt, but now I look at him and see proof of a life that was meant to be. We may have struggled at the start, but he's proof of our love then and now."

"Yes, he is." Rebecca lifted her hand and slid it along the back of his head, drawing him down so their lips could touch. She gave him several light kisses. "And I do love you very much."

Before he could respond, their kiss deepened and Alex decided to show her how much he loved her instead. As he pulled her close, he whispered a prayer of thanks that God had brought them together again and that against all odds, a spark of love had endured and now flourished between them.

The End

OTHER AVAILABLE TITLES

Marrying Kate

Faith, Hope & Love

Home Is Where the Heart Is (*Home to Collingsworth: 1*)
Home Away From Home (*Home to Collingsworth: 2*)
Love Makes a House a Home (*Home to Collingsworth: 3*)
The Long Road Home (*Home to Collingsworth: 4*)
Her Heart, His Home (*Home to Collingsworth: 5*)
Coming Home (*Home to Collingsworth: 6*)

This Time With Love (*The McKinleys: 1*)
Forever My Love (*The McKinleys: 2*)
When There is Love (*The McKinleys: 3*)

Guarding Her Heart (BlackThorpe Security: 1)
Signs of Love (BlackThorpe Security: 2)
A Matter of Trust (BlackThorpe Security: 3)
Proof of Life (BlackThorpe Security: 4)

For news on new releases and sales
sign up for Kimberly's newsletter

http://eepurl.com/WFhYr

Please visit Kimberly Rae Jordan on the web!
Website: www.kimberlyraejordan.com
Facebook: www.facebook.com/AuthorKimberlyRaeJordan
Twitter: twitter.com/KimberlyRJordan

Made in the USA
Las Vegas, NV
31 May 2023

72772006R00146